A Devon Midwinter Murder

By Stephanie Austin

a&b

A Devon Midwinter Murder

STEPHANIE AUSTIN

Allison & Busby Limited
11 Wardour Mews
London W1F 8AN
allisonandbusby.com

First published in Great Britain by Allison & Busby in 2023.
This paperback edition published by Allison & Busby in 2024.

A CIP catalogue record for this book is available from
the British Library.

10 9 8 7 6 5 4 3 2 1

ISBN 978-0-7490-3046-9

Typeset in 11/16 pt Sabon LT Pro by
Allison & Busby Ltd.

By choosing this product, you help take care of the world's forests.
Learn more: www.fsc.org.

Printed and bound by
CPI Group (UK) Ltd, Croydon, CR0 4YY

For Claire

CHAPTER ONE

It was a lovely day for a murder, bright blue and sharp cold, the sort of December day I thought I'd never see again. Devon winters have been so mild and soft over the last few years. I suspected nothing. When I awoke, I had no sense of foreknowledge, no ominous fluttering of foreboding. Despite my recent experiences of discovering dead bodies, I have not yet developed an early warning system. Instead, I was excited, looking forward to the day.

It was Sunday so I had no dogs to walk, but I got up early and dressed in the dark, pulling on a thick jumper in readiness for the cold outside. Bill, curled up warm in a furry circle on my bed, didn't even stir. I closed the door of the flat softly and tiptoed down the stairs, avoiding the treads that creaked. I didn't want to disturb Adam and Kate on the ground floor, although their Sunday morning lie-ins are a thing of the past since baby Noah arrived.

I opened the front door and the cold snatched my

breath. It was quiet, the little town of Ashburton still snug in its Sunday sleep, enfolded by the hills that rise up towards Dartmoor, undisturbed by the icy waters of the stream that burbles softly through its heart. The houses were in darkness, no lights showed; above their rooftops one laggard star remained that should have been in bed long ago. Not even the rooks roosting in the church tower had stirred their feathers yet. I rammed my woolly hat down over my hair and pulled on my gloves. The grass was crisp and crunched beneath my boots, ivy leaves sketched with chalk lines of frost. I love winter. Perhaps this Christmas, there would be snow, real snow.

I scraped a sparkling crust of ice from the windscreen of Van Blanc and headed for *Old Nick's*. There was no one about in town. I passed the Victoria Inn, the stream sneaking behind an old weavers' cottage, and drove through streets empty save for a solitary driver delivering Sunday papers to the co-op, stacking them in piles on the pavement by the door. I negotiated the cobbled ginnel of Shadow Lane, where my shop stands in splendid isolation – *Old Nick's*: antiques, crafts, paintings and second-hand books – source of constant angst and not much income. Not so much cash flow as cash drip.

I unlocked the door, pushed it open, and for a moment stood in the dark and listened. Sometimes, when I go into the shop first thing, I get a sense of Old Nick still being around.

I don't mean he's a ghost. I don't snatch glimpses of him from the corner of my eye, or hear the shuffle of his slippers on the stairs. He's not a presence exactly. But as I walk in the door, I get a feeling as if I've come in on the end of his laughter, just missed it. And the joke is always on me. I had a perfectly viable business as a Domestic Goddess, cleaning, gardening and walking dogs, before Nick left me the antique shop in his will. Now I have to juggle two businesses just to make enough to keep this one running. But I remember his chuckle and his wicked blue eyes and realise that I miss him. Poor murdered Nick. I haven't asked Sophie and Pat, who spend more time in the shop than I do, if they've experienced anything similar. Their imaginations are overactive as it is.

Boxes were packed and waiting inside, and I loaded them into my van, my breath puffing little clouds in the cold air at each trip; small antiques and collectibles for me, handicrafts and jewellery for Pat, paintings and display stands for Sophie. I locked them all in the back then headed up the hill towards Druid Lodge.

On the way I passed a number of posters tied to trees and telegraph poles, white rectangles in the thinning gloom, advertising today's event and pointing the way. I didn't need to read them because I'd helped to write them. *Victorian Christmas Fair in aid of Honeysuckle Farm Animal Sanctuary*, they announced proudly, *Fun for all the Family*.

That's what today was about. Pat, who sells her handiwork in my shop, runs Honeysuckle Farm, a sanctuary for abandoned animals and injured wildlife, along with her sister and brother-in-law. It costs them a fortune to run and they are always desperately short of funds. Today's event was about raising them some money, all profits going to support the animals.

I drove in through the gates of Druid Lodge and up the winding drive. As the house came into view, I could see there were lights on downstairs, so someone in that grand Georgian pile was up and about. Ricky and Morris are like vampires, they almost never sleep.

On the lawn stood two large marquees, ghostly white in the dimness, empty and waiting, like the animal pens in front of them, for their occupants to arrive. I'd parked Van Blanc and was still crunching my way across the gravel towards the house when the front door was flung open, revealing Ricky, tall and elegant in a silk dressing gown, one hand thrust into his pocket. 'The breakfast shift's arrived,' he announced to no one in particular. 'Hello, Princess! Watch these flagstones by the porch here, they might be a bit slippy. Bleedin' hell, it's cold!'

'Well, get inside, then.' I tugged the sleeve of his dressing gown as I entered the hall. 'You'll freeze in this thin thing.'

'Noel Coward wore this, I'll have you know,' he sniffed as he shut out the cold behind me.

'Onstage, maybe.' I stamped my boots on the doormat and pulled off my gloves and hat. 'I bet even Noel Coward had a fleecy one in real life.'

He cackled with laughter. 'As to that, I couldn't say. Come on in. *Maurice* is getting busy with a fry-up.'

I stuck my head into the kitchen. Morris threw me a glance, his bald head shining, his gold specs sliding down his nose as he jiggled sizzling pans on the Aga.

'Hello, Juno love.'

The fair was not due to start for hours. I'd arrived in time for breakfast because, despite weeks of preparation, there were last-minute things to sort out. On our way through the hall, we passed rails hanging with Victorian clothes. Ricky and Morris have run a hire company for years, renting out costumes to theatrical groups, and their stock takes up most of the house. They're always busy during the panto season, but a low demand for *A Christmas Carol* this year meant the Victorian department had enough left to provide costumes for today's stallholders and volunteers. Ricky held up a full-skirted dress in a startling blue and green tartan. 'We thought this would do for you.'

I gaped at it in horror. 'You want me to spend all day in a crinoline?'

'Now we agreed, Juno,' Morris reminded me, calling from the kitchen, 'all volunteers would wear Victorian costume.'

'Can't I get away with a mob cap and a shawl?'

Ricky raised an eyebrow. 'Who do you think you are, some old washerwoman?'

'Oh, do try it on, Juno,' Morris pleaded, coming to the kitchen door and wiping his hands on his apron, 'it will look gorgeous with your red hair.'

'I'll try it after breakfast,' I said, praying it wouldn't

fit. But of course it would fit. Ricky and Morris know what'll fit me, just by looking.

As I sat at the table, Ricky slipped his first fag of the day between his lips.

'Not till after breakfast.' Morris brandished a fish slice in his direction. 'You promised.'

'Oh, all right, *Maurice*.' He sighed and put the cigarette away. 'Tea or coffee?' he asked me sulkily.

'Coffee, thanks.' I dragged my list of what we had left to do out from my shoulder bag and flattened it out on the table so we could study it over breakfast. It contained the names of all the traders and volunteers, stewards and raffle-ticket sellers. It may be the nerd in me, but I do love a list. I'd also sketched out a plan of the layout of pitches for people who would be setting up their own stalls outside in the grounds. Santa's Grotto would be in the little wooded area next to the lake. The lights were already strung up in the trees, a job that had taken three days. Now they were just waiting to be switched on.

'Have we got much left to do, Juno?' Morris asked anxiously, as he placed a loaded breakfast plate in front of me. I crunched into a triangle of hot buttered toast.

'We've got to put up those parking signs out in next door's field,' I muttered.

Ricky rose to his feet as the doorbell rang. 'Then let's hope that's another volunteer.'

It was two, as it happened. Olly charged into the kitchen, looking taller than when I'd seen him three days ago. But adolescent boys are like that, they grow in sudden spurts. He was taking off a cycling helmet, his little face pinched with cold, the tip of his nose and his sticky-out ears glowing scarlet.

'Hello, Juno!' he grinned.

'You're bright and early.'

'Chris called for me at home and we rode up on our bikes,' he answered, his eyes alight with excitement. 'It was great, but it wasn't half cold. I wish I had an e-bike like Chris.' He sat down at the table and pinched a piece of toast. 'I promised Pat I'll give her a hand setting up the animal pens when she gets here.' He began the construction of an elaborate triple-decker fried-egg sandwich, layered with brown sauce. 'Aunt Lizzy's coming later.'

Aunt Lizzy was my friend, Elizabeth.

Chris Brownlow strolled in then. The son of doctors whose house I clean once a week in my job as a Domestic Goddess, he was several years older than Olly and back from university for the holidays. He and Olly had appeared together in Ricky and Morris's production of *A Midsummer Night's Dream* back in the summer and were easy in one another's company.

'So, what do stewards have to do?' he asked as he sat down.

'Make sure people park their cars sensibly,' Morris called out as he bustled back into the kitchen.

'Yeh, and take money as people come in,' Ricky went on, 'then we need a few wandering about the grounds, pointing everyone in the direction of the loos, Santa's Grotto, and just keeping an eye on people.' He grinned,

'Make sure no one falls in the lake.'

After breakfast I gave into pressure and tried on my costume. I stood in front of the mirror in the hall whilst Ricky raked fussy fingers through my curls.

'Tried a comb this morning, have we?' he asked waspishly, squashing a black velvet cap on my head and tying the long ribbons under my chin. I slapped his hands away, tried taking a few steps and felt the whalebone cage of the crinoline sway ominously.

'I'm not sure I can move in this.' I had visions of falling over and rolling down the slope of the lawn, caged in a tartan puffball, unable to stop myself and ending up in the lake.

'You'll get the hang of it.' He handed me a pair of fingerless mittens. 'And the long petticoats will keep you warm.'

So they might, but I was still keeping my leggings and boots on underneath. 'I'll put it on later,' I told him as I began to wriggle out of the skirt. 'I can't shift stock in all this clobber.' Through the window I could see the sky was lightening and glanced at the grandfather clock in the hall. Time to get going.

'Yeh, buzz off,' Ricky recommended.

I had to get my stall set out. I trudged back and forth from my van, carrying boxes of stuff that might loosely be described as 'collectibles' and dumped them on my trestle table. I put Sophie's paintings and easels on the table next to mine. Like Pat, she works in my shop, manning it when I'm not there, in return for free

14

working and selling space. Poor Sophie, she works so hard, but like a lot of talented people, her talent doesn't translate itself into much cash. Pat would have her own stall, for her jewellery and handicrafts, as well as an information board about the work of Honeysuckle Farm, with photographs of all those animals patiently waiting for good homes.

Her old estate car was already bumping across the lawn, the back of it filled with creatures in cages. Pygmy goats, rabbits, guinea pigs, chickens and ducks would sit in pens on the lawn in a well-behaved fashion and form the petting zoo. With any luck, some of them would have found new homes by the end of the day.

'Don't forget you've got to get into costume,' I reminded her.

She sniffed, her nose red with cold. 'What's the point of dressing me up?' She rolled her watery blue eyes. 'Well, if I feel chilly, I'm going to put my coat on over the top of it, whatever it is.'

As I walked back to the house to change, a petite figure came skipping towards me: Sophie, her short hair concealed by a bonnet, her dark eyes shining with excitement. She'd also appeared in the Shakespeare production back in the summer, was still a bit stage-struck, and had obviously decided changing into costume was a more important priority than getting her stall laid out. She wore a short velvet cape trimmed with fur, her blue dress revealing inches of lacy petticoat and pretty buttoned boots. I stared at the boots with envy.

Why couldn't I have some like that? The simple answer, I mused sadly, is they probably don't make any large enough to fit a female who's six feet tall.

'Aren't they lovely?' she cooed, coquettishly pointing the toe of one foot to be admired.

'Lovely,' I agreed sourly as she danced towards the marquee. Ah well, the tartan crinoline awaits.

I saw a skinny figure in a patched tailcoat, his battered top hat set at a rakish angle, chatting to Pat's sister Sue, who'd driven up from the farm in a horsebox: Olly, looking like the Artful Dodger.

'School breaks up on Tuesday,' I heard him telling her. 'I'll come up the farm on Wednesday and give you a hand.'

'Volunteers always welcome, Olly,' she told him.

He loped over towards me. 'Buy a raffle ticket from a poor boy, lady,' he snivelled pathetically. 'Only a pound a strip and we got some lovely prizes.'

We certainly had, and they were being kept safely on display in the tea tent. Lady Margaret Westershall had asked some of her well-heeled friends to donate prizes and she can be a formidable woman to say no to when the mood takes her.

There was a penny whistle sticking up from Olly's pocket. 'Aren't you supposed to be playing carols?' I asked.

'Yeh, soon as the blokes on the squeeze box and fiddle arrive. They're not here yet.'

'Well, good luck.' I looked at my watch. The fair was

open to the public from twelve o'clock but our Local Celebrities, retired television stars Digby Jerkin and Amanda Waft, almost certainly wouldn't turn up to cut the ribbon before the last minute.

I needed to get a move on, into the dreaded crinoline and back to my post. I didn't anticipate selling much, or spending much of the day manning my stall. Elizabeth would watch it for me. Mine was more of a roving brief, keeping an eye on things. And it was my job to collect the stall money.

By now the sun was up, the sky was blue and except in the odd obstinate corner, the morning frost had melted away. I directed the Victorian Sweet Shop man to his pitch on the far side of the rose bed, his barrow packed with jars of humbugs, gobstoppers, sugar mice and anything else Victorian kids liked to rot their teeth with. Some of the food stalls had fired up, and the air was growing sweet with the smell of roasting chestnuts, hot spiced punch and minced pies. Christmas smells. I could see the tall, striped booth of the Punch and Judy man as he set up on the lawn. I was sure it was going to be a wonderful day. Which only goes to show, you can never tell what's coming.

CHAPTER TWO

I was just getting the hang of the crinoline when Bob the Blacksmith turned up. His name isn't really Bob, it's Jeff; but Jeff the Blacksmith doesn't have quite the same ring about it somehow. He'd named himself after a famous nineteenth-century boxer who packed such a powerful punch it was claimed he hid a horseshoe inside his boxing glove. Perhaps Jeff thought he could borrow some of his kudos. Whatever, he prefers to be called Bob. He works out of the back of a specially fitted van which includes a gas-fired forge, allowing him to ply his farrier's trade around the farms and stables of Dartmoor. Back at his forge, he and his wife make fancy iron goods like weathervanes and sundials, and run courses for students.

Today, Bob arrived on foot, leading a black horse pulling an old-fashioned wagon. He had bought and restored a genuine American Civil War forge wagon, circa 1861, as he would proudly tell anyone who asked. His considerable bulk was squeezed into the dark blue uniform of a Yankee soldier. His uniform and wagon might fit perfectly into our Victorian theme, but the sight of them both made me shudder. I don't like to think about horses going into war.

I gave him a wave as he approached and pointed across the grass to the pitch where I wanted him to set up his forge, on a stretch of flat lawn. It was a little way away from the rest of the fair, on the other side of the drive, but Bob had been the last trader to book a space for the day and it was the only pitch left that was big enough. At least he would be the first pitch people saw on their way into the grounds and the last on the way out.

His wagon was followed by a van packed with goods for sale. The driver, it turned out, was not another Yankee soldier as first appeared, but Bob's wife Jackie, tendrils of black hair escaping from her soldier's cap, a Celtic iron cross dangling from one ear. I wondered if she'd forged it herself.

'D'you mind parking the van in the field next door once you've unloaded?' I asked and she gave me a thumbs up. Bob brought his horse and wagon to a halt and wavered slightly, grinning at me inanely from the depths of his bushy black beard.

'Is he all right?' I muttered to Jackie. 'He seems a bit . . . um . . .'

'He's been celebrating,' she laughed softly. 'It's his birthday.'

'He's not drunk, is he?' The thought of Bob drunk in charge of red-hot coals and sharp tools was not a comforting one, especially with members of the public about.

We watched him fumbling with the horse's bridle and

Jackie grinned. 'Nah, he'll be all right, you'll see,' she said, regarding him affectionately. 'Good as gold, my Bob.'

I wasn't sure I believed her, but I left them both to set up whilst I did a tour of the grounds, making sure traders arriving had all they needed. I almost didn't recognise Pat, in a high-necked gown and shawl, hair demurely concealed under a mob cap. Morris had finished making breakfasts apparently, because he was now walking about dressed as Mr Pickwick.

'Everything looks splendid, Juno, love.' He drew a gold pocket watch from his waistcoat and consulted it. 'All we need now is for the public to arrive.'

I glanced down the drive towards the gates where two stewards were waiting at a table to take the price of admission and realised what I'd forgotten. 'I've got to give them their float and make sure the credit card machine is working.' Admission to the fair might only be a pound, but you could bet some awkward bastard would want to pay by card.

'You go down there and check on the machine, my love,' Morris told me. 'I'll fetch the cash box. It's locked up in the kitchen.'

As I hurried down the drive, trying not to trip over my crinoline, a camper van swept in through the gates and drew to a halt right next to me, crunching on the gravel and sending up a spray of tiny stones.

'Sorry we're late!' Fizzy Izzy gave me a breathless smile as she stuck her head out of the window. She had a stall in the gift tent. The camper was being driven by her husband, Don.

I don't like Don much. He and I got off to a bad start. Fizz used to rent space at *Old Nick's*, and like me, she's tall with red hair. There the resemblance ends, but it was enough to get her mistaken for me and she nearly got murdered as a consequence. Fizz bears me no grudge whatsoever, unlike her husband. Don's resentment is understandable and I'm probably better off giving him a wide berth; but his hobby is woodturning, he produces fine work, and frankly, anyone who was prepared to cough up the fee for a stall today was welcome. Right now, though, he looked like thunder.

He leant across Fizz from the driver's seat and beckoned me close, glaring at me from fierce blue eyes, and jerked an aggressive thumb at where Bob was busy setting up his forge. 'What's that tosser doing here?' he demanded.

'Same as everyone else, I expect, here to sell his stuff. Why, is there a problem?'

'I've worked a few craft fairs he's been at,' he said with something like snarl, 'and he's always trouble. I don't like his attitude.'

I don't like yours either, I thought, but I ignored the waves of rampant hostility emanating in my direction, gave what I hoped was a serene smile and pointed him in the direction of the gift tent. 'You can drive up to the entrance to unload your stuff, and then if you don't mind, could you park—'

I didn't get to finish what I was saying. With a grinding of gears, the camper jerked forwards and off towards the tent, leaving me still pointing.

Morris arrived at my elbow, puffing slightly, cash box in

hand. 'Everything all right?' he asked.

'Of course,' I told him, although at that particular moment I couldn't swear to it. I tucked my arm in his and we strolled down to the gate together.

Between us, the stewards and I worked out that the credit card-reader was functioning. Chris Brownlow jogged by in a brightly coloured steward's coat, on his way to the car-parking field. He grinned at Morris. 'Can I keep this coat, after?'

I peeled back a fingerless mitten to peer at my watch. 'Aren't Amanda and Digby here yet?' There were only a few minutes to go before they were supposed to make their grand entrance.

'It won't matter,' Morris confided. 'They've already got their costumes. We sorted them out earlier in the week. Amanda wanted to choose hers herself.'

I laughed. 'I bet.'

'She's a vision in pink,' he added, giving me a sly nudge.

'Well, let's hope she's sober. I've already got my doubts about Bob the Blacksmith.'

His brow wrinkled in an anxious frown. 'Really?'

Ricky sauntered in our direction, dressed in a top hat and frock coat and twirling a silver-topped walking stick. 'What's up?'

'Juno was just saying she thinks Bob might be drunk.'

'Well, getting that way,' I said. 'It's his birthday, apparently.'

Ricky's eyes narrowed as he watched Bob staggering across the grass under the weight of an anvil, his mighty arms bent around it, clutching it close to his chest like a lover. He set it down on the ground with a grunt, then picked up a stone cider flagon and took a swig. 'We'll ask the stewards to keep an eye on him.' He smiled suddenly, pointing his walking stick towards a knot of people heading up the drive from the gate. 'Looks like our public is starting to arrive.'

It was another hour and a half before Digby and Amanda made their grand entrance, by which time, if the public wasn't exactly pouring in, at least there was a steady trickle.

Amanda swept in like a galleon in full sail, in an enormous pink crinoline. She had twisted her hair into ringlets, her face framed by a bonnet with curling ostrich feathers, tied becomingly beneath the chin with a cluster of ribbons. As with everything she wore, this would have looked better on a younger woman. She seemed to be carrying a polar bear wrapped around one arm, but this turned out to be a large fur muff. With the other hand she clung to Digby, her faithful swain, looking handsome and distinguished in a frock coat and beaver hat with a curling brim. To what extent he was actually holding Amanda upright wasn't apparent to the casual onlooker. But it was, I reminded myself cynically, still early in the day.

Morris watched as they made their way through a knot of clapping onlookers to a small platform especially set up for them. 'That's not our muff she's carrying, is it?' he asked.

'I've never seen it before,' I admitted.

Ricky grunted. 'Must be her own, then.'

Digby, his fruity voice slightly disembodied by a microphone, was giving a speech about how honoured he and Amanda were at being asked to open the fair, reminding everyone it was for a very worthy cause, and encouraging them to spend generously.

'Where'd they dig these two up from?' a girl in front of me whispered. 'Who are they?'

'They used to be on the telly, years ago,' her mother told her. 'Some sit-com, it was. Pair of old has-beens, if you ask me.'

Whilst this assessment was undoubtedly accurate, it was also a bit unfair. Digby and Amanda still have lots of fans, although most of them live in retirement homes by now. And even today there is probably a TV channel somewhere endlessly running repeats of *There's Only Room for Two*. I dared a glance at Ricky. He grinned at me and winked.

Amanda stepped forward, whipping a large pair of scissors from the confines of her muff, and with a little assistance from Digby, managed to cut the ribbon. 'I declare this fair open,' she announced graciously, ignoring the fact it had already been going strong for an hour and a half. 'Please, all of you, have a wonderful day,' she added, and threw the onlookers an airy kiss.

The three musicians struck up with 'Deck the Halls with Boughs of Holly' as Amanda handed the scissors to a waiting Digby and allowed Morris to lead them both over to the vendor of mulled wine for some much-needed refreshment. This would be the first stop on their tour of the fair. I decided I might tag along. That muff was worrying me.

CHAPTER THREE

I thought I'd better check in at the gift tent first. I hadn't been inside since I'd set my stall up and was relying on Sophie, Elizabeth or fellow antiques dealer Vicky to cope if I had any customers. It was already getting busy. Half of the tent was occupied by a children's workshop, a long table full of kids making Christmas decorations. Some of them were really getting into it, their clothes and hair smeared with glue and sparkling with glitter. A small gathering of people was listening to Pat talking about the animal sanctuary, and how the adoption scheme worked. 'Adopt one of our animals today,' she was telling them, in the slow deliberate voice of one who is trying to remember a script, 'and for a small sum each month, you will receive photographs, regular updates and a VIP pass to the farm to visit your adopted pet whenever you like. And o' course,' she added, coming off script completely, 'this makes a lovely Christmas present for the awkward bugger you don't know what to buy for.'

I needn't have worried about my stall. Elizabeth, Olly's

Aunt Lizzy, who helps out in *Old Nick's* now and again, had already arrived. Vicky seemed to be explaining to her the finer points of the stock laid out on my table. I wished I had time to stop and listen. She knows far more about the stuff I'm selling than I do. Looking at the two of them together, I realised how alike they were: both in their sixties, slim, elegant and silver-haired. Although Vicky's bobbed hair and long skirts were more relaxed in style than Elizabeth's usually smartly tailored appearance. Today, though, they were both in crinolines – Vicky in purple with a wide collar and cameo brooch at her throat, Elizabeth in a silver-grey with deep lace cuffs. Neither of them had been saddled with tartan, I noticed.

'You've just made your first sale of the day,' Elizabeth informed me with a smile. 'A little jug,' she indicated its size between her palms. 'Blue and brown.'

'Torquay pottery,' Vicky added with a twinkle. 'Hello, Juno.'

I knew the jug they meant. Not exactly a big sale, but better than nothing. 'Thank you, ladies,' I said. 'I'll be back later. Keep up the good work.'

Ricky and Morris would be busy shepherding dignitaries and chatting up potential donors all day, so I'd been given the job of visiting each of the stalls to collect fees; but I decided I'd let everyone settle down and make some sales first. There was plenty of time. Besides, I was on a mission.

Amanda and Digby hadn't made it into the gift tent; they were still outside. I needed to find them if I was to keep tabs on Amanda. I raised the edge of my crinoline to stop it dragging on the grass and hurried around a knot of families admiring the animals in the petting zoo, one little girl gently cuddling a duck in her arms. I glimpsed Amanda, her pink crinoline surrounding her, looking like a Barbie doll stuck in a blancmange. She was still attached to Digby's arm, listening with politely feigned interest to Bob the Blacksmith. He had shed his jacket, tied on a leather apron, and was holding forth in a loud voice about his war wagon.

'The coal box is at the back,' he said, laying a hand upon it. 'The bellows are inside the wagon and are pumped by this handle. The air is then piped through into the firebox at the front. Today, mind, I shall be using a furnace powered by bottled gas' – he pointed to the forge he had set up, looking like an antique barbeque, a basket of glowing red coals balanced on a sturdy oak barrel – 'for the simple reason it's quicker to get going, and the missus doesn't like having to pump these bellows all day long.' He laughed and the crowd laughed with him. There was no denying that Bob was an entertaining speaker. There was also no denying that, at this particular moment, his speech was ever-so-slightly slurred. Jackie was watching him keenly, standing in front of display boards hanging with barbeque tools, pokers, key rings and medieval-looking pendants on leather thongs – all items which the public could buy, or have a go at forging for themselves. There were also daggers, swords and axe heads I hoped no one would want to have a go at.

Whilst Bob's diction might be blurring around the edges, it didn't stop his flow. 'Now then, why do blacksmiths go to war?' he asked. 'To mend tools and weapons,' he went on before anyone had a chance to answer, 'but mostly because of these.' He held up an iron horseshoe in his ham-like fist. 'Horseshoes. And if any of you want, you can make a lucky horseshoe here today. Now, the horse doesn't feel a thing when his new shoe is fitted,' he went on, 'but we would, if we grabbed one of these shoes when it was red-hot, wouldn't we?' He pulled a long, pointed chisel from his tool belt. 'This 'ere is called a *pritchel*, ladies and gentlemen, and it has a very fine point' – he demonstrated by touching it with a thick, sausage-like finger – 'and this fits precisely into the holes on the horseshoe, allowing the blacksmith to carry the shoe from the forge and present it flat to the horse's hoof . . .'

By now, Amanda had had enough of smithing and drifted away with Digby towards the gift tent, dutifully stopping to coo over the animals in their pens on the way. I stuck close behind her. Apart from Digby, I was probably the only person who knew Amanda had form. She'd once been arrested for shoplifting, and although that was many years ago, I knew her kleptomaniac tendencies hadn't left her. She usually confined her light-fingered activities to the goods in my shop, but I was convinced the crowded tent with stalls crammed full of goodies would be too much temptation for her. I didn't want anyone getting robbed, but equally, I didn't want her getting caught. It would be a terrible humiliation for her and poor Digby, who suffered enough in my opinion, and would undoubtedly ruin the day. Also, I'd just glimpsed the burly figure of Detective Constable Dean Collins coming in the gate with his young family. He might be off duty, but if a crime was committed, he'd feel obliged to arrest the perpetrator. Worse, I'd seen Evie from the *Dartmoor Gazette*, her camera slung around her neck, here to cover the event for the local newspaper. I could just imagine the headlines if our Local Celebrities were Involved in a Nasty Occurrence. No, preventing crime before it happened was the only option as far as I was concerned. I was going to stick to Amanda like glue.

Unfortunately, I got stopped on my way into the tent by the arrival of Lady Margaret Westershall and her two bulldogs, Florence and Wesley. It wasn't so much her bearing down on me with a loud hail of 'Juno, my dear!' that impeded my movement, as an excited Wesley diving under my crinoline and nearly knocking me off my feet. Lady Margaret had been generous, not only in contributing funds for the fair, but in cajoling her contacts in various charitable organisations to provide lavish raffle prizes. I disentangled Wesley from my petticoats as I thanked her for all she'd done.

'Nonsense, the least I can do,' she responded briskly.

'The raffle prizes are superb,' I told her. 'We're selling lots of tickets.'

'Excellent.' She patted my arm. 'You look like a cat on hot bricks, my dear. I expect you've got loads to do. You carry on. Wesley, Florence and I are going into the tea tent for a spot of lunch. See you later.'

I didn't wait around to watch her go but plunged into the marquee. Digby and Amanda were standing by a stall selling handmade soaps and candles. Then, to my horror, I saw them stop at Don Drummond's table. *Please, please,* I prayed silently, *do not try to steal anything from Don Drummond.* He had beechwood platters and ash bowls on his table, too large to be picked up without notice, but I could also see bowls of wooden light-pulls and turned drawer knobs, and other items small enough to delight the pilfering finger. I tried to edge closer, but the tent was full by now, and squeezing through a crowd whilst wearing a tent of your own is not an easy matter. Muttering apologies, I forced my crinoline between members of the public. Amanda was as light-fingered and skilled as any Victorian pickpocket; I'd seen her at work before and knew what to look for. I saw that familiar movement, a quick whisk of her fingers and *something* disappeared inside her capacious muff.

Unfortunately, I wasn't the only one to spot the movement. Eagle-eyed Don Drummond had noticed it too. 'What did you do just then?' he demanded, glaring at Amanda.

She blinked at him like a startled owl. 'I beg your pardon?'

'You did something,' he insisted. 'Put something in that muff.'

'I'm afraid I don't know what you're talking about,'

she responded, her free hand fluttering nervously for a moment at her breast.

'I want to see what's inside.' He held out a hand, waggling his fingers as if he expected her to hand it over.

But Amanda was not an actress for nothing. She drew herself up to her full height and gave him her best haughty stare. She does a very good one, looks at people as if she'd only handle them with tongs. 'I don't know what you're implying,' she said.

'You know damn well what I'm implying.'

All around them the tent was falling silent. There was only one thing to do, and I had to do it fast. I trod on the hem of my crinoline and pretended to stumble, launching myself forward and reaching out with both arms to save myself. One hand caught at the edge of Don Drummond's table. I grabbed at the cloth covering it and pulled, dragging the bowls of small objects forward, upsetting them and tipping them over the edge. A cascade of small wooden knobs spilt everywhere. With my other hand I grabbed at Amanda's muff and managed to drag it from her sleeve before collapsing on the ground in a mushrooming cloud of tartan crinoline. 'Oh dear!' I cried out loudly as I fell. 'Oh, I'm so sorry!' I slid my hand into the muff's silk lining and my fingers closed on three small objects. One felt like a wooden drawer knob. I closed my fingers tightly around the rest and clutched them in my hand as Ricky, eyes narrowed in suspicion, stooped to help me up. Digby, meanwhile, was fussing around Amanda. 'I'm so sorry Amanda,' I exclaimed as I was hauled to my feet. 'I didn't hurt you, did I?'

'No, of course not,' she answered coolly.

'Don, was there some sort of problem?' I asked innocently. I held out the muff. 'Did you want to see this?'

Without a word he snatched it from me and plunged his hand inside. His fingers finding nothing, he glowered at me and then thrust the muff back at Amanda. He said nothing but I could see a pulse of anger beating in his cheek. He's not the sort of man to like being made a fool of.

Sophie, being a helpful sort, had hurried out from behind her table and begun picking up the fallen drawer knobs. She placed a handful on the cloth I had so clumsily disarranged and began to smooth it out. 'There,' she said innocently.

'Are you all right, Mandy?' Digby asked solicitously. 'And you, Juno, you didn't hurt yourself?'

'Only my dignity,' I assured him. 'Why don't you and Amanda go and visit the tea tent?' And for God's sake keep her away from the raffle prizes, I added privately.

'Good idea!' he agreed as Amanda slid the muff back on to her arm. He turned to Don. 'No damage done is there, old chap?' he asked. 'Nothing broken?'

'No,' Don answered between gritted teeth. 'Nothing broken.'

'What the hell was all that about?' Ricky muttered as Amanda and Digby glided away.

'Just me tripping over this damn crinoline you've made me wear.'

Ricky's not easily fooled. He eyed me for a moment,

clearly disbelieving, but decided to let it go, shook his head and walked on. I turned away and slyly opened my fingers to take a look at the tiny objects digging into my palm: a silver spoon, which I knew belonged to a mustard pot on Vicky's table, an old WWI service medal and a wooden drawer knob. What on earth could Amanda want with this odd assortment? Nothing, was the answer. She was driven by the compulsion to steal. It seemed it didn't matter what.

'Sorry,' I said, returning the spoon to Vicky. 'I must have knocked this off your table when I fell.' This clearly could not have been possible, but she made no comment, receiving the spoon with thanks and a bemused smile. I dropped the old WWI medal back on my own table, where it had come from. Elizabeth gave me a quizzical look but said nothing.

'Oh look!' I cried, bending down and pretending to pick something up from the ground. 'it's one of your drawer knobs, Don.' I placed the one I'd palmed from the muff down on his table with a smile. He didn't say anything either. Not even thank you.

The rest of the afternoon passed without incident, plenty of visitors arriving and tucking into the various eats on sale or making their way to the tea tent. By the middle of the afternoon the gift tent was heaving, with good sales reported by everyone inside. At the petting zoo, several guinea pigs had been earmarked for rehoming, Sue informed me happily, once they had been coaxed out of hiding under their straw.

I saw Dean Collin's eldest child, my little god-daughter Alice, her chubby legs astride the saddle of Maureen the donkey, shrieking with delight as the animal plodded along, Sue leading her, her father walking alongside holding her firmly in place on the saddle. Her baby sister, born on Hallowe'en, was wrapped up in a sling on her mother's chest, snug as a pea in a pod, only the fuzzy bobble of her hat visible to the naked eye. I waved to them, but didn't stop. I was clutching my clipboard with the list of stallholders, a bag of change and a receipt book, ready to take their money. It would take a while to get around all of them and I thought I'd start with Bob the Blacksmith, whilst he was still sober.

He was still on his feet, anyway, intently watching as a customer in leather gauntlets, his face half hidden by protective goggles, was striking at a piece of red-hot metal on the anvil, sending up glowing sparks. 'That's my dad,' a child in the crowd of onlookers pointed proudly.

'What's he making?' I asked.

'A sausage sizzler, for the barbecue.'

Bob felt it necessary to take over from dad at this point, hammered the metal with far more forceful blows and then returned it to the red-hot coals of the forge using tongs. He staggered slightly as he stepped back, bending to pick up his stone flagon from the grass and taking a lengthy swig. 'Thirsty work,' he nodded to the crowd as he wiped a hand across his mouth. There was a ripple of slightly uncomfortable laughter. After a few moments he withdrew the irons from the brazier, put them back on the anvil and handed the tongs to the customer. 'Give the end another bashing,' he recommended.

Satisfied Bob was still under Jackie's watchful eye, I collected the pitch money from her, wrote out a business receipt, then trailed my horrible crinoline back over the grass towards the food stalls. It seemed like a long time since breakfast and I was feeling peckish. A mince pie would go down nicely. I bumped into Ricky, apparently on his way to the loo. He grabbed my arm. 'Mandy up to her old tricks again?' he murmured, 'in the gift tent?'

I blinked at him for a moment. 'I didn't think you knew.'

'Oh, come on! Every time she and Digby come to the house another ornament goes missing.'

'Have you ever said anything?'

'Nah! Not worth it. Poor old Diggers, we wouldn't want to upset him. His life must be a nightmare as it is.' He tapped his hat in a mock salute as he hurried away. 'Must go,' he said. 'Carry on.'

As the afternoon sun was sinking lower, the air was turning chilly. I arrived at Neil and Carol's cider stall. They owned orchards at their farm near Widecombe. Dressed in old-fashioned farmers' smocks, breeches and floppy hats, their gloved hands were wrapped around styrofoam cups of steaming coffee.

'You will come to our wassail in January, won't you?' Carol asked. 'We're blessing the orchards, although,' she added with an uncertain smile, 'it is a pagan ritual, so I'm not sure if *blessing* is the right word.'

'It's just a laugh,' Neil told me, 'an excuse for drinking and dressing up.'

'Well, I'm all for that,' I said. 'I'd love to come.' I noticed some stone flagons on their stall. 'Did you sell one of those to Bob the Blacksmith earlier?'

He grinned. 'He was our first customer of the day. He hasn't started drinking it already, has he?'

'Afraid so. It's his birthday, apparently. Mind you, I think he'd already had a few before he left home.'

Neil laughed and shook his head. 'He's an idiot. Trouble is, he can get bolshy when he's drunk. He got into a fight with a fella at an agricultural fair back in the summer.'

'A fight? You mean proper fisticuffs?'

'Me and a few other guys had to pull them apart.' He nodded his head in the direction of the gift tent. 'He's in there, the bloke he fought with, I saw him when I went in for a look around.'

'Let me guess, Don Drummond?'

'The woodturner?'

'That's the fella!' I nodded. 'What were they fighting about?'

'God knows! Never found out, but they each blamed the other one for starting it.'

'Men!' Carol tutted, laughing. 'They're all the same.'

This earned her an astonished look from her husband. 'Excuse me?'

I decided it was time to leave them to their coffee and headed for the man with the barrow of Victorian sweets.

I'd like to have known more about Bob and Don's fight, though. From my very slight knowledge, I'd have said Don was the more aggressive of the two, more likely to start a fight, and Bob, the stronger one, more likely to finish it.

As the darkness of a winter afternoon closed in, the sky fading from blue to indigo, will-o-the-wisp lights twinkled in the wood and sparkled on the black water of the lake. At exactly four o'clock Father Christmas arrived on the cart drawn by Nosbert the steadfast carthorse, driven by Pat's brother-in-law, Ken, the bells on the harness jingling festively.

I wouldn't have recognised Morris. Apart from a magnificent scarlet robe and false beard, a wig of luxuriant silver curls covered his bald head and a Christmas crown, a wreath of holly and mistletoe twined with ivy, was set upon his brow. Waving and ho-ho-ho-ing, he rode down to his grotto, followed by a gaggle of excited children dragging their parents. At around the same time, Digby's voice came over the sound system, asking all those visiting Father Christmas in his grotto to stick to the lantern-lit path, as the garden was steep in places and we didn't want any accidents in the dark. He also announced that he and Amanda would shortly draw the raffle tickets and winners could collect their prizes from the tea tent. And finally, anyone who fancied a good old Christmas sing-song, please go down to the lake where a carol concert would be starting shortly, under the baton of Professor Jingle.

Professor Jingle, otherwise known as Ricky, would be

conducting from the keyboard of an ancient upright piano, which had been rolled out from somewhere, accompanied by the three roving musicians on accordion and fiddle, Olly swopping the penny whistle for his bassoon.

I wanted to go down and join in, but I still had money to collect.

The gift tent looked deserted now, most of the children dumping their Christmas decorations in favour of the trip to Santa. But the traders had taken enough money to keep them in festive spirit. Even Don had a smile on his face. He'd taken a commission from Neil and Carol apparently, who'd asked him to turn a special wooden drinking bowl for their wassail in January. The ladies of the antiques team, Elizabeth and Vicky, had deserted their posts and gone to the tea tent along with Sophie, leaving Vicky's husband Tom to man the stalls single-handedly.

After I'd finished taking stall money, I headed back to the house. I had Morris's spare back-door key hidden inside my mitten, ready to let myself in. Pat hurried after me so she could come in and change out of her costume. The residents of the petting zoo were caged up and she wanted to take them back to warmer quarters at the farm.

'We can't leave 'em out here now night's fallen. Thanks ever so much for organising all this, Juno,' she added. 'It's been wonderful.'

'It's Ricky and Morris you need to thank, I just had the idea.'

'I know, but it still wouldn't have happened without you.'

'It's not over yet.' The money from admission and raffle tickets would be going to the farm too. We were looking forward to counting up all the takings later.

'I'll come back here as soon as I've settled the animals down.' Pat hung up her dress and shrugged herself back into her old jacket. 'And I'll pack up my stall. Thanks for bringing my stuff from the shop this morning.'

'You had the animals to think about and I had to fetch mine and Soph's anyway.'

I followed her out of the house, locking the door behind me. As I came around to the front, I almost collided with one of the stewards holding a lantern.

'I don't think anyone else will be coming in through the gate now,' he said, 'so there's not much point hanging around.'

He was right. The public were already beginning to drift away and I knew the stallholders would start packing up soon. He handed me the cash box and credit card-reader. 'We've had a fair few in, though.' He rubbed his hands together. 'I'm going to catch a cuppa in that tea tent before I go home.'

I returned a pleasingly heavy cash box to the kitchen. It seemed the card-reader hadn't been needed much. Whilst I was inside the house, I changed back into my own clothes. There was really no point in staying in the stupid crinoline any longer. I wriggled out of it and hung it up, glad to see the back of it.

It was fully dark by now. A string of lanterns cast their light on the path leading down to the grotto. Families were still queuing to see Santa. At the back of the queue, I could make out the distant but unmistakeable figure of Dean Collins, carrying little Alice.

I looked behind me. The coals from Bob's forge glowed red in the darkness, although there was no sign of him. Perhaps he and Jackie had gone down the garden to join the carol singers, or to fetch their horse who had spent the day down in the paddock by the lake. 'God Rest Ye Merry, Gentlemen' started up from the far end of the garden. I gazed up at the dark sky, at the sharp icy splinter of a bright evening star. All we need now, I told it longingly, is snow.

Looking back on it, I wonder what might have happened if I hadn't gone down to join the carol singers. If it would have made any difference. As it was, I walked down the steep slope of the lawn, guided by the light from the lanterns, thankful I wasn't still wearing that damned crinoline. But I had to admit the carol singers looked lovely in their costumes. Sophie, Vicky, Elizabeth and Amanda were gathered together in a group, Digby holding a lantern raised over their heads. They could have come straight off a Christmas card.

As Santa's queue dwindled, the choir of singers swelled, parents bringing their children over to join in, including Dean Collins, who turned out to have a very decent baritone. I looked around for Lady Margaret and her two bulldogs, but she must have gone. I learnt later she had stayed only until the raffle had been drawn, just to satisfy herself the prizes were up to scratch, then declared she was off home to have a gin and put her feet up. I found I was standing next to Jackie. 'Bob not coming down for a sing-song?' I asked.

She smiled, raising her voice above 'We Three Kings', 'He's dealing with a last-minute customer. Some fella wanted to buy a Christmas present.'

The last child in the queue had received a present from his sack, so Father Christmas himself came to join in the singing. It was all joyful, festive and merry. There was only one thing missing, or rather one person: Daniel, my recently lost lover. I had no idea where he was at that moment, or how he might be faring, I just knew I missed him. I blinked the thought of him away.

'Excuse me.' One of the caterers from the tea tent was standing next to me. 'We've just packed everything away. As Ricky and Morris are busy, could we give the account to you?'

Reluctantly, I dragged myself away from the carols and accompanied her back up the garden to the light of the tea tent where she gave me the bill for their services. The catering corps had been hard at it, serving up huge numbers of turkey sandwiches and mince pies all through the day. I gaped at the amount that had been consumed. 'Do you want me to settle up now?'

'If you wouldn't mind.'

I walked back to the house, let myself in, extracted the necessary cash, locked up again and went back to the tea tent where I paid the lady, asked her to sign the receipt, then took it back into the house and put it in the cash box with the money. What with catering and lighting and hiring the marquees, the day must be costing Ricky and Morris a fortune. And I knew they wouldn't accept a penny in expenses, because doing so would take money from the farm. I felt a sudden stab of guilt. Because they hadn't held the fair only to help Pat and the animals. They'd done it for me, because I'd asked them.

People were already leaving, carrying raffle prizes and tiny children who should already be in bed. In the gift tent, the stallholders were packing up too, Fizz and Don carefully wrapping things in bubble wrap. Pat had returned as she had promised and was boxing up her own stuff.

'I'll keep an eye on your things and Sophie's,' she promised, nodding in the direction of our two tables, 'until you come back. I'll pack your stuff up for you, if you want.'

'You'll do no such thing,' I told her. 'You've had a long day. You need to go home. Don't worry about my stuff, I'll be back in a few minutes.'

I went out back into the garden because something was niggling at me, something I'd noticed during my trips back and forth to the house, but which hadn't consciously registered. The drive was in blackness. There should have been lanterns shining, lighting the way, and there was no light at all. Unlike the string of lanterns that lit the path to the grotto, and were wired into the system, these lanterns were battery-powered, so they could be carried about. I knew the batteries had been checked this morning, I'd watched Ricky doing it; which meant these lanterns had been switched off. Who would have done such a stupid thing? The only light was the red glow coming from the coals of Bob's forge. But there was no sign of Bob, or anyone else. His last-minute customer must have gone. Would he have left the forge unattended, still burning?

I crossed the grass, grabbed a lantern from the nearest empty stall and walked back. The display boards were still up. I'd seen Jackie down at the carol concert. I didn't think she would have left goods on display for anyone to help themselves to, especially the weapons. So presumably, Bob was meant to be here. Perhaps he'd fallen down drunk.

I called his name, holding up the lantern. There was no response, so I yelled a little louder. 'Bob?' I moved in closer, holding up the lantern to light my way. The anvil was around here somewhere and I didn't want to bump into the damn thing or trip over his blasted cider flagon.

What I nearly tripped over was Bob himself. He was sitting bolt upright, his back against the anvil, dead asleep. I shone the lantern on him and felt my stomach clench in a sick knot. For what seemed like a long moment I felt frozen, unable to move. Then, slowly, I lowered myself to a crouch and held the light closer. Bob's head was resting against the anvil, his eyes closed. A trail of blood, black in the orange lantern glow, had flowed over his neck and shoulders and on to the leather of his apron. I felt for a pulse at his wrist. There was none.

Feeling queasy, I stood up and backed away. There

was a sudden noise, a rustling close by.

I swung the lantern around, straining to see into the blackness. 'Hello?' I called. There was no answer. But it came again, the rustling sound. Someone, something, was moving in the darkness, moving fast. I held the lantern up, peered at the thick, dark mass of shrubbery between the drive and the garden wall. 'Is anyone there?'

Suddenly, a light was bobbing up the drive towards me and I could make out the bright colours of a steward's coat. 'Hey!' I called out, my voice gone suddenly wobbly. I ran towards the approaching figure, my breath coming in little gasps as I ran.

It was Chris Brownlow who called back. 'Juno?' He slowed to a stop. 'Are you okay?'

I grabbed his arm. For a moment I couldn't speak.

'What's up?' he asked. 'You're shaking.'

'Did you see anyone just now?'

'Where? What do you mean?'

'Anyone, going out down the drive?'

'There've been a few people coming out. Why?'

'It's Bob,' I managed at last. 'He's dead.'

'Dead? Are you sure?' He took a step towards the forge, but I put a hand against his chest, holding him back. 'Don't. There's nothing you can do . . . I think he fell, hit his head against the anvil . . .' I took a breath. 'Listen, you know Dean Collins? The policeman? He's down there, singing carols . . . I want you to . . . I'll stay here, guard the . . . guard Bob. I want you to find Dean and bring him back here. Discreetly. Don't let anyone else come . . . don't let him bring his family. And don't let Jackie hear you. Tell him, there's been—'

'Shouldn't we phone for an ambulance?' Chris interrupted.

'In a minute. Get Dean up here now. Tell him there's been an accident.'

I watched him run off down the slope of the lawn, then turned back to where Bob lay. I couldn't leave him, couldn't risk anyone else coming up here and stumbling upon him.

I crouched again and shone the lantern over his body. There were gouge marks on the chest of his leather apron and a scattering of small, bloody punctures around his collarbone. He didn't get those in a fall. He was clutching an iron horseshoe, his fists gripped round either end. If he'd been holding it when he'd fallen, wouldn't he have let go of it, at least with one hand, reached out to try to save himself? Unless someone placed the horseshoe in his hands afterwards. There was something else, a small sprig shoved through one of the nail holes, a few shrivelled flowers hanging from one end. I stood up, shone the lantern around me, still nervous about that rustling in the dark.

Feet pounded across the gravel path behind me, keys jingling in a pocket with each step. I turned in time to see Dean Collins, Chris following close behind.

'What's up, Juno?' he asked, stopping a moment to catch his breath after his run up the steep lawn. 'Chris says there's been an accident.'

'I don't think it is an accident.' I tried to stop the lantern from trembling in my hand. 'I think it's murder.'

CHAPTER FOUR

Detective Inspector Ford stirred his coffee with slow deliberation, laying the spoon gently in the delicate porcelain saucer before looking up at me from beneath his jutting, sandy brows. He sighed as he sat back and stared down the gleaming mahogany surface of Ricky and Morris's dining table. The interview was taking place in their formal dining room. Members of the public had gone, directed away from the fair by uniformed officers. Dean Collins had secured the scene of the crime. The volunteers and stallholders, their names and phone numbers taken, had been allowed to change out of their costumes and go home. All anyone had been told was there had been a tragic accident. Even Jackie, shocked into a frozen stillness more worrying than any sobbing, had been told the same. She had not been allowed to see her husband's body but had been driven home by a family liaison officer, where a doctor would attend. Accident was what she'd been told, what everyone had been told. Only the police and I knew any different. And the murderer of course.

'Now, Juno, can we go through this all once more, please?' the inspector said at last. 'Start when you first went back into the house.'

'I went in to put the stallholders' money away. Pat came with me. She wanted to change her clothes. Then I came out . . .'

'Did you and Miss Giddings leave the house together?'

'Yes. But Pat went to the car park to fetch her car so she could take the animals home.'

'She walked down the drive?'

'Yes, that's where I saw the steward. He was coming to give me the admission takings.'

'And you stopped and had a conversation.'

'Briefly.'

'You must have been quite close to Bob Millard's forge at this point. His pitch is right by the drive. Neither you nor this steward . . .' he paused and looked down at my list of names, spread out on the table before him.

'I think his name is Joe,' I said, trying to be helpful.

'Ah yes.' He tapped at a name with his forefinger. 'You and this Joe didn't notice anything amiss at the time?'

'I certainly didn't notice a murder going on.'

The inspector frowned and sipped his coffee.

'Sorry,' I went on, 'that sounded trite. No, I didn't notice anything. I must have been aware of the darkness, but Joe was holding the lantern up quite close to our faces, and I couldn't really see anything beyond it, if you know what I mean. I didn't register that Bob wasn't around until I came out for the second time.'

'You went back into the house?'

'Yes, with the money Joe had given me. He went off towards the tea tent. I put the money in the kitchen and stopped to change my clothes.'

'How long do you think you were indoors?'

How long had it taken me to wriggle out of that damn crinoline and hang it up? 'A few minutes, I suppose. Five, not much more.'

'And when you came out, you noticed neither Bob nor Jackie Millard were on their pitch?'

'I couldn't see them. I thought they might have gone down to the bottom of the garden to join in the carols, or perhaps to the paddock to fetch their horse.'

The inspector turned to Detective Sergeant deVille, seated at his elbow, primly taking notes.

'Have we resolved the problem of the horse, Sergeant?'

She looked up, favouring me with a brief glance of loathing from her violet-coloured eyes. 'Yes, sir. Mr Ken Roach is returning with a horse box and will stable the animal at Honeysuckle Farm until Mrs Millard is ready to have it returned to her.'

'Excellent.'

Cruella looked smug, as if it had been her idea, not Pat's.

The inspector rubbed his chin. 'I can't help wondering what these stewards were up to. Shouldn't they have been making sure everywhere was well-lit?'

'To be fair, people were beginning to drift away,' I

said. 'They were probably concentrating on the car park, lighting the way across the field for people to get to their cars safely. And I know two of them were down in the grotto, making sure everyone kept to the path.'

'Apart, that is, from his friend Joe, who'd nipped off for a cup of tea.' The inspector was thoughtful for a moment. 'How are these lanterns powered, anyway?'

'Batteries. The candle flame looks realistic but you can turn it on and off with a switch underneath.'

'I see. And then where did you go?'

'Down the garden to join the carol singers. That's where I saw Jackie and she told me Bob was still at the forge dealing with a last-minute customer.'

'And do you remember who else you saw there?'

He knew I did. I'd been through the names once already. I listed them again – all the people who couldn't have murdered Bob Millard because they were down by the lake, singing carols.

'Then one of the catering firm approached me and asked if I could settle the bill. So, we went back up to the tea tent together . . .'

Inspector Ford permitted himself a little grunt of amusement. 'You certainly did some toing and froing this afternoon.'

Tell me about it. 'Anyway, I collected her money from the house, took it to her in the tea tent, got her to sign a receipt, took that back to the house. Then I went back to the gift tent and had a brief word with Pat – Miss Giddings . . .'

'Who had returned by this time. She didn't remark on noticing anything unusual?'

'No, but she would have driven her car up the drive this time, in order to load up. She wouldn't have been walking.'

'Ah! And who else did you see in the tent?'

'Fizz and Don – Mr and Mrs Drummond, I mean – they were packing up, and Tom Smithson from Exeter. He was packing up their stock whilst Vicky – she's his wife – was down at the carols. Then I went outside because . . .' I hesitated. Why *had* I gone back out? 'because I suppose finally it had got through to my dim brain something was the matter.'

A nasty smirk tugged at the corner of Sergeant deVille's little mouth. Cruella doesn't like me and the feeling is mutual.

'I'd registered it *consciously*, if you know what I mean. There were no lanterns, Bob's pitch was in blackness, there was no one around. Even if he'd finished with this last-minute customer, he shouldn't have left the furnace burning unattended. And the display boards were still up with all their stock hanging on. Anything could have been stolen.'

'Interestingly,' the inspector responded, 'nothing has been stolen. At least, there are no empty hooks on those display boards and there are a couple of very nasty-looking swords and daggers hanging there, which leads me to wonder about the murder weapon.'

'It could have been wiped and put back, sir,' Cruella suggested.

50

'In which case forensics will pick it up.' The inspector folded his arms in thought and gazed up at the ceiling. 'But would you, though?' he asked after a moment's silence. 'It's dark, there's lots of shrubbery around, wouldn't you drop it somewhere, dump it? You've just attacked someone with a sharp implement, and either by accident or design, that person has fallen and struck their head a fatal blow against an anvil. Would you calmly wipe the weapon and put it back? You'd have to have some nerve.'

'Whoever it was had nerve enough to place the horseshoe in his hands,' Cruella pointed out.

'Yes, and the damn sprig of ivy or whatever it is!' The inspector scowled. 'What the devil's all that about? Is the killer trying to send us a message or—'

'I think you should look for the pritchel,' I interrupted.

The inspector stared. 'Pritchel?' he repeated.

'Bob was showing it to the crowd this afternoon. It's a tool a blacksmith uses to present the horseshoe to the hoof whilst the shoe is still hot. It's like a long chisel,' I measured its length in the air between my palms, 'with a sharp point. It can fit in the hole where the nail will go. I saw those wounds around Bob's neck,' I added, feeling a bit queasy at the memory. 'I think they could have been made by a pritchel.'

'Go and inform the scene of crime officer, would you, Christine?' the inspector asked. 'Tell him to start a search for it.' Cruella nodded and stood up. I wondered how much effort of will it cost the inspector to remember to use her proper Christian name. 'Oh, and ask Messrs Steiner and Gold to join us in here, would you?'

'Sir,' she said, and left the room.

'What about this noise you say you heard, just before you met up with young Chris Brownlow?'

'Just a rustling noise, as if someone was creeping about. I didn't see anyone. There's a lot of shrubbery just there, thick bushes. I suppose it could have been an animal but I . . .' The inspector was staring at me, waiting for me to finish.

'But you don't think it was?' he encouraged me.

I shook my head. 'I don't know. I just got a sense it was someone, rather than something, but I was a bit shaken up after finding Bob's body.'

'Of course.'

'There's something else I ought to tell you. Probably before Ricky and Morris get in here.'

'Something you've just remembered?'

'Not really. It was something one of the stallholders told me – Neil, he and his wife own Cold East Farm near Widecombe. They were here today selling cider. Neil told me he'd once seen Bob fighting with another person who was here today, Don Drummond, the woodturner.'

'When you say fight, you mean a quarrel?'

'Apparently it became quite physical. They had to be pulled apart.'

'When was this?'

'Back in the summer, I believe, at an agricultural show.' I felt a bit of a rat repeating what I'd heard. I don't like telling tales, even on someone like Don Drummond. But I reckoned it was bound to come out anyway, and from what Neil had said it had been a fairly public brawl.

There was a knock on the door at that moment, Ricky and Morris waiting outside.

'Not a word of what you've just told me, Miss Browne,' the inspector warned me in a low voice, 'and not a word about the horseshoe, either. So far, the only people who know about it are us and the person who placed it there.'

I nodded mutely. Ricky and Morris came in and sat at the table, next to me. They had changed their Victorian attire for casual slacks and sweaters and Ricky had a thin cigarette clamped at the corner of his mouth. Inspector Ford eyed him with disapproval but I don't suppose he was going to order him not to smoke in his own home. 'You will be aware by now this is a potential murder enquiry?'

'Yes, Inspector,' Morris said solemnly.

'Yes Inspector,' Ricky agreed, narrowing his eyes in the cigarette smoke. 'If this was just an accident the grounds wouldn't still be crawling with police.'

'As I say, it's a potential murder enquiry and I would appreciate your discretion until we are able to inform the victim's family for certain.'

Morris shook his head. 'Poor Jackie!'

'Now, the three of you were responsible for organising today's event,' the inspector went on, 'was anyone else involved?'

'Pat and Ken and Sue because it was their place we're raising the money for,' Ricky answered. 'Mag-bags – sorry, I mean Lady Margaret Westershall, was involved in the planning stage. But we three saw to all the practical things – setting it all up, finding volunteers, and people to rent stalls.' He flicked a glance at me, 'Juno found a lot of those.'

'So how come Bob Millard rented a pitch here?' the inspector asked. 'This isn't his usual sort of event, is it? I would have thought the agricultural shows back in the summer were his sort of thing, but isn't this Victorian fair – forgive me – not quite his style?'

'I think it was the Victorian theme which appealed to him, Inspector,' Morris told him. 'It's the right period for the American Civil War, you see.'

'And Bob just loves showing off that war wagon,' Ricky paused to blow smoke above our heads. 'It's his pride and joy. He belongs to some society of people who restore them, apparently. Always going over to America, for conventions.'

'I think Bob was a bit infatuated with anything American,' Morris added a trifle awkwardly. 'I've heard Jackie say they wanted to live there.'

'How well would you say you knew Bob and Jackie Millard?'

Ricky shrugged. 'We've met him at a few fundraising events.'

'I've talked to Jackie more than Bob,' Morris put in. 'She's a nice girl.'

The inspector directed his gaze towards me. 'I'd never met either of them before today.'

There was a knock on the door and Dean put his head around it. 'The DS has finished now, sir. He says the body can be removed to the morgue.'

'Thank you, Collins.' The inspector didn't bother to look over his shoulder, and the door closed again. 'So, who invited Bob to come to this event?'

'He rang me up and asked if he could come,' I told him. 'Or rather, Jackie did. It was all last minute. She said they'd only just learnt about the fair and asked if there was still room for them. That's how they ended up with the pitch on the other side of the drive. It was the only one left.'

'What I suppose I'm getting at,' the inspector continued deliberately, 'is this. Who else would have known Bob was going to be here today?'

'You mean if someone was planning to murder him?' Morris and I looked at each other and Ricky gave a silent shrug. 'I don't know,' I admitted. 'I don't know if he and Jackie had heard about today from another trader or just seen a poster somewhere. She didn't say.'

The inspector sighed. 'I see. Thank you. Would you mind if I held on to these very useful lists of names and contact numbers of yours?' he asked me.

'Not at all.' I knew those lists would come in handy.

He smiled. 'In that case, I think you can go home now, Juno.'

He has a warm smile, the inspector, and I don't see it often enough. But I didn't let it fool me, this wasn't a suggestion, this was a command. He didn't want me hanging around with Morris and Ricky, discussing the case. 'Oh!' I said, suddenly remembering. 'What's happened to Sophie? She's not still here, is she? Her mum dropped her off this morning and I was supposed to be taking her home.'

'Don't worry,' Morris smiled. 'Elizabeth gave her a lift. She's also packed all your stuff up and says she'll drop it off at the shop in the morning.'

'Oh, that's good of her!' I could have cried with gratitude. The thought of having to pack up the goods on my stall and load all the boxes into my van before I could go home was just too much.

Ricky and Morris saw me to the door. 'What a terrible end to a lovely day.' Morris looked almost tearful. 'I was so looking forward to our sitting down together and counting all the money, finding out how much we'd made for the animals.'

'We'll do it tomorrow,' I told him, squeezing his arm. 'Tomorrow evening, I'll come around after the shop's shut.'

Ricky searched my face. 'Are you okay, Juno, love?' he asked. 'It must have been horrible, finding poor old Bob like that.'

'I'm all right.' I was trying not to think about it.

'You can stay the night, if you want,' Morris added.

'I don't think the inspector would approve. Besides,

what I really want is a hot bath and my own bed.'

Morris dropped his voice to a whisper. 'I hear Mandy has been at it again.'

I nodded. 'I didn't realise she's pinched stuff from you, though.'

He sighed. 'It doesn't really matter. It's just annoying when she pinches one item from a set of things – like that silver fish fork. I'd rather she pinched the whole set, really.'

I made sympathetic murmurs and kissed them both goodbye.

I opened the door, surprised to find a uniformed policeman outside it, apparently waiting for me.

'I'll walk you to your car, miss.'

'I can find my own way,' I assured him.

He glanced over at where white arc lights lit up the scene of the crime, a small blue tent erected over it, to keep out prying eyes. 'I think that's what the inspector is afraid of, miss,' he said.

CHAPTER FIVE

'What's an honest copper got to do to get a cuppa tea around here?'

Detective Constable Dean Collins' considerable bulk seemed to fill up the whole of *Old Nick's*. It had been less than forty-eight hours since the Christmas Fair had ended and already it was all around the town of Ashburton that Bob the Blacksmith had been murdered. At least, the town was rife with *speculation* he'd been murdered; the official cause of death had still not been revealed by the police and despite constant pestering by Evie from the *Dartmoor Gazette*, who was kicking herself because she'd gone home just before it all happened, I couldn't tell her any different.

I'd only just arrived myself. I'd spent the morning on Domestic Goddess duties, shopping for Maisie and exercising her horrid little terrier, Jacko. I managed to drag him around the town without him attacking anything, although it was a near thing with a motorbike parked by a kerb. I was worried about Maisie. Her stone cottage was freezing cold, which is not good for a ninety-seven-year-old. The central heating had packed up.

'I don't know what it wants to go breaking down for,' she'd complained loudly, swaddled in an eiderdown. 'It's new.'

I looked at the yellowed, paint-chipped radiators. 'When did you have it put in?'

After a lot of deliberation, she'd concluded it had been installed when her daughter, Our Janet, was in the sixth form at school, about fifty years ago. Either the radiators needed replacing or Maisie needed a new boiler. I spent an hour on the phone trying to find someone who could come out and take a look at it, preferably today, as her only other forms of heating were a couple of feeble blow heaters and an ancient electric fire. I eventually found someone who promised to call that evening. 'You know, you'd stay warmer if you went back to bed,' I told her.

'I'm not spending the day in bed!' she protested, looking up from her copy of *The People's Friend*. 'What do you think I am?'

'An old woman with nothing whatever to do?' I suggested.

'Cheek!' She waggled her head in indignation.

I made her a hot drink, poured more tea into a thermos, settled her down with an extra cardigan, blankets and hot-water bottle and promised I'd pop back later when the central heating man arrived. If he couldn't fix the problem, then it would mean a long phone call to discuss the situation with Our Janet up in Heck-as-Like where, according to Maisie, they already had snow.

'Why can't I have a real fire?' she complained. 'Bring in coal, like we used to?'

'Well, for a start, I don't suppose your chimney's been swept in twenty years.' The thought of an unsteady Maisie toddling about trying to strike matches and get a blaze going didn't bear thinking about. On my way out, I called on her nearest neighbour, and asked him if he wouldn't mind looking in on her in a couple of hours. He promised he would, but warned me that if that bloody dog tried to bite him again, he'd sue.

All this meant I was late getting to the shop for my afternoon shift, so Sophie and Pat were still both there when Dean arrived. 'It was you two ladies I wanted to see, anyway,' he told them. 'Just to take a quick statement from you both about Sunday.'

'Any news?' I asked.

He shook his head. 'I've just been around the *Gazette* offices, going through the pictures their photographer took on Sunday. I'm supposed to be searching for anyone looking suspicious, but amongst a lot of damn fools in fancy dress, nobody stands out.'

'I've got lots of pictures from Sunday,' Sophie volunteered, looking up from her painting, 'on my phone.'

'They won't be much good,' I told her. 'They're all selfies of you in your costume.'

'They are not!' her dark eyes flashed indignantly.

'Well, all right, perhaps most of them are. But you can look at them if you want,' she added to Dean graciously.

'I just need to ask you and Pat a few questions.' He looked around him. 'Is there a room we can use, Juno?'

'Well, if you must be all hush-hush about it, you can use the kitchen upstairs. Sophie can make you a cup of tea.' After a moment I called up to her. 'Don't let him eat all the biscuits.'

'I hope they're not going to be too long,' Pat muttered. 'I want to get away in a minute.'

'I don't think Soph's got much to tell him.' We'd already had a long discussion about the events of Sunday. Like everyone else, Sophie had been blissfully unaware there had been anything amiss until it was too late. She'd spent most of her time selling her wares in the gift tent, and apart from a look around the fair in the early afternoon and a visit to the tea tent later, hadn't strayed from there until she went down to the end of the garden to join in the carol-singing.

'Well, I can't tell him anything neither,' Pat said. 'I was busy all day, talking my head off about the animals.' Her thin shoulders shuddered. 'It's spoilt everything, all this.'

'It certainly spoilt things for Bob.'

'Oh, I know! O'course, I'm sorry for Bob and that poor wife of his. What I meant was, it was such a wonderful day. Everyone was having such a lovely time.'

'And we made a lot of money, don't forget,' I reminded her, in an effort to cheer her up.

I hadn't been up to Druid Lodge the evening before for the official totting up of the profits, as planned. Apparently, there was a policeman on the gate trying to keep the press and any other prying eyes away from the crime scene. Ricky and Morris thought it was unlikely I'd be allowed in. Instead, they came to me. We sat around my kitchen table, gobbling the wine and cake they'd bought, and added everything up. Altogether, we'd raised over two thousand pounds for the animal sanctuary, and several animals had been rehomed or would be having their keep contributed to under the new adoption scheme. The sponsorships, Pat told me, would help towards the animals' winter feed and the cash we'd raised would pay for the repair of old fences.

I had a sudden thought. 'Are you still looking after Bob's horse?'

Pat sniffed. 'Yes. Noddy's no trouble. Least we can do, if it'll help the poor girl out.'

'How is Jackie? Does anyone know?'

Pat shook her head. 'I don't know how she's going to run the forge now. Not on her own. I mean, I know she makes the jewellery and other stuff, but she can't make a living without the farrier side of the business, I wouldn't have thought.'

'No, I suppose not,' I agreed, sighing.

The shop door opened just then, and Digby Jerkin walked in, rubbing his gloved hands together. He was sufficiently old-world and charming enough to remove his hat. 'Good afternoon, ladies,' he said with a smile.

'Goodness, it's chilly out there!'

'I'm afraid there's no news,' I told him.

'Er . . . no, I hadn't actually called to talk about the . . . er . . .' He flicked an uneasy glance at Pat. 'I wonder if I could have a quiet word with you, Juno?'

'Of course.' I gestured towards the back room. 'We can go in there.'

'Excuse us, Miss Giddings,' Digby said politely, and followed me down the hall.

'Amanda's well, I hope?' I asked, waiting for him to tell me what he wanted.

'She's fine,' he assured me. He lowered his voice. 'But it was the incident on Sunday that I wanted to talk with you about.'

'Oh?'

'This is very awkward.' He hesitated, his eyes downcast. He was clutching a shopping bag, his fingers convulsively gripping the handle, and looked as if he wanted the ground to swallow him up. 'You see, I couldn't help but notice . . . well, what was going on with the muff . . .'

'Oh Digby!' I began. 'You don't have to say anything.'

The poor man's cheeks flushed scarlet. 'No, please hear me out. It's not the first time it has happened and you have intervened. I shudder to think what the consequences might have been if Mandy's . . . momentary lapse . . . had been discovered. She'll never thank you herself, of course, . . . but I just wanted to say thank you, for what you did for Mandy. Not everyone would have the same attitude as you.' He dared a glance at me, his slightly bulbous eyes shiny with tears. 'She's such a silly sausage but she really doesn't mean anything by it, you know.'

'I know.' I squeezed his arm. 'Please don't give it another thought.'

'She can't help herself. It's an illness.'

'I understand that, Digby.'

'I'm always finding things that she . . . well, she has these little hiding places all over the house. After the event on Sunday, I made her turn them all out. I felt like a brute but . . .' he indicated the shopping bag he was carrying, 'I found some more.'

'You mean, more from Sunday?' I asked.

'Oh yes. I'm afraid that almost being discovered was not enough to deter her.' He shook his head sadly. 'It never is.'

He dived into the bag and pulled out two wrapped, scented candles that had come from a stall in the gift tent. 'These belong to those two lovely girls who run the shop in town. I'll take them back, of course, and try to explain . . .'

I felt so sorry for him. 'Why don't you let me take them back?'

His eyes widened. 'But why should you?'

'Because they won't think anything of it if I do. They could easily have left them behind when they were packing up their stall, people forget all sorts of stuff. I'll just say I found them when we were clearing away after everyone had gone.' He didn't look convinced. 'And it will save Mandy any embarrassment,' I added.

'Thank you, Juno. That is most kind.'

'Has she ever had any kind of treatment,' I asked carefully, 'for her illness?'

'Oh, years with the shrink but to no avail.' He sighed. 'But there are drugs now, apparently, which limit impulse control, and I told her that after Sunday's episode . . .' As he moved in agitation, something in the shopping bag clinked. 'Oh dear,' he said. 'I'm forgetting, there's more. Mandy admitted she's had these quite some time. She can't remember which shops she took them from, but she thinks they were here in Ashburton.' He pulled out a silver napkin ring, hallmarked Chester and embellished with a crest, an art deco card case, and finally a small Beswick figure of a sheepdog, which I strongly suspected was mine. I didn't say so, though. 'I could ask around about these, too,' I offered, picking up the silver. 'You know, in antique shops, we get offered stolen items.' Usually, I added silently, by lurky-looking drug addict types desperate for money. 'Again, no one will think anything of it if I ask the other antiques dealers in Ashburton if they've had these items stolen.'

Digby looked overcome with emotion. 'Are you sure?'

'Perfectly.'

He felt around again in the bottom of the bag. 'Oh dear, here's one more.' He held up a silver, pearl-handled fish fork and I took it from him with a smile. 'No need to worry about this one,' I told him. 'I know exactly where this came from.'

'Thank you, my dear.' Digby gave me a quick, apologetic kiss on the cheek, and hurried away up the hall, almost colliding with Sophie coming down the stairs. 'Excuse me,' he muttered into his handkerchief.

'What's up with him?' she asked, watching him depart.

'Nothing. Is it Pat's turn to be interrogated?'

'Yes,' she said, calling out for her to go up. 'Dean has cleaned the biscuits out of the tin,' she added to me, 'but I kept the new packet out of sight in the cupboard.'

'Good girl.'

Pat rolled her eyes as she passed us and plodded heavily up the stairs.

'Well, I'm going home now if you're here,' Sophie added cheerfully. She sat down briefly to rinse out her paintbrush, and frowned, critically studying her watercolour of Dartmoor ponies on Bell Tor. 'Elizabeth unpacked all your stock from the fair, did you see?'

'Yes. That was kind of her.'

'She says she's sorry if she hasn't put everything back in the right place.'

'She's probably arranged it better than I would.'

'Probably,' Sophie agreed artlessly. She looked at her watch. 'Look, do you mind if I go? Only, I've been offered a waitressing shift at the hotel this evening, and I need the money, quite frankly, so . . .'

'Yes, of course,' I told her. 'You go.'

A few minutes later Pat came down from the kitchen. 'I told you I wouldn't be able to tell him nothing. Same stupid questions he asked me the other day.'

'He has to ask them, though, Pat.'

'I s'pose.' She put away her handiwork and shrugged on her coat. 'I'm going now.'

'Rats deserting the sinking ship.' I sighed. 'Have I sold anything today?'

She thought about it for a moment. 'No.'

'Nice to be consistent.'

'You got most of the afternoon yet. You never know.'

'Oh, I think I do.'

A few moments after Pat had gone, Dean joined me down in the shop.

'So, how's it going?' I asked.

He sat in Sophie's chair. 'You might as well know, there will be a press release in the morning. Bob Millard was murdered.'

'I think I'd already worked that out for myself.'

He ignored my comment and carried on. 'We're asking members of the public who attended the fair to send us any photos they might have taken of Bob.' He sighed. 'Another lot of pictures to trawl through.'

'You think you might spot his killer in the crowd?'

'Trouble is, Bob was known as a drinker and a womaniser who was handy with his fists. There's any number of people who might have had it in for him.'

'Enough to kill him?'

He shrugged his broad shoulders. 'Perhaps they didn't mean to. It was hitting his head against the anvil killed him.'

'But someone attacked him with a pritchel.'

'It might have been an argument that went too far.'

'What about the pritchel, have you found it?'

'No. But the pathologist got hold of an identical one and confirmed it would have been the implement that made those wounds around the victim's shoulders. He said whoever had made them had been shorter than Bob – mind you, most people are – and a bit feeble. The wounds weren't very deep, apparently, despite its being a sharp implement. Could have been a woman.'

'Jackie said the last-minute customer was a man.'

'We sent an officer to her place this morning, in the hope she can put together a photofit of this person . . . if he exists.'

'You think she made him up?' I asked, astonished. 'She's not a suspect, surely?'

He raised his eyebrows. 'Why not? The husband or wife is always the most likely suspect in a murder, you know that.'

'Well, for one thing, she adored him. I could tell by the way she looked at him.'

'Yes, and maybe she didn't like him having so many lady friends. According to people who knew the couple well, they had a very volatile relationship. They reckon Bob's dodged more dinner plates than he's had cooked dinners.'

'But she couldn't have done it. I saw her down at the other end of the garden, singing carols.'

'Ah well, you see,' Dean held up an admonishing finger, 'it's the time frame that's the problem. The pathologist can't narrow the time of Bob's death down beyond an hour, more or less. Now, Ricky told us the carol-singing was supposed to begin at 4 p.m., but they decided to delay the start of it because the raffle prizes were still being drawn in the tea tent.'

'That's right. Amanda and Digby took ages picking the winning the tickets.'

'So, they waited for them to finish, but no one is exactly sure what time it was. Now Jackie states that when she last saw Bob, with this last-minute customer, the lanterns around their pitch were still burning. Yet when Lady Margaret Westershall walked up the drive on her way home shortly after all the prizes had been drawn, she complained the pitch was in darkness. She also stated that when they walked past the forge – remember the coals were still burning, so she could see that all right – her dogs started growling, which, apparently, is very uncharacteristic behaviour. It even led her to call out and ask if anyone was there. But there was no response so she didn't investigate. She says she saw a steward with a lantern further down the drive and,' he gave a chuckle, '*hallooed* him to come and light her way.'

I smiled. 'She would. She's got a voice like a foghorn.'

'Point is,' he added more seriously, 'we don't know how long those lanterns were out for.'

'Have you found them?'

'Three of them, all switched off. So, we've got an unspecified period when anyone could have attacked Bob and then switched off the lanterns to cover up the crime. Even Jackie could have done it and nipped down to join the carols, with no one any the wiser.'

I thought about Jackie, standing next to me among the carollers, singing away so brightly. There was no way she could have been standing there so carefree if she'd just murdered her husband.

'What about Don Drummond?' I asked. 'Where was he whilst all this was going on?'

'In the gift tent, you saw him there yourself.'

'All the time?'

'According to him, he slipped out once to fetch his wife a hot drink. He says he was only gone a few minutes. And Fizz confirms it, but then, she would.'

'What about the other stallholders?'

'Busy with customers. No one was paying much attention to when people nipped in and out or how long they were away, people were doing it all afternoon.'

'So, he could have murdered Bob?'

Dean grunted. 'Possibly.'

'Do we know why he and Bob fought?'

'*We* do not.' Despite discussing the case with me, Dean likes to remind me now and then of my lowly civilian status. 'Drummond said the matter was personal and he didn't care to go into it. But now this is officially a murder investigation, we shall be asking him again.'

I linked my hands behind my head, considering. 'I can't see Don Drummond being stupid enough to put a horseshoe in Bob's hands. It's like advertising *this is a murder*. And what about the stem threaded through the nail hole, those flowers?'

'They're elderflowers.'

I frowned. 'Where do you get elderflowers at this time of year?'

'These were dried.'

'But no one would just happen to be carrying them about. The murderer must have come prepared, so the crime was premeditated.'

'Looks like it.'

'But what's the significance of elderflowers? What message is the killer trying to send?'

The shop bell jangled just then as two ladies let themselves in and began to look around.

Dean stood up. 'That's for us to find out, Sunshine,' he grinned as he headed for the door. 'You just attend to your customers.'

Pat was right, I did make a sale during the afternoon – a copper picture frame and a tortoiseshell snuffbox – both to the same customer. Her friend bought a silver thimble and a decorative butter pat. In fact, it turned into quite a busy afternoon. But as it wore on it got chilly in the shop, and I was looking forward to going home. Except I couldn't go home, could I, because I had to meet the man who was fixing Maisie's heating. With any luck.

He'd been there over an hour when I arrived. He told me he'd bled all the radiators and stripped down the boiler, replaced one of its original parts and got it going again, but he wasn't prepared to swear it would keep going indefinitely. 'It might last a year or it could break down again tomorrow. The whole thing needs replacing, really.'

'You mean the whole boiler?'

He pulled a grimace. 'The whole system, to be honest. I'm surprised it's lasted this long.'

The agency carer arrived to put Maisie to bed, so I decided to go home to break the bad news to Our Janet. It was easier to have a conversation on the phone without Maisie squawking in the background like a parrot.

Janet sighed as I explained the situation. 'I'll have to drive down and fetch her, bring her up here to stay with us for Christmas, it's the only way I'm going to have any peace of mind. I know she won't want to come – she never wants to come – but she can't stay in the cottage if she's got no heating. Perhaps we could get the work done whilst she's up here.'

'I did ask Malcolm what his availability was,' I told her. 'He said he could get it done in the new year, but not before.' I gave Janet his phone number so they could talk about costs.

'You could keep an eye on him, could you, Juno?' she asked. 'Let him have a key and so on?'

'Yes, of course.'

'You are a star! Oh, God,' she moaned. 'I suppose we'll have to have that bloody awful dog as well.'

Jacko, the bloody awful dog, was one of the reasons Maisie didn't want to stay with her daughter for Christmas in the first place. She didn't like the family's refusal to accept that Jacko was only playing whenever he nipped the grandchildren, or growled at anyone who dared to move in their own house without his permission. She also didn't like boisterous, noisy kids running around or sulky teenagers who refused to engage in conversation and spent all their time staring at their phones. 'I'd much rather be quiet and cosy in my own home,' she told me after last Christmas. 'I go to church on Christmas morning and the social club does us a lovely Christmas lunch and they bring me home afterwards. And Jacko and I can watch what we want on the telly. We're perfectly happy.'

Cosy was the operative word in this case. It might not be. We couldn't risk her dying of hypothermia if her heating broke down over the Christmas holiday. Maisie was going to spend the festive season with her nearest and dearest whether she liked it or not, and make the trip to Heck-as-Like.

'And what are you doing for Christmas, Juno?' Our Janet enquired politely.

'I don't know yet,' I admitted. 'I haven't made up my mind.' I'd had all the usual invitations from friends prepared to take pity on a single female spending Christmas Day on her own: Ricky and Morris, Olly and Elizabeth, Sophie and her mum, Pat and family, not to mention some old college friends. The exception was Kate and Adam, who would be away for once, taking new baby Noah on a tour of his grandparents in Norfolk and Sussex. The house would be empty, apart from Bill, who was currently curled up asleep on my lap.

I'd also been invited to spend Christmas with my cousin Brian who'd just taken up his diplomatic posting in Paris. Christmas in Paris, wouldn't that be wonderful? So why didn't I want to go, apart from the fact Brian's wife, the adder-tongued Marcia, would be having her two daughters and their husbands to stay. They were worse snobs than she was and there's only so much supercilious amusement about the lives of ordinary people I could take. The truth was I wanted to stay in Ashburton for Christmas. Just in case.

'Juno, are you still there?'

I must have been silent during all these musings. 'Sorry, Janet, I was miles away. Tell me, have you really had snow?'

CHAPTER SIX

We might not have had any snow but the weather was biting cold. The prevailing front was coming from Russia, apparently. I'd taken the Tribe out early, and three of them – Schnitzel, E.B. and Boog – had been dressed by their owners in warm coats for protection. Shaggy-haired German Shepherd Dylan didn't seem worried by the icy temperature and Nookie the Husky was positively energised by it, friskier than usual. We walked beneath the leaden grey sky of a winter's early morning, skeletal forms of frozen hogweed and teasels standing stiff and spiky in the hedgerow. Puddles in the deeply rutted lane shone with ice. I cracked one with my boot, just to hear the thin crust snap and see it splinter like a pane of glass. But it was too cold to linger, my cheeks and ears stinging in the icy air, and after a brisk walk and a run around a frosty field lobbing balls for them to chase, I took the dogs back to their homes.

I called into *Old Nick's* to make sure the gas bottle in the heater didn't need replacing and wouldn't run out on Sophie and Pat during the afternoon. I paid a visit to my friends Ron and Sheila in *Keepsakes* antique shop, who immediately recognised the silver napkin ring as one missing from a set of six, and also the card case. I concocted a story about being offered them by a suspicious-looking teenager who seemed desperate to get rid of them, and only paying him a couple of pounds for them. I then had the problem of Ron and Sheila wanting to pay me back, money I tried to refuse, but they insisted. I surreptitiously slipped it into the charity box on their counter on my way out. *Oh, what a tangled web we weave . . .*

I decided to visit to *Fizzy Izzy's* silk gallery in North Street. If Don was being tight-lipped with the police about why he and Bob had quarrelled, I might be able to find out something from Fizz. I was pretty certain the obnoxious Don would not be present, as he worked for Aigler Wealth Management, a firm of financial consultants in Exeter; his woodturning was just a hobby.

I experienced a definite sense of déjà vu as I walked into Fizz's place. For a start, there was no one around in the empty shop and loud music was playing from somewhere upstairs. It reminded me of when she used to rent a room at *Old Nick's*, leaving the shop unattended for anyone to rob whilst she worked on her silk paintings upstairs, blissfully unaware of customers waiting downstairs. It had been a relief when she'd decided to get a place of her own.

I pinged the little bell on the counter and waited,

gazing around at the stunning silk paintings that adorned the walls: hummingbirds zipping through green rainforests, glimmering fish swimming among coral reefs, exotic hothouse flowers. I pinged the bell again, my eye caught by a range of coloured silk bags and scarves with expensive price tags. There was still no response to the bell. After waiting a little longer, I headed to the back of the shop, flung open a door and yelled 'Shop!' up the stairs.

The music stopped abruptly. 'Hello?' Fizz's voice called uncertainly.

'Hello!' I called back.

'I'll be with you in just a moment,' she responded, and I wandered back into the shop.

It was considerably more than a moment before Fizz appeared, tucking a wayward strand of auburn hair into her messy bun. 'So sorry,' she said, smiling, 'but I had to get the colour on whilst the silk was still wet, you see, or the painting would be ruined.' Her smile vanished when she saw it was me. 'Oh. Hello, Juno.'

'You've made this place look really lovely,' I told her.

'Thank you. I have plenty of room to spread my stuff in here.' In *Old Nick's* she'd had a tendency to spread her stuff over everyone else's. She flashed an awkward grin. She seemed strangely on edge, not her usual blithe and breezy self. 'Don says I'll always fill up all the space, no matter how much room you give me.'

'But you've found room for his stuff too.' I indicated a collection of vessels in various woods, set out on a long bench; there were platters and bowls, but also beautiful abstract shapes in wood. I couldn't deny the bastard was talented. 'I hear he's going to make a drinking bowl for Neil and Carol's wassail in January.'

She relaxed into a smile. 'Oh yes, he's thrilled.'

The thought of Don being thrilled was difficult for my brain to cope with. He always seemed a grumpy sod to me. I would have thought a slow, ancient, meditative craft, turning wood on a lathe, would have a calming effect on anyone who practised it, but not on Don, it seemed. Perhaps it was the stress of managing all that wealth.

'I just called around to tell you how much we made for Honeysuckle Farm on Sunday,' I lied. I gave her the figures. 'I thought everyone would be interested to know.'

'Oh thanks, Juno. I'm so glad the sanctuary did well.'

'Did you have a good day?' I asked, as casually as I could. 'You and Don?'

'Well, yes, yes, very good thank you, until that awful . . . I mean, the murder.' Her brown eyes widened. 'Have they caught who did it yet?'

'Hardly. I don't think the police have much to go on. They're looking for someone with a motive. Of course, I didn't know Bob personally, I'd only just met him. Neil and Carol were saying they'd come across him before at an agricultural fair. Did you know him at all?'

To my horror, she burst into tears. 'Oh dear!' I cried as she hunted in her pockets for a handkerchief. 'What's the matter?'

'Everyone thinks Don did it!' she gulped between sobs. 'Killed Bob!'

For a moment I didn't know what to say. 'I'm sure they don't,' I managed at last. I put an arm around her shoulders and steered her towards a chair. 'Why would anyone think so?'

'Because he punched him.' She hiccupped. 'Don punched Bob, last year, at the Honiton show. Everyone saw him.'

'I see. Well, just because you punch—'

'The police think he did it.' Fizz sniffed dolefully. 'They asked him to volunteer a DNA sample. Why would they do that if they didn't think he was a suspect?'

'I expect they're just being . . . um . . . well, why did Don punch Bob?'

'Because,' an arctic voice cut in, 'he was poking his nose into things that were none of his concern.' I turned to see Don standing in the doorway, dressed in a sharp grey business suit and blue tie. Early return from work or late start? Whatever, he wasn't in the office now. 'A bit like someone else around here,' he added, his blue eyes boring into mine.

'Hello!' I began weakly. 'I just came to—'

'I told the police it was none of their business and I'm damn sure it's none of yours.' He held the door open wide. 'And as you seem to be upsetting my wife, I'd like you to leave.'

'Oh, Don!' Fizz protested. 'It wasn't like that. Juno was just—'

'I know what Juno was *just*,' he snarled.

Unfortunately, he had me bang to rights. I couldn't deny information was precisely what I'd been fishing for. I could feel a hot blush rising to my cheeks. 'I'd better go,' I murmured to Fizz and squeezed her arm. 'I am sorry.'

Don held the door wide, his hostile vibes quivering in the air. I had to resist the temptation to edge by him on tiptoe as if I was creeping past a tiger.

'I've said it before, you're a menace!' he growled. 'You stay away from me in future, and my wife.'

'I'll stay away from you with pleasure,' I told him, stopping in the doorway and meeting his gaze with far more defiance than I felt. 'As for your wife,' I turned to look at Fizz, tears on her cheeks, staring at us both wide-eyed in horror, as if she expected us to start trading punches at any moment, 'you know where I am if you need me.'

I could feel Don's blazing blue gaze burning into my back as I turned out of the shop and strode away, trying to look confident. In fact, my knees were trembling. I always find that man intimidating. I headed back to the sanctuary of *Old Nick's* for a calming cuppa before I went off to check on Maisie's heating situation and get on with the rest of my day.

But if I thought I was going to find an oasis of calm in *Old Nick's*, I was sadly mistaken.

Sophie flashed me a look of indignation as soon as I got in the door. 'You never told us about this!' she accused me, sweeping her hand across the newspaper she had spread out on the counter.

'About what?'

'All this! In the *Dartmoor Gazette*. It says here Bob had . . .' she paused whilst she looked down and found her place on the page, prodding at it with her finger, 'Multiple stab wounds made with a sharp implement, believed to be a *pritchel*.' She wrinkled her nose. 'What's a pritchel? Anyway, you didn't tell us that. You said he'd just bashed his head on the anvil. And,' she went on, pushing her red-framed spectacles back up the bridge of her titchy nose, 'it says here he was found with a horseshoe in his hands, which, it says '*must have been placed there by the killer*.' You didn't tell us that bit either!'

'No, you didn't,' Pat nodded, knitting needles never missing a click.

'No, I didn't,' I agreed, peeling off my coat and throwing it over the back of a chair, 'because Inspector Ford swore me to secrecy. I didn't tell anyone because no one was supposed to know. Here,' I indicated the newspaper, 'let me see that.'

Sophie slid it across the counter towards me. With an increasingly queasy feeling in my stomach, I read an article which revealed almost all of the details of Bob's murder. The only thing that wasn't mentioned was the sprig of elder. By the end of it, I felt quite sick.

'How did they get hold of all this?' I certainly hadn't told anyone and now the police would think I had. I could be arrested, although I wasn't sure on what charge. Did giving out secret information to the press count as hindering an investigation?

I rang Guy Mitchell, editor of the *Gazette*. Mitch is a very amiable fellow, but he laughed down the phone when I demanded to know where he got his information from.

'You know I can't reveal my source. I can't tell you who it is. I can't tell the police who it is either.'

'Fine,' I snapped. 'As long as you're prepared to tell them who it *isn't*.'

'Come again?'

'That it isn't *me*.'

He sounded surprised. 'Why would it be you?'

'Because I found—' I stopped myself, but not soon enough.

'Oh, did you?' I could hear the rising interest in his voice. 'You found the body? Ashburton's Famous Amateur Sleuth has been at it again! In that case, perhaps you'd like to confirm these details are true.'

My turn to laugh down the phone. Just before I slammed down the receiver.

'Buggeration,' I muttered.

In a thoroughly bad temper, I stomped down to Maisie's cottage in Brook Lane. Her heating was working, at least. In fact, her cottage was toasty, the radiators fairly throbbing with heat. She must have turned the thermostat right up. I wasn't sure the system could take it, at least not for long. She was in a mood to match my own and told me in no uncertain terms she was not going up to Heck-as-Like for Christmas. 'It's colder up there than down here,' she complained. 'They've already got snow.'

'They had a few light showers, that's all. Janet told me. It hasn't settled and they're not expecting any more.'

Maisie snorted. 'Expecting! The weather could turn nasty any time.'

'Yes, and so could your central heating. And if you go and stay with Janet,' I went on in a wheedling voice, 'just think what you'll save on your heating bills.'

'I don't care.' She shook her permed apricot curls. 'I'm staying here.'

'Maisie, it makes sense to go up there for a few days and have your heating replaced whilst you're away. You won't like being here when the work's being done, all the radiators and pipes will have to be replaced, your floorboards will have to come up. And you know how Jacko feels about workmen in the house.' We stared across at him, sleeping in his basket, keeping up a growly monologue even as he slept, his bristly snout twitching and revealing odd glimpses of fang.

Maisie thought about this for a few moments, turning her cough sweet over in her mouth. 'I still want my Christmas tree up,' she insisted petulantly. 'Why haven't you put my decorations up yet? Where are they?'

'You haven't asked me to put them up.' I'd been hoping to avoid digging her boxes of crushed and dusty paper chains out of the loft and looping them around the picture rails. They must be older than her central heating. Each year more links broke off and the chains got shorter and shorter.

'Well, I'm asking you now,' she responded belligerently. 'And I want my tree up.'

'That ratty, bent, bald thing that only had a few branches left?' I asked. 'Last year we threw it away.'

'Then I want a new one,' she insisted, her voice rising in agitation. 'I want a proper one, not some plastic thing, I want a real one.'

'But you always complain you can't put up with pine needles dropping on the carpet.'

Maisie's eucalyptus cough drop clacked against her dentures, her mouth working furiously as she thought what to say next.

'And unless you buy a rooted tree and plant it in the garden afterwards,' I went on, 'there's the problem of disposing of it afterwards.'

Maisie fidgeted in silence, her lips pursed, her knobbly fingers pulling at the cuff of her cardigan. I took pity on her. 'Look, why don't we buy a new tree, an artificial one that will fold up and go in the loft? You can get some really realistic ones these days. I could take you out to that big garden centre and you could choose one.'

She was silent a moment. 'The garden centre with the nice cafe?' she asked. I knew she wouldn't be able to resist a trip out. 'Well, all right.' She hunched a shoulder. 'Course, I don't want a big one.'

'No, of course not.'

She shot me a venomous look. 'And don't think you're buttering me up, sly puss! This doesn't mean I'm going to stay with Our Janet. If I've got a nice tree up, I might as well stay here over Christmas and enjoy it.'

'Of course, Maisie,' I said.

When I got back to the shop late in the afternoon, ready to cash up, Pat and Sophie had both gone home. I found Elizabeth sitting behind the counter. There was an air of discontent about her, which is strange for Elizabeth, usually the essence of calm.

'I've had a slight run-in with Olly,' she admitted.

This was unusual too. The two of them usually get along very well. 'What's the problem?' I asked.

'He wants an e-bike.'

I laughed. 'Like Chris Brownlow.'

'Exactly.'

'Don't they cost thousands of pounds?'

'Yes, and in a way,' she answered, sighing, 'I'd rather he spent thousands of pounds. As you know, he was left all of his grandparents' money as well as the house, and he has plenty in the bank, far too much than is healthy for a boy of his age.'

'He's always been pretty careful with it, though,' I reminded her.

'Yes, if you don't count buying himself little treats like drones and motion-sensor cameras. Oh, and a saxophone, which he almost never plays. But Olly being Olly, he doesn't want to spend the money on a new bike.

He wants to buy a conversion kit for his existing bike. He's seen them on the internet.'

'You know how he loves messing about with things, especially anything technical.'

'Yes, but I've read up on these things myself and I'm not convinced these kits are safe. The bicycle batteries can't cope with much charge, apparently, and there are horrible stories of people plugging the charger into an ordinary socket, leaving it on charge overnight and catching the house on fire. One can buy a safe charger with a control that switches itself off as soon as the batteries are fully charged,' she went on, 'but that can cost as much as the kit itself. And when I pointed this out, and told him he couldn't buy the kit unless he bought the charger too, I was told in no uncertain terms that I had no right to tell him what he could spend his money on. Which is true, of course. I haven't. I am not, as he reminded me, his *real* aunt.'

'Oh dear.' I could see she was upset. She had arrived in Ashburton with little more than the clothes she stood up in, running away to avoid her late husband's unscrupulous creditors and living in her car with her cat. She needed a roof over her head and a new identity. I'd introduced her to Olly. He had been brought up by his great-grandmother, the indomitable Dolly, who had died the year before, leaving him in the house alone. He was fourteen at the time, terrified he would be found out and taken into care, and happy to accept Elizabeth to live with him as his 'aunt', and thus evade the attentions of social services. He had accepted her *in loco parentis* almost meekly, and seemed to feel secure with the sense of order she brought into his life. Perhaps he had grown used to it now, but he was growing up, and it seemed he was testing the boundaries.

'If he insists on buying the wretched kit, I'll be forced to buy him the battery-charger, which is more than I can afford. I'm not in a position to forbid him to do anything,' she added. 'In fact, once he's sixteen, he can throw me out any time he likes.'

It was true that she was in a uniquely vulnerable position. 'But you do have a hold over him,' I reminded her. In fact, we both did.

She raised her eyebrows. 'You mean because he buried his great-grandmother in the back garden? Well, he was a minor at the time and only complying with her wishes. I'm the one who's committed a crime, obtaining a false death certificate.'

'Only so he could legally inherit what was his.'

'I doubt if the law will see it that way. In any case, if he doesn't want me around, I'm not going to blackmail him into letting me stay.'

'I really don't think it'll come to that,' I said. 'Olly's just kicking against the fences, behaving like a teenage boy.'

'I know he won't want me to live with him forever. What young man would? And I certainly don't intend to be dependent upon him, financially or emotionally. But I was hoping for a year or two's grace before I have to look for another home.'

'Olly is very fond of you, Elizabeth.'

'Perhaps.' She shook her head. 'It's my own fault. I expect I mishandled the situation. I'd already told him off once this morning.'

'Why?'

'Yesterday he promised Susan and Ken that he'd go up to Honeysuckle Farm and help out. You know, he often does. But he didn't go. Chris Brownlow asked him if he'd like to go cycling to Dartmeet and he went with him instead.'

'He forgot the farm?'

'No. That wouldn't have been so bad. He just decided he'd go on another day instead.'

'I don't suppose Sue and Ken mind.'

'No, but that's not the point. He didn't phone them. If you promise to do something on a certain day, you should do it. And if you're forced to let people down, then at least you can do them the courtesy of letting them know. And that's what I told Olly. It's just basic good manners.' She caught me smiling at her and laughed. 'I *sound* like a great aunt, don't I?'

'No. You sound like a grandmother.'

For a moment she looked taken aback. 'Well,' she added, clearing her throat, 'I'm probably making a mountain out of a molehill, but I'm just not used to Olly speaking to me that way, and I don't intend to put up with it.'

* * *

I got as far as the evening without being arrested so I imagined the police weren't blaming me for leaking the details of Bob's murder to the *Dartmoor Gazette*. But just to be on the safe side, I phoned Dean Collins.

'No, of course we don't think it was you,' he told me.

'Good.'

'Mind, Cruella had a go at trying to persuade the boss it *was* you,' he added, 'but she couldn't convince him you were quite so stupid.'

'Well, that's comforting,' I snapped as he chuckled down the phone. 'But it means someone else must know the details. It's not likely to be someone on the force giving away this kind of information, is it?'

'It's not totally unknown,' he admitted glumly, 'but in this case, we think there might be a leak at the mortuary.'

'Yuck!'

'I'm not talking about leaky drains. You have to think who else could have had access to the body. Apart from ourselves and the murderer, no one saw Bob after he'd been killed, which narrows it down a bit. Possibly a mortuary technician.'

'Is that likely, if he wants to keep his job?'

'Like I say, it's not unknown. In any case, Mitch says this was an anonymous tip-off.'

'He doesn't know who his source was?'

'No.'

So, why hadn't he told me that? Perhaps he was just trying to wind me up. 'Then it could have been the killer?'

'Juno . . .' There was a warning note in Dean's voice.

I ignored him. 'He wants to draw attention to his crime. That's why he leaves the horseshoe on Bob's body and that's why he phones the newspaper.'

'Juno!' Dean barked at me. 'Just listen a minute. Now, I'm not saying you're wrong or right, but don't go repeating your theories to all and sundry, that's all I'm asking.'

'So, it *is* what you think.' I couldn't prevent a note of satisfaction creeping into my voice.

'But if you're going to leak details to the press, why not leak them all? The horseshoe was mentioned, but not the sprig of elderflowers.'

'Well, maybe he, or she, is saving that juicy titbit of information for later,' Dean replied. 'Who knows what goes on in the mind of a killer?'

Surely Don or Jackie wouldn't have phoned the press? They wouldn't be that stupid. 'Doesn't this point to our last-minute customer being the murderer?' I asked.

'Or it might be a clever smokescreen, intended to throw us off the scent.'

I laughed. 'Sending you round in circles looking for a homicidal collector of botanical samples?'

Dean snorted down the phone like a disgruntled horse. 'Something like that.'

CHAPTER SEVEN

'The police have removed their dinky little blue tent from our garden,' Ricky told me the following day as he lounged in the back room of *Old Nick's*, perched on a pretty Arts and Crafts table I was hoping to sell, if he didn't manage to break it first. 'They've finished with the crime scene. They've taken the anvil away, and a few of Bob's tools and left us with all the rest.'

'You mean Bob's war wagon?'

'His war wagon,' he repeated, 'the mobile forge, the display boards, Jackie's van and everything that was packed into it. Thank God, Ken took the horse.'

'How's Jackie going to get it all back?' I asked. 'If her van is at your place . . .'

'Ah!' he held up a finger. 'I've just spoken to Pat, and she says Ken will bring the horse and put him between the shafts of the war wagon and walk him back to Jackie's place. It'll take a couple of hours, but she says he won't mind.'

'What about the rest?'

Ricky grinned. 'We were hoping you might drive the van back to Jackie's.'

'Me?'

'We thought it might give you an opportunity to have a few words with her, if you know what I mean. We thought you might like that.'

'I would,' I admitted. I didn't really know her well enough to feel I could risk just turning up and intruding on her grief, but I wanted to ask her about Bob and Don Drummond. Returning Bob's stuff to her would give me the opening I needed. 'Then, how do I get back?'

Ricky wiggled his eyebrows as if he was about to reveal the crucial secret element of a cunning plan. 'We follow you in the Saab.'

'I see.'

'Point is, Princess, we know you're busy, so when do you want to do it?'

I heard the bell ring in the shop, and a few moments later, Morris's cheery greeting to Sophie and Pat.

'Tomorrow?' Ricky suggested.

'Hang on!' I protested. 'Give me a moment to think. I've got clients all day tomorrow. It'll have to be Saturday, and it'll have to be the morning, because I'm taking Maisie shopping for a Christmas tree in the afternoon.'

His voice cracked with laughter. 'Good luck with that.'

Morris bustled into the back room just then, loaded down with bags of shopping. 'All set?' he asked, beaming.

'Yeh,' Ricky told him. 'All set for Saturday. I'll just use your loo before we go.'

After Ricky and Morris had cleared off, I looked at the shop rota. I was supposed to be manning it on Saturday, all day, as I usually did. I'd already cajoled Elizabeth into coming in to cover the afternoon so I could take Maisie shopping. I smiled sweetly at Sophie, who'd seen me staring at the rota and was regarding me with the utmost suspicion. 'You couldn't cover for me Saturday morning, could you?' I asked. 'Ricky and Morris want me to help with taking Bob's stuff back to Jackie's.'

She rolled her dark eyes in exasperation and heaved a dramatic sigh. 'I suppose!'

'You're a star, Soph!'

She pulled a face. 'I spend my whole life in this place. One day I'm going to be discovered dead in this chair, covered in cobwebs, like Miss Havisham in . . .' her brow wrinkled in a frown, 'whichever Dickens book it was.'

'It was *Great Expectations*, and she wasn't found dead in a chair, her dress caught fire.' I looked around. 'This place could do with a dust, now you mention it. Look, why don't you go home now? I'll stay and lock up.'

'Okay, thanks.' She rinsed her paintbrush thoughtfully. 'Actually,' she began,' I need to have a little chat with you.'

'Oh? You all right Soph?'

'Well, I'm really grateful to you for letting me work here and display my stuff,' she began awkwardly. 'You know I'd never be able to afford my own studio, set up in business for myself. You pay all the business rates and electricity and so on . . . and I do feel guilty . . .'

'Well, don't. I'm the one who feels guilty because you and Pat look after the shop all day and I don't pay you anything.'

'We don't expect to be paid. But money is a problem. I contribute hardly anything at home. Mum never says anything, but the odd painting sale just isn't enough. I need to be earning regular money. Unless things improve soon, I'm just going to have to leave and get a job. I am sorry.'

'I understand, Soph.' I was sorry too. It would be awful if Sophie had to leave, not just for me, but for her. It would be tragic if she had to abandon her painting to go and flip burgers or something.

'I've been offered more shifts at the hotel,' she admitted.

'Well, take them. You can't afford to let them go. Don't worry about this place. Pat and I will manage.'

She nodded sadly. 'Thanks, Juno.'

I gave her a hug. She pulled on her coat and scarf and was out of the shop in seconds.

I looked at my watch. There was at least another hour till closing time but in narrow Shadow Lane we had already lost the sun. It was dark outside. I wondered if we'd get any more customers this late in the afternoon. I could either spend the remaining hour writing the Christmas cards I'd finally remembered to buy, or I could save them up for a thrilling evening ahead, get out the beeswax and give that Arts and Crafts table another polish. I'd just about decided on buffing the table up when the shop doorbell rang and a woman stepped inside. She was about fifty, greying curls escaping from beneath a yellow beret, a purple wool shawl flung over the shoulders of her coat. She stood before me at the counter, smiling up from a bright, enquiring face. 'Hello, Juno!'

I stared at her for a moment.

'Don't you remember me?' she asked, looking slightly hurt. 'It's Penny. Penny Anderson.'

Suddenly I was taken back years, to the little New Age shop in Totnes where I'd spent my school holidays, back to my cousin, Cordelia. 'Penny?' I stared as she nodded, her blue eyes crinkling as she laughed. 'Good Lord!' I came around the counter as she held out her arms and we hugged. Scents of neroli and geranium rose up from her scarf. Aromatherapy, I remembered, she was into aromatherapy. 'I haven't seen you since . . .'

'Since Cordelia's funeral,' she told me. 'Twelve years ago.'

She said it kindly, but I felt I'd been rebuked. Cordelia had been killed by a van rounding a bend too fast to stop. Penny had been a fellow astrologer and her closest friend. I'd never even sent her a Christmas card since. She pulled back, still holding on to my arms and stared up at me. 'You are so like her. The hair . . . she wasn't this glorious red, of course, but she had this magnificent mane of curls, just like you.'

'I'm sorry I never kept in touch.'

'You were in pieces, my dear,' she smiled sadly, 'I understand. You needed to get away and there was nothing left in Totnes for you to stay for. And you were studying at university as I remember.' She frowned. 'Weren't you just about to take your exams?'

'My finals, yes,' I said with a laugh. 'I managed to screw them up good and proper . . . at least, I didn't get the grades I was expected to get.'

'Not surprising under the circumstances. Couldn't you have taken them again?'

I shrugged. 'I didn't want to. I no longer cared.' I pointed her towards a chair and we sat down.

'I used to think you had a funny childhood,' she admitted. 'That exclusive boarding school during term time and then home to Cordelia and her old hippy friends in Totnes during the holidays. That's what you used to call us, a bunch of old hippies.'

'I must have been an obnoxious brat.'

She shook her head. 'You were questioning, and youngsters should be full of questions. Besides, old hippies were exactly what we were . . . are. We still meet, the same group who used to get together at Cordelia's place. Well, those of us who are still around. We're a bit thinner on the ground these days.'

I remembered that group. Totnes was the citadel of the New Age in those days, second only to Glastonbury for weirdness. Every Wednesday evening Cordelia's tiny flat above the shop was full of friends involved in everything from astrology, tarot and crystals, to reiki, shamanism, spirit healing, past-life regression and reading the aura. The air would be smoky with incense and heavy with the scent of ylang-ylang and patchouli, intense discussions going on long into the night about crop circles and visits from aliens. I remember being fascinated by these people, sopping up their ideas like a sponge, whilst never quite losing the still, small voice inside of me that reminded me they were all nuts.

'It's lovely to see you,' I said. 'But how did you find me?'

Penny laughed. 'You're very easy to find, Juno, if you read the *Dartmoor Gazette* – *famous amateur sleuth*,' she quoted.

I groaned. 'Please don't believe everything you read.'

'Oh, but I do, and that, in part, is why I've come to see you.' For a moment she looked grave, hesitant. 'I knew you'd be absolutely the right person to speak to.' She clasped her gloved hands in her lap, suddenly deadly serious. 'You see . . .'

The shop bell jangled and four teenage girls in school uniform trailed into the shop, noisy as squabbling starlings. They were a regular crowd, coming in every week after school to buy earrings. They were harmless, but they would still manage to wreck half the shop if left to their own devices. I'd have to keep an eye on them.

'Perhaps not here,' Penny went on. 'Somewhere

private. Would you like to come to my place? I'm only around the corner.'

'You live here, in Ashburton? You've moved from Totnes?'

She gave an irritated little sigh. 'After fifteen years my landlord decided he could make more money from short-term holiday lets than long-term tenants. Threw us all out. Well, you know how difficult it is finding rented accommodation around here. There was nothing in Totnes. Luckily for me, a friend of a friend had heard about a place here in Ashburton. I only moved in a few weeks ago, but I love it. I never realised it was such a fascinating little town.'

She scribbled down her address, whilst I kept my eye on the giggling gaggle of girls surrounding Pat's table. They were unhooking earrings from the black velvet display stands and holding them up to their ears, jostling for a place before the mirror.

I looked back at Penny. 'You said I'd be the right person to speak to. Was there something particular you wanted to talk about?'

She glanced in the direction of the schoolgirls and hesitated, lowering her voice to a whisper. 'Murder, my dear,' she said. 'I want to talk to you about murder.'

I found it difficult to concentrate on writing Christmas cards that evening. But I was already late for posting and it would be a miracle if any of them arrived in time for the big day. Luckily, I could deliver the majority by hand. I kept thinking about Penny. Her arrival brought back a host of forgotten memories. My mother died when I was barely three, from heart failure following a drug overdose. I don't remember her, and I've never known who my father was. Cousin Brian had paid for my boarding-school education and Cordelia had given me a home in the holidays, because there were no other family members I could go to. Brian was working abroad. He wasn't married to Marcia back then, or I'd probably have been packed off to camp or summer school during the holidays, like most of my boarding schoolfriends, who spent their holidays much like their term time, miserably missing their families. I'd certainly never have been allowed anywhere near an old hippy like Cordelia. And if the contrast between school and home was extreme, as a child I loved both. My school world was orderly, disciplined, polite and gave me a sense of structure and security; my holiday world gave me freedom to roam the wild places of Dartmoor and the wilder ideas of Cordelia's consciousness-raising, spirituality-seeking friends.

Penny said she wanted to talk about murder and she seemed serious. Perhaps she just wanted to gossip, to hear the gory details that weren't printed in the newspaper. I didn't get that impression, but I wouldn't be able to get round to see her before Sunday at the earliest, so I'd just have to wait to find out.

CHAPTER EIGHT

People deal with their grief in different ways. Jackie Millard dealt with hers by banging the hell out of red-hot metal with a hammer. That's what she was doing when I arrived at Bob's forge on Saturday morning. The war wagon had already been delivered by Ken. There was no sign of Noddy the horse, but the wagon itself was standing on the gravel forecourt outside of the showroom. The forge was housed in an old cattle shed painted white, 'The Country Blacksmith' in black iron letters mounted on one wall, clearly visible from the road. Wrought iron gates and railings were stacked outside, with garden seats and rose arches, advertising what was manufactured within. A weathervane on the roof showed a blacksmith working at his anvil.

Inside, the showroom was freshly painted and clean, a range of wood-burning stoves and chimneys as well as firedogs, door knockers, light fittings and fancy iron brackets on display. The clang of metal on metal echoed from the workshop beyond.

I wandered through to where Jackie was working at an anvil, a slim, athletic figure in dungarees and a leather apron, with bare bronzed arms, her eyes hidden by safety goggles. Sparks flew up at each echoing blow, the air above the hot coals quivering with heat. Whilst I waited for her to stop hammering, I studied some framed photographs hanging on the walls, pictures of Jackie and Bob astride powerful motorbikes, burning blue sky and desert scrub behind them. Bob was grinning, sporting a stars and stripes bandana and aviator shades. But what drew me more was a tiny print, taken from an illuminated manuscript. It showed women dressed in long skirts, their hair bound in medieval coifs, working at a forge. Women, it seemed, had been blacksmiths for centuries.

'They were allowed to join the Guilds back in the Middle Ages.' Jackie had paused in her work and was watching me. 'The widows of blacksmiths were permitted to carry on their husbands' trades, to register their own mark.'

'I had no idea,' I said, still staring at the picture.

She gave a slight laugh. 'Women have always forged chains and nails. Back in the eighteenth century, women nailers outnumbered men.'

I'd never thought about it before. Was any of the antique furniture in my shop held together with nails forged by women? I turned to look at Jackie. 'How are you?'

She took off her goggles, leaving a faint outline of grime around eyes red from shedding tears. 'I'm all right,' she said flatly, though her face was pale. She pushed back her spiky dark fringe with her forearm. 'I'm keeping busy. Thanks for bringing the van over.'

'No problem. We packed the stuff in as best we could.'

'I'm sure it will be fine.'

'You'll carry on here, then, at the forge?' I asked.

'I'm selling the farrier side of the business to another smith, but I'll carry on here with the metal work. It's what I trained for. I've always done most of the fancy stuff. And I've got an apprentice, Ryan. He's a great help.' She was silent a moment as if she was making up her mind whether to speak. 'You haven't heard any more about Bob?'

'No, no I haven't.'

'I thought you might . . . I thought the police might tell you things they wouldn't tell me.'

I smiled. 'In general, they try not to.'

'They haven't arrested Don Drummond, then?' Her voice suddenly broke with emotion and she turned away. I groped in my pockets for a tissue and held one out to her, feeling stupidly inadequate. She took it, blowing her nose before she turned back to face me again. 'Thanks,' she muttered.

'Do you really think Don killed Bob?'

She didn't answer, just gave a bitter laugh.

'I know they fought,' I added. 'What was it all about?'

She dashed angry tears away with the back of her hand. 'You want to ask Don.'

I'd rather not. 'What do you mean?'

'Ask him about his brother, Gary.'

'I didn't know Don had a brother.' I said it in the hope Jackie might be more forthcoming. After a moment, she decided to open up.

'Gary and Bob were mates,' she went on, 'but Gary had a problem with drugs. He was a bit of a sad soul, to be honest, vulnerable, always turning up to crash on our sofa or cadge some cash. Don had washed his hands of him, thrown him out, left him to live on the streets. And after a year or two of living rough, the poor sod died. So yeah, Bob had a go at Don, told him how many sorts of a bastard he thought he was.'

'And you think they fought again? At the fair?'

She eyed me defiantly. 'No one else had any reason to kill Bob.'

Whilst I could see why Don had accused Bob of poking his nose into his personal business, it was hardly a motive for murder. But Don was quick-tempered, Bob was far from sober and too handy with his fists. An argument could have got out of hand, as it had before, with unintended consequences. 'What about this last-minute customer of Bob's?' I asked. 'You don't know who it was?'

She shrugged. 'Just some bloke, ordinary, inoffensive-looking.'

'And you hadn't seen him before? Hanging around?'

'Well, if he was, I didn't notice him.'

From outside came the scrunch of wheels on gravel, the sound of a car drawing up on the forecourt. 'That's probably my ride home,' I told her as I turned towards the door. 'Perhaps you'd better come and look at what's in the van, make sure we haven't left anything behind.'

Jackie grabbed my arm, delaying me, her grip firm and strong. 'I want you to swear to me, Juno. You will tell me, won't you, if you find out anything?' She stared intently into my face, and the wild gleam in her eyes made me uneasy. 'Any proof it's him?'

'The only people likely to find that out are the police,' I told her carefully. At least that was true. If there was any trace of Don's DNA on Bob's body, forensics would find it, eventually. 'And in the meantime, Jackie, I'll be honest with you, I intend to steer well clear of Don Drummond. And,' I added as Ricky and Morris's voices sounded in the showroom, 'I think you should do the same.'

'I thought she was flippin' scary, if you want to know the truth,' I told them as I rode home in the back of the Saab.

Ricky half turned in the front passenger seat to look at me. 'You think she could be out for revenge?'

'I think she's a bit of a wild one.' I remembered what Dean had told me about Jackie and Bob's stormy relationship. I didn't know if the police were right to consider her a suspect. Perhaps she had killed Bob and that was why she was so keen to throw suspicion on Don Drummond. Could she have stabbed her drunken husband with a pritchel, pushed him so hard he fell and hit his head? She was certainly strong enough, but I couldn't see it myself. And why would she place a horseshoe in his hands, threaded with a sprig of elder?

'I know there's a lot of gossip about how she and Bob used to fight,' Morris glanced at me in the rear-view mirror, 'but some couples fight all the time. It doesn't mean they don't love each other, or that either of them is capable of murder.'

'How long had they been married, do we know?'

'A few years.' Ricky answered. 'I was having a chat with someone at the farmers' market yesterday – course, everyone was talking about Bob – and he remembered a story about Jackie chucking him out of the house because she caught him around the back of the pub with one of his lady friends.'

'But she took him back again,' Morris pointed out.

'More than once, from what I heard.'

'Then she must have loved him,' he insisted.

'Perhaps she loved him too much. Jealousy got the better of her.' Ricky chuckled. 'It was a crime of passion.'

'It's no laughing matter.' Morris changed gear with rather too much feeling. 'I think it's horrible. Everyone singing carols, whilst poor Bob was fighting for his life. I can't bear to think about it.'

This wasn't the first body to have been found in the grounds of Druid Lodge, so I could understand Morris feeling upset. He's very sensitive.

'It is horrible,' I agreed. Jackie had been singing carols down there with the rest of us. I remembered her face in the light of the lantern. Even if she'd had the opportunity, the motive, I didn't believe she could look so relaxed, so carefree, if she had just murdered her husband. Even if he was a bastard and she'd hated him. Which brought us back to Don Drummond and the inoffensive last-minute customer.

I didn't get home again until the evening, following a long afternoon at the garden centre with Maisie. She was ready and waiting when I went to pick her up, dressed in her best coat and black velvet beret as if she was going to church, and refusing to consider using the wheelchair. 'I don't want to go in that thing. I'm all right with my walking frame.'

'But it will be very crowded there this afternoon,' I pointed out. 'It's the last Saturday before Christmas. We don't know how far away we may have to park, and we might have to wait a long time at the checkouts to pay. You know you can't stand for long.'

After a lot more argument, she grudgingly agreed to take the wheelchair with us.

I was grateful I'd won the day. The garden centre is an enormous indoor and outdoor complex including a gift shop, cafe, aquatic and pet department, an outdoor-wear franchise, and a food hall selling very expensive and beautifully packaged local produce. Maisie wanted to see it all, tutting over every label and price tag, and complaining when anyone got in her way.

The Christmas tree department was like an indoor forest. We must have spent at least an hour in there, Maisie demanding to know the price of every single tree, including ones that were too tall to fit in her living room without sawing a hole in the ceiling. She considered silver trees, gold trees, trees with fibre-optic lights or artificial snow, before being persuaded into a modestly priced, sensibly sized green one with a few fir cones attached. We spent another half hour deciding on a new string of fairy lights before she announced, 'I want new baubles an' all.'

A well-deserved cup of tea and slice of Christmas frangipane came after fifteen minutes queuing at the cafe counter. We did a quick race around the gift shop and food hall, the inconveniently long box containing the tree balanced across the arms of Maisie's wheelchair and getting in the way of all the other shoppers. I managed to grab a few gifts for friends before we ran the gauntlet of the checkouts and escaped out into the car park, where the next challenge was to locate Van Blanc in the failing light and the sleety rain we didn't realise had started whilst we were inside. Eventually I got Maisie loaded into the front, her wheelchair, tree and other parcels into the back and we set off thankfully for home.

At least, for Maisie's home. Back at the cottage I unloaded her and everything else, considerably hampered by Jacko who took exception to the large box containing the tree and even graver exception to the big green bristly thing I eventually wrestled out of it, barking and growling until Maisie silenced him with a swipe across the snout from a roll of wrapping paper. After I'd made us another cup of tea, I set up the tree in the required corner, unreeled the new lights and draped them on the branches and found the setting that allowed the colours to gradually change without the whole set flashing on and off and giving Maisie a headache. 'Would you like me to put the baubles on for you?' I asked her.

'Well, who else is going to do it?' she responded graciously, and then proceeded to criticise the placement of every single one. But by the time I finished I could tell she was pleased with the result, and I was glad I'd overcome the urge to strangle her with tinsel.

'It looks lovely, Juno. Thank you ever so much.'

'You're welcome, Maisie,' I told her, placing my hand on the nearest radiator and burning my fingers. The central heating was still holding up. Thank God.

I was just getting my teeth into the chunk of leftover hazelnut and cranberry roast Adam and Kate had brought me back from *Sunflowers* when the phone rang. I'd barely sat down. I'd bumped into Kate on my way indoors and spent twenty minutes walking around the kitchen, jigging a grizzly baby Noah in my arms whilst she put her groceries away. Then we'd had a glass of wine whilst I told her about my thrilling afternoon. Adam returned from the cafe, bearing leftovers wrapped in foil, like one of the three kings arriving at the manger, and I'd come upstairs gleefully clutching my booty. Cafe owners definitely make the best landlords.

I was looking forward to an evening munching festive fare in front of some old film whilst I finished writing my cards and wrapped a few presents in the ridiculously expensive paper I had just bought. No such luck. The phone rang and when I picked up, the voice of an ancient banshee wailed down the line. 'It's broke again!'

'What? Maisie?'

'It went clunk and now it's freezing in here.'

'Are you sure it's not just the timer?'

'Eh?'

What was the point in trying to explain? If the timer was the problem, she wouldn't be able to deal with it anyway. 'I'll be around in half an hour,' I promised. I thought I had as much chance of getting Malcolm the heating engineer to come out on a Saturday night as hell freezing over, but it turned out he was only too happy to have an excuse to get away from the in-laws who'd just arrived for the Christmas holidays. He met me at Maisie's cottage, where after shaking his head in a sorry fashion over the innards of her boiler, declared this time, there was nothing he could do. Her agency carer arrived to put Maisie to bed. At least her bed was warm, courtesy of a new electric blanket, and I felt happy enough to leave her for the night and come home.

I phoned Our Janet up in Heck-as-Like and gave her the bad news. She was already planning on driving down next day to pick her mother up. 'It's about a six-hour drive,' she sighed down the phone. 'I'll set off early. I should be with you by lunchtime.'

'I'll make sure she's packed and ready,' I promised. 'And Jacko.'

'Juno, you are a star.'

'Oh yeah,' I agreed ironically, as I put the phone down. 'Star o'wonder, me.'

CHAPTER NINE

It was the middle of the next afternoon before I made it to Penny's place. I'd never heard of Loft Cottage, although I must have walked past the address she had given me on East Street hundreds of times. It was a large townhouse, probably Georgian, and slightly run-down, its white walls dulling to grey, its front door opening straight on to the pavement, the jumble of assorted doorbells indicating the building had been divided into several flats. Taking Penny's advice, I walked straight in. A long corridor took me past the entrance to two flats, and through a half-glass door into an outer courtyard where bins and bicycles were stored. A flight of twisting stone steps led me up into a tiny surprise garden, a square patch of ground enclosed by stone walls, the grey tiles of rooftops sloping down low to meet them. I found myself staring through the ramshackle window of an adjacent house at the lights of a Christmas tree. I turned around. I was surrounded by rooftops, seemingly leaning in towards me, some tall and pointed, others long and sagging, their ancient tiles green with moss, little windows peeping between them here and there. I loved it. I was right in the middle of the town and yet I had no idea this secret place existed. The garden itself was dull and winter bare, a few straggly dried stems sticking up in terracotta pots, except in one corner where a glorious old rose had spread itself, its flowers long shrivelled, brightening the grey walls with bulbous, orange hips.

A wooden sign on the wall proclaimed Loft Cottage. I couldn't see a front door. The only way in seemed to be through a pair of French windows opening directly onto the garden, and I knocked on the glass. It was growing dim and the lights were on inside, a shaded Tiffany lamp throwing a glow of colours across a polished wood floor, a large rag rug taking up its centre.

It was a long room, with open beams, bookshelves, a desk, two sofas facing each other, and what appeared to be a small, modern kitchen area behind. Penny came through a door at the back and smiled when she saw me, beckoning me in. I opened the window and stepped into the welcoming warmth of a woodburning stove and the scent of clove and cinnamon coming from joss-sticks burning on a low table. 'This place is lovely!' I told her as I closed the window behind me.

She nodded. 'I'm lucky, aren't I? The landlord had just done it up before I moved in.' She swept an arm around the room. 'This is more or less all of it. There's a tiny bedroom with an even tinier bathroom at the back. But there's more than enough space for me.'

She offered to take my coat, advised me to kick off my

shoes, and I settled myself on one of her low sofas. Hanging loosely around her neck was a silk scarf, in shades of blue and turquoise. 'Isn't that one of Fizzy Izzy's scarves?' I asked.

She laughed, looking down at it and fingering the silk fringe. 'I bought it in that gallery in North Street.'

I nodded. 'That's the one.'

'I just loved these colours. It's a Christmas present to myself. It cost me an arm and a leg, but it will go with so many things.' Whilst she made tea, I studied the books on the shelves opposite, mostly astrology books, so many of the titles familiar because Cordelia had owned them too and they were still stored in boxes under my bed.

'Do you still practise?' I asked.

'Oh yes,' Penny called back from the kitchen. 'Not as much as I did, these days, but I still give the occasional consultation. I don't do the magazines anymore.' She came in, handed me a mug and sat down on the sofa next to me. 'I used to do horoscopes for some of the monthlies. "What's in the stars for your sign this month?" sort of thing. Very looked down upon I was, by some of our astrological brethren, giving serious astrology a bad name.'

'Why? People love horoscopes.'

'They do. But you know that if I want to cast an accurate birth chart for someone, I need their time and place of birth as well as the full date. Trying to make a generalised forecast for everyone born within a thirty-day period can never be accurate, which is what leads some people to dismiss astrology as rubbish. And, sadly, it's still the case that anyone can call themselves an astrologer without any training or experience. You should see some of the rubbish out there on social media.' She gave a wry little smile. 'I used to call myself Isis in those days.' Her bright eyes danced. 'Not such a good idea now.'

'Isn't this her?' I pointed to a small statuette on her desk, an Egyptian figure with wings.

'Yes, that's Isis. Egyptian goddess of healing and magic.' A certain dreaminess crept into her eyes. 'I love Egypt.'

'You and Cordelia went together,' I remembered.

She nodded. 'When we were young. I want to go again before I'm finished,' she added wistfully. 'It's on my bucket list.' She patted my knee. 'But I want to know all about you. What did you do after university?'

'Not a lot,' I confessed. 'Travelled a bit.'

'You had a boyfriend at the time.'

I nodded. 'We split up after a year. I tried out various jobs, all of which I hated. Went through a couple of relationships but nothing seemed to work out. After wandering about like a lost soul for a few years, I decided the only place I really felt happy was at home.' I shrugged. 'Home for me had always meant Cordelia. I came back to live in Totnes. But of course, the shop had been sold. I couldn't find a job, couldn't find anywhere to live . . .'

'You should have come to me,' Penny said reproachfully.

'Yes,' I nodded. 'Perhaps I should.' I didn't mention that I found just being in the town unbearably painful. 'But then I might not have ended up here in Ashburton.'

'And are you happy here?'

'I love it.'

'And, if I may ask,' she ventured tentatively, 'is there no one in your life at the moment?'

Now there's a question, I asked myself. Is there? I hesitated. 'It's complicated.'

'And you'd rather not talk about it.'

'Not just now.'

'Fair enough.' She smiled. 'Don't mind me, I'm incurably nosy. Typical Gemini. I have a mind like a magpie, not content unless I'm gathering bits of information.'

We both sipped our tea. There was silence for a while, the only sounds the crackle of the fire and some faintly mystic music playing in the background. But I could sense Penny's restlessness, her desire to talk, a fizzing energy building up inside her.

'You mentioned in the shop you wanted to talk about murder,' I prompted.

She put down her mug and took a deep breath. 'Yes, I do. It's difficult. But the police won't take me seriously, despite having called upon my services as an astrologer on more than one occasion.'

'Really?'

'Oh yes! I don't mean here, in Devon. But there have been occasions in the past when they've sought out my professional services. They'd deny it, of course. Anyway,' she threw up her hands, a quick darting gesture, 'that's neither here nor there. I read in the paper about the murder of that poor blacksmith. What started my alarm bells ringing was that it mentioned the day he died was his birthday, is that correct?'

'Yes, it was.' I don't know what was alarming about it. There are only three hundred and sixty-five days to choose from. Lots of people have died on their birthdays, Shakespeare for one.

'Making this blacksmith a Sagittarius.' Penny nodded to herself, as if confirming some inner knowledge. I waited. She looked up at me and smiled, a little nervously I thought, unconsciously fiddling with the fringe of her scarf. 'Tell me what you remember about the sign of Sagittarius.'

I laughed. 'Is this a test?'

'Call it a game.'

'Okay, I'll play.' I thought for a moment. 'Well, it's a fire sign and it's ruled by Jupiter, so Sagittarians are generally jolly, fun-loving people, expansive, love to travel,' all the things I knew about Bob, when I thought about it. 'They're also inclined to be hot-tempered . . .' I shrugged, that was all I could think of. 'The sign is represented by the archer.'

Penny nodded. 'But not just any old archer.'

'No. The centaur, half man, half horse.' All this was vaguely interesting but I had no idea where Penny was going with it. 'So, what's all this got to do with Bob's murder?'

'The sign has always had an affinity with travel, with speed – nowadays, we might think about fast cars or aeroplanes.'

'Or motorbikes,' I added, thinking of the photos I'd seen at Jackie's forge.

Penny nodded. 'But throughout millennia, Sagittarius has been associated with the horse. So, for a Sagittarian blacksmith to be murdered on his birthday, whilst the sun is in the sign of Sagittarius and for that . . .' she hesitated, searching for a word, '*Association* to be pressed home by the leaving of the horseshoe . . . well, it set my alarm bells ringing.'

I must have looked blank.

'Well, it's all too . . . apt,' she went on. 'The timing, the manner of death . . . the horseshoe, it's all too perfect.'

'You think Bob was murdered because he was a Sagittarius?' I asked incredulously.

'Not exactly. I don't know *why* he was murdered,' she stressed. 'But I think there is an astrological connection.'

'Surely it's nothing but coincidence,' I responded. 'I suppose the murderer might have been making some kind of sick joke about the fact horseshoes are supposed to be lucky.' Not lucky for Bob, as it turned out.

She shook her head. 'No, no. There are just too many parallels with the others.'

'Others?' I repeated.

'The other murders.'

I blinked at her. 'What other murders?'

She gave an intriguing little smile. 'I think it's time for another cup of tea.'

'It began with the death of a scientist at the university.' Penny had made tea and settled down again. 'I was still working there then. My job was only clerical, part-time, but even so, I kept my astrological activities to myself.'

'You think you'd have been disapproved of?'

116

She laughed. 'Oh, my dear, I was working in a science department!'

I grinned. I could imagine how some scientists might react to an astrologer in their midst. 'So, your colleagues never knew they were working with Isis?'

'Never. Even though,' she added with an impish smile, 'I once caught one of them reading my column. Anyway, the research going on in the department was into the beneficial effects of natural toxins – in particular, scorpion venom.'

I couldn't imagine there were many benefits to being stung by a scorpion myself.

'There are medical applications,' she went on enthusiastically. 'Chemical compounds in some scorpion venom kill harmful bacteria. In the laboratory, they were researching its use in the treatment of tuberculosis, diabetes, even certain cancer cells.'

Well, it was nice to know the crawly little buggers were good for something.

'Gordon Peters was a scientist involved in this research. He worked with scorpions every day in the lab.' She glanced down briefly, her fingers still twisting in the ends of her scarf. 'He died after being stung.'

'In the lab?'

'No.' She sighed. 'That was one of the odd things about it. He was at home. There was an investigation into his death, of course. The conclusion it came to was that a scorpion had escaped, unnoticed – although it's difficult to believe it could, because they were so careful in the lab, had so many safeguards – and it had either got onto Gordon's clothes, or into his open briefcase and he'd carried it home himself.' She shook her head. 'I can't go along with the clothes theory. Scorpions don't sting unless they feel threatened, but I'm sure his movements as he drove his car home would have been enough to antagonise it.'

'So, you think he took it home in his briefcase?'

'Or someone put it in there, hoping the next time he put his hand in, he'd be stung.'

'Then you think someone was trying to kill him. But that means it could only be someone in the lab, someone who had access to the scorpion. Did you suspect anyone?'

She shook her head. 'No. Everyone loved Gordon. Besides, it isn't what happened. He must have opened the case and the scorpion escaped because it was found inside his shoe. Scorpions like places to hide in. Shoes are ideal.'

'This thing couldn't have been very big, then.'

'No, it was a Deathstalker.'

'Great name!' I blurted out before I could stop myself, but my tactlessness didn't seem to bother Penny. She carried on.

'It's only about two inches long. And its sting is not usually lethal. It wouldn't kill a healthy adult, although it would be agonisingly painful, but it could kill a child, or an elderly person, or someone with a weak heart, like Gordon. Its venom induces tachycardia, you see, accelerated heart rate, and breathing difficulties. If only it had happened in the lab,' she cried tearfully, 'with other people there to help, but Gordon lived alone. When he didn't come in to work next day, we were worried. It wasn't like him to miss work without phoning or communicating in some way. We phoned, but when there was no response, a couple of colleagues went round to his flat and broke in. They found him dead.'

And one squashed scorpion, I added privately. Nasty. 'You said you thought someone might have put the scorpion in his briefcase deliberately. There's no possibility he would have taken it himself?'

She shook her head vehemently. 'Absolutely none.' She turned a serious gaze on me. 'This happened in November and Gordon was a Scorpio.'

'Well, there's certainly a horrible irony in the way he died,' I conceded, 'but no more than that, surely? And you say you don't know anyone who had a motive for wanting him dead?'

She shook her head. 'No, I don't.' She gave me an uncertain glance. 'You probably think I'm as crazy as the police do.'

'No, of course not,' I assured her, fingers mentally crossed, 'but it seems to me Gordon's death could just have been a terrible accident.'

'I know,' she sighed. 'And I know on its own, it may not seem like much. But Gordon's death made me think about Professor Gideon and what happened to him the year before.'

'Did he work with scorpions too?'

'Oh no,' she shook her head, 'he worked in psychiatry. He was a Pisces, and as you might remember,' she added, with a little smile, 'Pisces rules the twelfth house, the House of the Unconscious Mind. A great number of Pisceans work in mental health, in fact, in all the healing professions. Anyway, Professor Gideon went missing. He kept a sailing boat down at Dartmouth. It was found one night, just offshore, floating in the fog. His body didn't turn up until days later, washed up on a beach some miles down the coast. They found drugs in his system and, of course, his death was dismissed as a tragic accident. He'd gone sailing whilst under the influence, fallen off into the water and drowned.'

'But you don't think so?'

'No. I mean, who goes sailing alone, at night, in fog?'

'You said yourself he was under the influence.'

Penny hunched a shoulder. 'He smoked a bit of pot. It wouldn't have rendered him incapable.'

'You don't think it was suicide?'

'No,' she said definitely.

'Then someone else must have been on board.'

'I believe so.'

'I take it there's an astrological connection here?'

'This happened at end of February, in Pisces.'

'Which is a water sign.'

'Yes,' she agreed. 'But it's not just water.' She stood and began to pace restlessly, fired up by her passion for her subject. 'Pisces is ruled by Neptune – or Poseidon, to give him his other name, god of seas, rivers, even mists and fogs.' She fixed me with her blue eyes. 'It's the symbolism which is so striking in this case, you see. This disappearance into the fog is intensely symbolic of how Neptune works . . .'

'Just hold on a minute, Penny,' I begged her. I was getting lost in the fog myself. 'What you seem to be leading up to is that behind these murders – both of which could be dismissed as accidents,' I added, holding up a defensive palm, 'there is a mind with astrological knowledge at work?'

She gave an emphatic little nod. 'Yes.'

'Right.' I took a breath. 'How long ago was all this?'

'Oh, Professor Gideon drowned seven years ago.'

'As long ago as that?' From the way she'd been talking I'd thought it was a far more recent event.

She nodded. 'And Gordon the following year.' She hesitated a moment. 'But it was what happened to poor Dorothy only last year that convinced me that whoever had killed them was still . . . well . . . at it.'

'Dorothy?' There was another murder coming up?

'Would you like another tea?' Penny asked.

'Got anything stronger?'

'Definitely,' she made a beeline for the fridge in the kitchen.

I leant back against the sofa cushions and puffed out my cheeks in a sigh. Across the room, shelves of astrology books faced me, and I gazed at them absently. I reached the same conclusion I had years ago when Cordelia was alive. No matter how fascinating, engrossing and truly mind-blowing a subject astrology might be, study it for too long and it will drive you bonkers in the end.

CHAPTER TEN

'Dorothy had been retired about a year. She used to work in the vice chancellor's office.' Penny smiled sadly. 'I don't think she'd ever worked anywhere else. She was a shy woman, lived with her mother until the old lady died, and was a keen forager, always out picking free food from the hedgerow. She used to document her finds in a diary, drew the most detailed illustrations. I believe she was planning to publish a book one day. Her notes, like her drawings, were meticulous. She was always most careful, precise, as she had been in her job at the university.'

'A Virgo by any chance?' I suggested.

'Yes.' Penny bit her lip, smiling. 'And probably a virgin too.'

'And she died at the end of the summer?'

'And, as you've no doubt guessed, she was poisoned.'

'She picked the wrong kind of mushroom?'

'No, fungi had nothing to do with it. And in any case,

Dorothy was too experienced a forager to make such an elementary mistake. No, it was the Naked Lady that killed her.'

I blinked at the image this presented. 'Sorry?'

'It's another name for the autumn crocus. It's easy to mistake its flowers for ransoms, apparently, because they are vaguely alike, but again, I can't see Dorothy making a mistake like that. The point is, the seeds of the plant are lethal. Just a few grams can kill an adult and there is no antidote. The central nervous system breaks down, leading to seizures, vomiting, internal bleeding – death usually results from shock. I'm afraid poor Dorothy suffered horribly.' Tears welled up in her eyes and I gave her a moment to gather herself.

'I'm sorry,' I said, after she'd wiped away a tear and blown her nose.

'So, if she didn't pick the plant herself,' I asked, 'do we know how she came to ingest these seeds?'

Penny shook her head. 'The police treated her death as suspicious. There was a full autopsy and an inquest. It looked as if she had shared her last meal with someone, or at least, the table was laid for two and there were two plates left on it after the meal. There were remains of what they'd eaten in a dish in the kitchen but none of the toxin was found in it. Yet the fatal compound – colchicine – was detected in her body.'

'And no one else died from the meal? So, what was the verdict at the inquest?'

'Death by misadventure.'

'But you think her death was the work of our astrological killer.'

'I know it's horrible, but Virgo rules the stomach, you see, and so poisoning . . . well, it's cynical and vile to say so, but it *is* appropriate. Also, here in Western society we think of the virgin as just an inexperienced young girl. But to the ancient Babylonians and to the Greeks, she was Ceres, Goddess of the Harvest, which is why she is always shown holding a sheaf of corn.'

'So, Dorothy's harvesting habit fits her nicely.'

'Indeed.'

I sat back and thought. 'And you think Bob's murder falls into the same category?'

'It fits the same pattern.'

'Does it? What about the horseshoe? None of the previous victims had any kind of symbol left on their body, did they?'

'Not that I know of.'

'You see, Penny, what strikes me,' I began as tactfully as I could, 'is that if you're right, over a period of several years, your astrologer-murderer has successfully got away with passing three murders off as accidents. He's committed the perfect crimes, if you like. But in Bob's case, murder was obvious. Bob's death was violent and the murderer left the horseshoe in his hands, almost as if he wanted to make sure everyone knew it *wasn't* an accident.'

Penny frowned. 'Could Bob not have been clutching it when he fell?'

I was forced to keep to myself any mention of the

sprig of elder. 'No,' I said. 'It was deliberately placed, as if his killer left it as a calling card. But if you've already got away with murder three times, why would you do that? And those murders were a long time ago. Why should the killer suddenly start again?'

'Perhaps he thinks it's time he got some recognition for his work.' She spoke in perfect seriousness, but after a moment we both laughed at the idea. 'And in any case,' she added more seriously, 'we don't *know* he ever stopped. Perhaps he's kept going but we just don't know who his victims were.'

'Is he planning to murder his way around the zodiac? Who's next, d'you think?' A Leo zookeeper torn apart by lions, I wondered privately, a Cancerian nibbled to death by crabs?

'You don't take me seriously,' Penny said sadly. 'Do you?'

I reached out and placed a hand on hers. 'Of course I do. It's just . . . there has to be some reason for all this killing. The murderer has to have a motive. At least your three victims were connected by working at the same university, even if they were in different departments. But that doesn't apply to Bob.'

'No, I suppose not.' She smiled again. 'Thanks for listening to me, Juno. I know I chatter on.'

'My pleasure,' I assured her. 'It's all been fascinating.'

'But not convincing?'

'I'm not saying that.' I hesitated. 'I just need to mull it over.'

'It has been lovely seeing you again.'

We stood up and gave each other a hug. 'Well, now we're such near neighbours . . .'

'Listen,' she said, as if struck by a sudden thought. 'After Christmas I'm having a meeting here of the old gang – well, those of us who are left – who used to meet up at Cordelia's. We haven't got together in a while. Why don't you come? They'd all love to see you.'

'Well, . . .' I began, fumbling for an excuse.

'Please. I know you think we're all loonies, but we are harmless, really.'

'I'd love to come,' I lied bravely. 'Thanks.'

We said our goodbyes and I made my way through the garden and back out on to the street. I really didn't want to get involved with Cordelia's old cronies again. As I remembered, some of them were certainly loonies. Harmless? I wasn't so sure.

By the time I reached home I was in a foul temper. It took me a while, not to mention a glass of red, to work out what was going on inside of me. It was Penny I was angry with. I really didn't want all this information she'd laid on me. What was I supposed to do about it? Her astrological murder theory was mad. But she was Cordelia's dearest friend, and I knew Cordelia would have wanted me to listen to her. I felt obliged to take her seriously, even though it seemed to me that what she had told me about was just a series of horrible accidents. It was the sense of obligation that was chafing me. I didn't want to go to this meeting, but for Penny's sake I felt obliged to attend.

I told Bill all this as he trod up and down the sofa, crossing my lap at each turn and allowing me to stroke his spine all the way to the tip of his tail. Then he settled down on my lap, purring. 'You're right,' I told him. 'It's time to stop fretting and chill out.' I took another sip of wine and reached for my diary, just to check I had cleared all my commitments before Christmas. Maisie had been safely packed off to Heck-as-Like, along with Jacko and the long-suffering Janet. There were just three days to go and as far as I was concerned, my diary should be clear. I wouldn't walk the Tribe over the holidays, and I had told my Domestic Goddess clients I wouldn't be working again until after Christmas. This left me three days to devote myself to the shop, enjoy a jolly festive time working in there with Sophie and Pat and hopefully make some jolly festive sales of antiques.

I flicked through the pages of my diary. All satisfyingly blank except for three small letters scrawled in pencil for December 23rd. C.B.S. I puzzled over them for a moment. They looked innocent enough, but what did they mean? C.B.S? I shrieked and leapt up from the sofa, discomforting poor Bill who'd just nodded off. I grabbed my coat and my keys and headed for the door. C.B.S! How in the hell could I have forgotten Chloe Berkeley-Smythe?

CHAPTER ELEVEN

Mrs Chloe Berkeley-Smythe is one of my long-standing clients and pays me a healthy retainer to look after her property whilst she is away cruising – which is most of the time. She would, if she could, spend her whole life floating about on a luxury cruise, and as it is, her stays on land are as infrequent and brief as she can make them. In return for this retainer, I keep her cottage clean, water her plants, tidy her garden, take in and sort her avalanches of mail, and always get shopping in ready for her return. She also expects me to devote my time to her pretty exclusively for the first two or three days after she arrives home, driving her to her various appointments, unpacking and laundering all the clothes that don't get sent to the dry-cleaner, and packing them up ready for her next voyage. She is without doubt one of the most good-natured and generous women I have ever met. She is also the most indolent, entirely devoted to her own pleasure. She's great fun and I love her dearly. And I had almost screwed up our harmonious arrangement by completely forgetting that this Christmas, just for once, she would be coming home.

I headed for Stapledon Lane and let myself in through the door of her handsome cottage, quickly punching in the burglar alarm code to silence the beeping in the hall. I switched on the lights. Fortunately, I am very conscientious when it comes to Chloe's cottage, and I had come in to water the plants and tidy the garden only a few days ago. The place didn't look too bad. It just needed a quick dust and whizz around with the Dyson, which I would do in the morning. The first, most essential thing was to pump up the central heating. I'd put it on to a frost setting when the weather had turned cold, but it was a stone building and needed a couple of days to warm through properly. Chloe was coming back after weeks in the heat of the Caribbean; she would expect her place to be warm. I adjusted the thermostat and turned up all the radiators.

Then I plugged in her fridge-freezer, which I always empty and defrost whenever she goes away. The cottage, silent and empty for weeks, began to hum with the sounds of returning life. I made up her bed, then checked her larder for ground coffee and counted the bottles of sherry. Tomorrow I would shop for her other essentials – prawns, smoked salmon, brioche, and coffee ice cream. I sorted the new mail in the porch into piles that were easily identifiable as Christmas cards, bills, medical appointments and letters from her stockbroker. There was a small pile for *other*. I checked my watch. It was already ten o'clock. I'd leave calling on her neighbour until the morning and collect up all the parcels she would have taken in for Chloe whilst she was away. Chloe was addicted to TV shopping channels.

I gazed around her living room. I don't think I had forgotten anything. I'd have to give all her blasted horse brasses a rub over in the morning as well. From the depths of my pocket, my phone rang. I almost laughed out loud when I saw who was calling. 'Mrs Berkeley-Smythe!' I cried, as I connected. 'What a surprise!'

'Hello, Juno, my dear!' came the plummy response and she launched into a fulsome apology for having forgotten to ring me to remind me she was coming home; which to be fair, she normally does. 'It never entered my silly head until a moment ago,' she admitted, 'and I'll be back tomorrow evening.'

'No problem. I had it written in my diary,' I told her smugly, not mentioning the gasping panic that had washed over me when I read it, or that I was standing in her living room with a cloth in hand as we spoke. 'Everything's ready.'

'Juno, you are wonderful! I can't wait to see my little cottage again.' She always says this. Within a week she'll be gagging to get back on the water. 'I don't suppose there's any chance of visiting the bank before Christmas?'

'Well, it's getting a bit close, but I'll try to make an

appointment.' We no longer have a bank in Ashburton. Two mobile banks visit on a weekly basis, calling in to the car park for a couple of hours, but Chloe likes to speak to a manager which always means a trip to her branch in Exeter.

'Oh no, too exhausting!' she moaned. 'We'll leave it until afterwards! The Plymouth One is after my money.' She gave a wicked chuckle. 'That's why he's invited me for Christmas. He wants to grab some of it before it's all gone.'

Chloe had two sons, both now middle-aged, the Plymouth One and the Other One. I forget what their real names are. She has never got on with either of them, admits to having been an appallingly negligent mother, and is unrepentantly spending her way through the considerable inheritance left by her husband. But, she points out, both boys were left fortunes by other relatives, have devoted their careers to amassing piles of filthy lucre, and have plenty of money of their own. 'They can keep their grubby hands off mine,' she says, whenever the subject comes up. She promised she would phone me as soon as she arrived in Ashburton, and I promised her I would come straight round.

I reset the burglar alarm and let myself out, standing for a moment in the lane. The stars above my head looked sharp and cold, a ring of ice crystals formed around a silver moon. I shivered and hunched into my coat, shrugging the wide collar up around my neck. At least Chloe's arrival had offered a brief diversion from

Penny and her astrological murders. To me, the most interesting thing about the victims was that they had all worked at the university at one time. It seemed to be the only real connection between them. Apart, of course, from Penny herself.

'Oh, there you are!' There was an almost accusatory tone in Sophie's voice when I finally fell in through the doorway of *Old Nick's* near lunchtime next day, as if she'd been waiting for me all morning.

'Sorry! Chloe's blasted horse brasses took longer than I thought. And she texted me this morning, she wanted me to buy her a bottle of Dartmoor gin.' I'd also bought her a plant, a red poinsettia, which I'd placed in a brass pot on her coffee table, just to welcome her home. It brightened the place up a bit. Then I'd popped into *Sunflowers* and bought Christmas flapjacks for us shop staff to enjoy with our coffee.

Pat was busy stitching a Santa hat onto a fluffy owl. 'I don't know what you're moaning about, Soph. You've got to get your painting finished for that customer before you can go anywhere. You wanna get on with it.'

'I am getting on with it,' she responded, dark eyes flashing indignantly. 'And I need to get to the framers with it. That's the point.'

'Well, I'm here now,' I said.

'You've just had a very nice sale, Juno,' Pat told me. 'One of them Della Whatsit plaques with the cherubs on.'

'The della Robbia?' I'd sold most of a collection of della Robbia pottery at auction recently and I only had a few small pieces left. I wasn't selling them cheap, so it was good to have sold another one. I looked over Sophie's shoulder at the painting she had almost finished, an ancient clapper bridge across a stream, with a lonely thorn tree in the foreground. It might have been an advert for the Dartmoor Tourist Board. I pointed to the bridge. 'Is this the one at Scorhill?'

Before she could answer, the shop bell jangled and the door opened, letting in a man with two small boys – *let's see if we can find a nice present for Mummy* – followed by friendly farmer, Carol.

She plonked a bottle of Cold East Farm Cider on the counter. 'Merry Christmas!' she said. 'I'm afraid this is last year's pressing. We're saving the new stuff for our wassail. It should be ready in time.'

'Oh yes, the wassail!' I said, just remembering she'd invited me.

'We wanted to hold it on Old Twelvey Night,' she explained, 'but we want the Border Morris to play for us and they're booked up almost every night in January, so we've had to go for the sixth.' She laughed, flicking her fringe of short blonde hair out of her eyes. Carol is what you might call a modern farmer. In other words, the reason for this wassail was not simply to bless the apple orchards so they bring forth a good crop, in accordance with ancient tradition, but also to impress the visitors she had staying in the farm's newly converted self-catering holiday accommodation. A few photos of folk merrily wassailing under the apple trees would not go amiss on its website. 'It seems wassailing goes on all through the month in these parts.'

Pat sniffed and nodded. 'Starts around the middle of December.' She was keeping her eye on the man with the two small boys as they tried to decide which colour earrings Mummy would like best.

Sophie looked up from her painting, her brow furrowed. 'When's Old Twelvey Night again?'

'The seventeenth,' I reminded her. 'Old Twelvey Night is when people used to celebrate Twelfth Night before the calendar was changed to the Gregorian calendar we use today.'

'When was that? When it changed, I mean?'

'Back in seventeen-hundred-and-something,' I said vaguely. 'That year they lost the month of September in the swop.' Tough luck on Virgos.

'I don't think Mummy likes purple,' a small voice objected softly.

'What about these pretty blue ones?' Daddy asked.

'Anyway,' Carol went on. 'I just popped in to give you the date and the bottle. I've got to go around to *Fizzy Izzy's*. The photographer from the local paper will be there shortly to take a picture of me and Don with the new wassail bowl he's made for us. They think it might make a good photo for their new year edition.'

I pulled a face. Would Don Drummond be at the wassail? That would take the gloss off my evening.

'Talking of Don,' I said, lowering my voice slightly, 'you remember you said he and Bob had been in a fight at an agricultural show back in the summer. Were you there when it happened?'

She nodded. 'Neil was one of the people who had to pitch in and pull the two of them apart.'

'Do you know who started it?'

'I don't, but Bob did a lot of the shouting.'

'What about?'

She shrugged.

'He didn't mention Don's brother at all?'

'To be honest, I don't remember. But it all got very nasty. I know Bob's a big man, fists like sledgehammers, but I don't think he stood much of a chance against Don. He was so much quicker. I think he must have studied martial arts or something. I honestly thought he might kill him.' A hand went to her mouth as if she realised what she'd just said. 'I don't mean that literally, of course.'

I think you do, I thought.

'Is there any news about Bob?' she asked.

'I haven't heard anything.'

'Poor Jackie. She won't be playing at our wassail now.'

'Playing?' I repeated.

'She plays the fiddle with the Border Morris,' Carol explained.

'Jackie plays the fiddle? I didn't know.'

'Yes, you do,' Sophie's voice piped up. 'She was in

135

that folk group we went to see at the arts centre last year.'

I remembered a couple of demon lady fiddlers. I just hadn't realised Jackie was one of them.

Carol nipped off for her appointment with the *Dartmoor Gazette* photographer, Daddy and the boys decided Mummy would like the blue earrings best and bought a pretty knitted scarf to match, and Sophie finally signed her name at the corner of her painting and rushed around to the framers with it. The shop was busy for the rest of the day. I sold an English stoneware beer mug and there was a sudden run on Delft meat platters, as if everyone had just found out their existing serving plates weren't going to be big enough for the turkey. But I kept thinking back to Jackie. Lady blacksmith, demon fiddler, a woman of many talents, obviously. Was murder one of them? I wondered.

'I'm in here, Juno, my dear,' a feeble voice called from the living room as I let myself in to Chloe's cottage that evening, mountaineering my way over the piles of suitcases left scattered in the hall. 'I'm shattered, absolutely shattered.'

Chloe was lying prostrate on her chaise-longue, feet up, eyes closed. She let out a shuddering sigh. 'Travelling does exhaust me so.'

Which kind of travelling, I wondered, biting back a smile. Floating around the world on a cruise liner or being driven back from Southampton in a chauffeur-driven limousine, which of those two was more exhausting? I bent down to kiss her well-rounded and fragrantly powdered cheek. 'Hello Chloe! Welcome home.'

'Thank you, my dear,' she responded. 'I just came in here and collapsed after poor Charles brought in the luggage.'

Charles was her regular chauffeur, poor man, who picked her up and drove her home from every cruise. She always insisted on having him, but she did tip him generously. 'Since then, I just haven't been able to do a thing.'

Except open the sherry, I noticed. There was a large, empty schooner clutched to her chest. 'Another?' I suggested.

Her eyes flew open. 'Oh, would you mind, Juno dear?' She gave me her glass and heaved herself into a more upright position. 'Pour one for yourself, of course.' She began to look around her. 'Now, there's a present for you somewhere. Where did I put it? It's in a carrier bag. I'm afraid it's only perfume from the duty-free. I couldn't think of anything else.'

Perfume from the duty-free would do very nicely. 'Thank you.' I handed her the sherry. 'I'll look for it later.'

I sat down and listened to what an exhausting time she'd had on her cruise and we planned her itinerary for the next few days, although most of what she wanted to do would have to wait until after Christmas now. 'I'm spending Christmas Day with the Plymouth

One,' she told me, pulling a face. 'That's why I asked you to get me the gin, I thought I'd better get him a present. He's up to something, though,' she told me, wagging a heavily ringed finger. 'He hasn't invited me for years.'

'You are usually on the high seas at Christmas,' I pointed out.

'Doesn't stop him inviting me, though, does it? No, he's after money, you'll see. Anyway, never mind about him!' She dismissed him with a wave of her hand, 'Tell me what's been going on whilst I've been away. That peculiar couple aren't still about, are they?'

'You mean the peculiar couple you met on a cruise and told them how wonderful Ashburton was and they decided to come and live here?'

'They're the ones!' She frowned. 'Actors or something. They didn't settle here, did they?'

'Digby and Amanda? Yes, they are still here. They've recently bought a house, but not in Ashburton itself, a mile away, near Landscove.'

'Well, as long as they don't want to visit.' Chloe suppressed a shudder, a hand clutched to her cashmere bosom. 'Visitors are just too exhausting.'

'Don't worry. They don't know you're back and I won't tell them.'

She sipped her sherry and cogitated. 'And what about that man you met? Tall, good-looking, dark, extremely rude as I remember. Had a house up on the moor somewhere. You started going out with him, didn't you?'

'Daniel Thorncroft,' I answered, trying to keep my voice as even as possible.

'Yes, what's happening with him?' she asked innocently.

'He's not around at the moment,' I said evasively. 'Look, why don't I start on your unpacking?'

'Oh, let it wait until the morning, dear,' Chloe dismissed the suggestion with a wave of her hand. 'It's too tiring to even think about now.'

We chatted for a little longer before I made my excuses. I knew she'd sleep late into the morning and didn't want to disturb her, so I said I'd see her the following lunchtime. This would at least give me the morning in the shop.

I got home just in time to meet Kate coming out of my flat. 'Sorry to let myself in, but I wanted to put some leftovers from the cafe into your fridge. I didn't know what time you'd be back and we're off early tomorrow morning.'

I nodded. 'Long drive.' I told her to wait and handed her the presents I'd wrapped for baby Noah.

'Thanks, Juno. I've put all Bill's food on the counter in the kitchen.' Kate tilted her head enquiringly. 'Are you still okay about feeding him whilst we're away? Well, he practically lives with you, anyway.' I detected a slight note of pique in her voice, as if I had deliberately stolen their cat. I can't help it if he's got taste. 'So, where are you spending Christmas Day?'

'I haven't made up my mind,' I responded honestly.

'Well, you'd better get a move on.' Her dark eyes suddenly grew round with horror. 'You're not thinking of spending it here, are you? On your own?'

'No of course not.'

'You'd better not be.' She shook her head, swinging her long, black plait over her shoulder in the process. 'You should have gone to Paris,' she told me bluntly.

She was right, of course. I should have gone to Paris. I closed the door of my flat and settled down on the sofa, quickly joined by Bill. And why hadn't I gone to Paris? I asked myself. Because of the man Chloe had been asking about: Daniel Thorncroft, my ex-lover, who after our last parting had gone away to sort his head out. Did I really think he'd come home at Christmas, appear on the doorstep like at the end of some sentimental, romantic film? Or Santa would drop him down the chimney like a gift? I had no idea where he was right now. He could be in a temple up a mountain in Tibet or he could be as close as the next village. I didn't know. I didn't know if I would ever see him again. I just knew if there was the slightest chance he might come home, I wanted to be here.

CHAPTER TWELVE

On Christmas Eve I'd stayed in the shop until closing time. Sophie, Pat and I enjoyed a convivial day, working our way through a bottle of Christmas liqueur while the customers came and went, some buying, and some not. By the end of the day, we had each racked up a decent, if not exactly exciting, number of sales. Pat left for the farm early, to meet up with someone interested in offering a home to a dog, and Sophie went off to waitress for double pay at the hotel, leaving me to cash up on my ownsome. But not for long.

A few minutes before closing time, Olly burst in through the door with a wild look of panic in his eye and collapsed against the door frame. 'I thought you might be closed.'

'Not quite,' I said, as he came in and shut the door behind him. 'What's up?'

'I need a present for Aunt Lizzie.'

I glanced at the clock. 'You're leaving it a bit late, aren't you?'

'No. I've got her some little things. Like, I got some of

that funny-smelling soap they make in that shop around the corner.'

'Funny smelling?'

'Well, it smells funny to me. Nan only ever used Lifebuoy. And I got her some chocolates. But those are just little things. I want to get her a proper present, but I couldn't think what. And then I thought, I'd get her a bottle of gin. She likes that. But I'm too young to buy gin, so will you come to the shop and get it for me?'

'Well, of course I will, but—'

'I've got the money. And I want a good one. And I thought you'd know which one she'd like.'

'Hold on a moment.' I got up, flipped the sign on the door to *Closed* and turned the key in the lock. 'Come back here,' I told him and led him through to my antiques room at the back.

I pointed to a pretty Edwardian dressing-table mirror that Elizabeth had admired when I'd bought it for the shop. 'I was going to give her this. But why don't you give it to her? I'll let you have it for whatever you were going to spend on the gin.'

He wrinkled his face in disgust. 'A mirror?'

'Yes. Listen, tell me something. Just between us. Do you still want Elizabeth living with you?'

'Yeh!' He hunched a shoulder. 'Course.'

'You don't want her to go?'

He looked horrified. 'No. why would I?'

'Okay. Just checking.'

'Is this about the bike?' he asked awkwardly.

'No. It's about the way you spoke to her.'

'Well, I know . . . and I'm sorry. That's why I want to get her something nice.'

'When she had to give up her home, she lost everything, remember? All her possessions. She hasn't got any of those things that make a woman's house her home. I think she'd really like this mirror. And I think she'd love it if *you* gave it to her.'

Olly scratched his ear, considering. 'Well, if you think so.'

'I do.'

'All right.' He grinned suddenly. 'Sold! Wrap it up.'

'Certainly sir.'

He followed me through to the front of the shop and I placed the mirror on the counter so I could hunt for bubble wrap.

'Are you cycling home?' I asked and he nodded. 'Don't drop this, then.'

'Course not. Seven years bad luck,' he added, a superstition I suspected his nan had encouraged him to believe in. 'Here,' he added, as if struck by a sudden thought. 'If I'm giving Lizzie this, what are you going to give her?'

'Oh, that's easy,' I told him. 'I'll get her a bottle of gin.'

When I'd sent Olly off with the mirror and locked up the shop, I took my god-daughter and her little sister their presents. It was a good pretext for visiting their father, aka Detective Constable Dean Collins, to try to find out whether the police were making any progress with the murder investigation.

We talked in the kitchen as the living room was occupied by Gemma packing last-minute presents, excited toddler Alice doing her best to wreck the Christmas tree, and baby Hannah occupying the sofa, miraculously sleeping through all the noise.

I was curious to know whether Jackie Millard had told the police all she told me.

'About Bob fighting with Don Drummond?' Dean brushed his hand over his stubbly hair thoughtfully. 'Apparently Bob told Don a few home truths about his brother which Don didn't take well. But unless forensics can come up with any of his DNA on Bob's body, there's nothing to link him to the crime.'

'But he's still a suspect?'

Dean showed his palm in a non-committal waggle of the hand. 'Let's just say he's a person of interest.'

'Any others?' I asked.

He grinned at me. 'None that I'm prepared to discuss with you, Miss Browne.'

This was supposed to put me in my place. 'What about Bob's old girlfriends?' I asked.

His eyes narrowed. 'What about them?'

It seemed I might have scored a hit. 'Well, there were a few of them, from what I hear.'

'There's one who took him to court a few years ago,' he admitted.

'Why?'

'Paternity suit.'

'No! What happened?'

'She insisted he was the father of her child. He denied it. The court ordered a DNA test but he refused to take one.'

This is not an area I know much about. 'The court couldn't force him to take a test?'

'The man can refuse to take a test, but his refusal is often seen as an admission of guilt. In most cases the court will legally declare him the father.'

'Is that what happened to Bob?'

'No.' Dean chuckled. 'But he could see that's what would happen if he refused to take the test so he admitted liability. But he claimed he and the lady concerned had only had a brief fling and they weren't in a steady relationship. Apparently, she's threatened him with the law on a regular basis over the years to get him to keep up with his paternity payments. She must often have felt like murdering him, but on the night in question . . .'

'She has an alibi.'

'And a good 'un, maid of honour at some fancy wedding in Exeter Cathedral. Over two hundred witnesses.' He pulled a grimace. 'Although what a posh bird like her ever saw in a slob like Millard beats me. She must have fancied a bit of rough.'

This sounded interesting. 'Posh bird, was she?'

He nodded. 'She met him when he came to Daddy's stables to shoe some of the horses.'

'What's her name?'

Dean flinched, as if he suddenly realised that he'd let

his tongue run away with him. 'No, don't go there, Juno. Daddy's a friend of the chief constable.'

'Hmmm! Interesting.'

He looked alarmed. 'I told you, she's got an alibi, so forget all about her.'

I decided to let it go, for the moment. 'No one else?'

'No.'

'It's unlikely Bob's killing was random, though, isn't it?'

Dean shrugged. 'We know Bob was a bit drunk. He could have got into an argument with this last-minute customer.'

'Which might have led to a bit of pushing and shoving,' I agreed. 'But whoever killed Bob tried to stab him with a pritchel. That's a bit extreme for an argument over a sausage sizzler. There must have been another reason.'

'Yeh. The killer was a nutter.'

The man I'd heard rustling in the bushes close by me, not a nice thought.

'There's nothing to link this murder to any others, is there?' I asked after a moment.

Dean frowned. 'How do you mean?'

For a moment I considered telling him what Penny had told me; how she'd linked Bob's murder to the three university deaths because of its astrological aptness, but I decided against it. He thinks I'm barmy as it is.

We abandoned talk of murder. I let Dean pour me a drink and we joined Gemma and the gleefully destructive Alice, who was still too young to understand what was going on but was excited anyway and played until it was her bedtime, when we put a mince pie and carrots by the fireplace for Santa and his reindeer, and tucked her up in bed.

The person most liable to know about who is likely to be marrying who, or should I say *whom*, at a society wedding in Exeter Cathedral on the day of our fair, would be Lady Margaret Westershall. But somehow, I doubted if she'd welcome a phone call about it on Christmas Eve. I reckoned she'd either be at a church service or some charity-raising bash, if she wasn't already tucked up in bed with a nightcap and Florence and Wesley.

So, I was left with the good old internet, which never sleeps and doesn't care what day it is.

I went straight to the website of the most exclusive monthly county magazine. But the wedding was only two weeks ago and I realised it wouldn't be reported until the issue for the following month; so I started to trawl the Exeter papers until I found coverage of a wedding in the cathedral on the right date with a whole page of colour pictures. This had to be the one: the wedding of the Hon. Tamsin Angelica Richmond-Crick to Mr Clive Jeremy Von Hoorn – a very attractive couple, judging by their photographs. There was a picture of the bride surrounded by a whole flock of bridesmaids. Does anyone really need eight? Perhaps they were family and the bride didn't dare leave any of them out. Finally, I found the picture I was looking for. The Honourable Tamsin standing with a woman of about her age, wearing a simpler, more elegant version of the bridesmaids' dresses but carrying a larger bouquet. The caption beneath the photograph declared her to be the Maid of Honour, Ms Lily Marwood. I stared at her slim figure, her poise, her face intelligent rather than pretty. Anyone less likely to have been attracted to Bob the Blacksmith I couldn't imagine. Still, it takes all sorts. The rest of the photos were of the assembled guests and so, apart from the hats, not of a great deal of interest.

I went back to my search, and googled Lily Marwood, adding in Devon. I struck gold instantly. Her picture, her light brown hair dressed more simply than at the wedding, came up straight away. She was sitting at a desk with a pen in her right hand. Lily Marwood, the caption declared, was the daughter of famous racehorse owner, Gen. Sir George Marwood. He sounded like the kind of man who'd be pally with a chief constable. Lily worked as an independent speech and language therapist, her website went on to tell me, and detailed a list of her services. She lives in Devon with her young son, Oscar, and their dog, Ruffles. There was a picture of her sitting on the grass in bright sunshine, a golden retriever lying by her side, and a little boy in her arms, a solid, chunky-looking lad with dark hair, who looked as if he might grow up to make a good rugby player. Or blacksmith. Well, well. They say opposites attract. But fascinated as I was, it seemed Lily Marwood had an alibi, which ruled her out as a suspect, and I had no reason to pry into her love life. As I closed the window on her website, the page of her friend's wedding pictures came up again, the groups of smiling guests.

Underneath a rather stunning hat, my eye lighted on a face I recognised. Perhaps I did have a way to find out more about Lily Marwood, after all.

At midnight, I did something really stupid. I shrugged on my coat and went out. I got in my van and drove up to Halshanger Common, to Daniel's farmhouse. I knew going there would do me no good, I'd come away feeling worse than I already did, but I had to do it. I needed to stand in front of that empty half-derelict building and see for myself he wasn't there, acknowledge to myself that he might never come back.

So, I drove up to the common in the dark, trying to ignore the dim flickering hope that when I got to his place there might be a light in a window, I might hear his dog, darling Lottie, barking in welcome as I arrived. But the only thing that greeted me was a dark and lonely shell, the old house still caged in scaffolding from the repair to the roof, begun before Daniel had decided to leave. All work had now stopped. The caravan he bought to live in whilst the restoration was carried out was still there, a silent metal box.

I love you, I told him silently. And I miss you. I missed his storm-grey eyes, that looked so cold and hard, and turned warm and tender whenever he looked at Lottie, and even warmer when they turned their gaze on me. I missed the cynical line of his mouth and the smile that altered everything. And I missed his lean, hard body in my bed and the way he thrust his fingers through my curls, and called me *Miss Browne with an e*, even when we were making love.

I don't know how long I stood there, long enough for the cold wind to find its way through my jacket and chill me to the bone. Eventually I decided to stop tormenting myself and turned my back on the place, got back in dear old Van Blanc and drove back down into Ashburton. Back to the warmth and safety of my flat.

Bill was still curled up on the sofa where I had left him. I poured myself a glass of wine and snuggled down next to him. 'What an idiot I am,' I told him, stroking his ears. He murmured but didn't argue. I sighed as I kicked off my shoes and put my feet up. I should have gone to Paris.

For Bill's Christmas morning treat, I opened him a tin of pilchards. It was strange being in the house without Kate and Adam, knowing there was no one downstairs. Invariably the source of noise and delicious cooking smells, it was weird for their flat to be quiet and empty. I'd even got used to Noah crying.

Breakfast was followed by a FaceTime call from Brian in Paris, wishing me a happy Christmas and pointing out there was still time to hop on a Eurostar. He forgets that getting to London from Devon can be a day's journey in itself. And there are no flights to Paris direct from Exeter at the moment. He'd sent me a swanky new phone as a present. It was time I had something decent, he said. I thanked him and explained I was having lunch with friends. I opened gifts from Kate, Sophie and Pat, dolled myself in true Christmas fashion and went forth into the world, leaving Bill to sleep off his pilchards in peace. Alas, there was no snow, but the day was bright and clear, the sky blue, the bells of St Andrew's Church were ringing out in celebration and really, what more can you ask for on a Christmas morning? Except snow.

Ricky and Morris don't celebrate Christmas. They throw a huge party every Boxing Day, which coincides with the end of Hanukkah, but they don't really celebrate the Jewish festival either. They're what you might call *lapsed*. They usually keep open house all day, with a running buffet of festive eats, much musical entertainment and, traditionally, charades. This year, perhaps out of respect for Bob's murder having been committed in the garden, it was to be a more low-key affair, and only a few people had been invited.

'You will be coming, won't you, Princess?' Ricky asked, when I turned up on Christmas morning with their presents: a bottle of their favourite port and an interesting-looking book on Tudor tailoring.

'Course I will. Try to keep me away.' Judging by the smells coming out of the kitchen, cooking for the day was under way already. 'I could come up early, if you like, lend a hand.'

He dismissed my offer with a wave of his hand. 'Nah, we got it all under control.'

'But you can still come early if you want to, Juno.' Morris hated to think of me spending any part of the festivities on my own. He handed me a large, wrapped parcel. 'From us,' he said simply, kissing me on the cheek. They always give me fab presents and I tore it open with what might be described as unseemly haste. Rivers of dark green velvet fell out of it. It was a wrap-around cape, lined in gold silk, roughly triangular in shape, the pointy end finishing in a heavily beaded tassel. I took off my coat and flung it around my shoulders. Morris hastily steered me in front of the mirror.

'It's gorgeous!' I told him, admiring my reflection. God knows when I will ever get to wear such a thing, but who cares? It made up for the tartan crinoline.

'I knew forest green would be right,' Ricky nodded approvingly.

'I love this tassel.' I fingered its heavily beaded fringe, weighed it in my hand. It was as heavy as a cricket ball.

'Yeh, just watch you don't knock anyone's eye out with it, swinging it over your shoulder like that.'

I stopped for a sherry and told them about my discovery – Bob's old flame, the genteel Lily Marwood.

'I bet they sent her to an all-girls' boarding school!' Ricky pronounced, a reckless glint in his eye.

'What's that got to do with anything?' I asked him.

'They come out of school, these girls, and boys are still a mystery. Their heads are full of romance. They're gagging for it!'

'Excuse me,' I objected, 'but I went to an all-girls boarding school.'

'Then you know what I'm on about,' he continued unabashed. 'See, if they sent them to mixed schools, they'd soon realise what horrible, spotty adolescent boys are like . . .'

'Excuse me!' I said again. 'I have never heard such rubbish! You honestly think it was because she might have gone to an all-girls' school that Lily Marwood fell for Bob the Blacksmith?'

'Take no notice of him, Juno,' Morris recommended. 'That's his third Bloody Mary since breakfast.'

Ricky shrugged. 'Why not?'

'Well, for one thing, I don't think she was just a silly schoolgirl at the time, and I doubt if Bob the Blacksmith was ever likely to inspire romantic notions in any young woman's head, however many years ago this was.'

He pulled a face. 'Must just have been the sex, then.'

'Probably.' I wished I'd never mentioned Lily now.

'Excuse me a moment,' he said, rising a little unsteadily to his feet. 'I must just visit the uh . . .' He disappeared off in the direction of the downstairs cloakroom.

'Again?' Morris called after him. He turned to me and shook his head.

'Is he all right?' I asked, my voice dropping to a whisper.

'He's got a problem with his waterworks,' he hissed. 'I expect his prostate needs looking at, but can I get him to go to the doctor?' He rolled his eyes in exasperation.

We heard the flush then and changed the subject as Ricky strolled back into the room. I told them about the arrival of Chloe Berkeley-Smythe.

'Is she coming here tomorrow?' Morris asked. 'She's more than welcome.'

'I think she'll still be with her son,' I told him, 'the Plymouth One. He's picking her up this morning to take her to lunch and she's supposed to be spending the night with him and his wife, although she hates the idea.'

'What's brought this on, then?' Ricky demanded. 'I thought they hardly spoke.'

'Chloe thinks he's after her money.'

Morris nodded wisely. 'She's probably right.'

'Apparently, he's lost a lot recently. Moved his pension on the advice of his financial consultant and it turned out to be bad advice.'

Morris frowned. 'I wonder if it was that firm of consultants in Exeter? There was an article in the paper the other day about some firm in trouble because of it. Aiglee something?'

'Well, whatever it was, the Plymouth One won't get much change out of Chloe,' Ricky chuckled. 'She might like to pretend she's clueless but she's pretty canny when it comes to the old shekels.'

If I wasn't careful, I was going to be late for my lunch. I kissed them both goodbye and promised to see them tomorrow. As I drove off in my van, still wearing my wonderful cape, something jolted my memory. *Aiglee* something, Morris had said. Did he mean Aigler Wealth Management? They were based in Exeter. And they were also the firm Don Drummond worked for.

'You don't think this idea has any validity,' Elizabeth asked me, as we sat together at the kitchen table, contemplating the remains of our Christmas lunch, 'this astrology theory of Penny's?'

We were alone. Olly had taken Elizabeth's friend Tom into the garden shed to show him the conversion kit for his bike, his Christmas present to himself.

'He bought it, then,' I said, once they were out of the door.

'And I bought him the battery-charger.' She smiled. 'Thank you for the gin, by the way. And the mirror.'

'Olly paid for it.'

'Yes, but I doubt if he'd have thought of it on his own.'

'Perhaps not, but he wanted to get you something special.'

'Well, that was very sweet of him, but there was no need.'

'I gather peace has been restored?'

'Oh yes.' She raised an ironic eyebrow. 'For the time being. But he's had to agree that he only charges the bike up in the shed, and that we install a smoke alarm in there.'

We had volunteered to wash up, largely because Tom, after his recent hip operation, couldn't stand for long, and because Olly had cooked most of the lunch. He'd made a great job of it. The air in the kitchen was redolent with the aroma of roasted veg, chestnut stuffing and a sweet, sticky red cabbage he had let cook for two days on the Aga. The table was a wreck of pudding dishes and the remains of his home-made crackers scattered across the cloth. Elizabeth removed her paper hat and smoothed her hair. I realised I still had mine perched on my head and removed it too.

I shrugged in answer to her original question. 'I think Penny's theory is all coincidence.'

'Rather too much coincidence, don't you think?'

Elizabeth is one of my favourite people because she is thoughtful and calm, and the person most likely to give an unbiased opinion on any subject asked. So I was surprised she thought Penny's theory might be worth considering. She got up to clear the pudding dishes, to add them to the pile of sticky plates already stacked on the draining board waiting to be washed. There was no point in putting it off any longer. I turned on the tap.

It snowed at last, on Boxing Day, late at night. Like most of Ricky and Morris's guests, I knew it was time to go home, but I was stuffed too full of delicious food, rounded off with coffee and liqueurs, to want to move from the fireside. We had already been entertained by an impromptu concert by Sauce and Slander, Ricky and Morris's alter egos and the names under which they perform onstage. Ricky played the piano as they sang some very funny, very dirty songs. Digby and Amanda also performed a song – 'I Remember It Well,' from *Gigi*. It's about a pair of old lovers reminiscing about their youth. The title was quite apt as Amanda forgot a line and had to be prompted. Her forgetfulness could have been due to the lateness of the hour, overconsumption of alcohol in various forms, or underconsumption of everything else. I have never yet seen that woman eat. No wonder she's stick-thin. Their performance was rapturously received by their tiny audience, but I had to resist the temptation to keep staring at her, to wonder what she might have slipped into her pockets. Now we sat in the glow of the firelight, listening to Morris telling us a ghost story. He always tells a ghost story at Christmas.

He had got to the bit where the new young vicar of an ancient church had descended into the crypt, a solitary candle to light his way, and heard a long, drawn-out ghostly wail in the darkness around him, when Ricky cried out 'Look at that!'

We all jumped. Amanda was shocked into hiccups. He was pointing through the French windows, not at a ghostly apparition, but at snow falling gently in the garden outside, white feathers whirling in the breeze like fairy thistledown, too light to settle. We opened the windows. Olly, Sophie and I raced outside, holding our hands palms upwards to catch the snowflakes as they fell. We ran about like children, turning up our faces as they landed on our eyebrows, and we tasted cold snow on our lips. The more sensible adults stayed inside.

'Come inside, you lot!' Ricky called out after a few minutes. 'You're going to get wet out there.'

We ignored him, of course, but the little squall soon blew away and the snow stopped falling. He was right. We had quickly got wet and cold, and we bundled back inside, shivering.

'What was that?' It was Tom Carter who called out suddenly. He was leaning on a walking stick, standing by the windows with Elizabeth and the others. He pointed.

'There it goes again. Did you see it,' he asked Ricky, 'a flash of light over there?'

It was Digby who answered him. 'I saw it, just for a moment, a beam of white light. Car headlight probably, a vehicle going past on the road.'

Ricky shook his head. 'You wouldn't see it from here. Must be someone on the drive.'

I saw it then, a glimpse of white light wavering between the dark leaves of the thick rhododendron bushes edging the lawn.

'Must be someone with a torch,' Tom said. 'You expecting more guests?'

'Perhaps someone's lost,' Morris suggested, 'or their car's broken down. We ought to go and see.'

'I'll go,' Ricky said.

Olly volunteered to go with him. 'It could be a burglar.'

'We outnumber him if it is,' I pointed out.

'I'll go,' Digby insisted. 'Olly and Tom, you stay here and guard the ladies.'

There were various protests of indignation from ladies who felt perfectly able to guard themselves.

'Look, it's probably just someone who's lost,' Ricky said as Morris produced a torch from the kitchen. He snatched it from him. 'There's no point in us all going out there.'

'He's right!' Amanda managed to gasp between hiccups.

'Yes, he is,' Elizabeth agreed sensibly. 'Tom, there's no need for you to go.'

He chuckled. 'I wasn't planning to.'

Morris, meanwhile, had walked out onto the lawn,

trying to peer through the bushes. 'Hello?' he called out. 'Anyone there?'

There was no reply. The light went out abruptly. Ricky and Digby walked out to join him and the three of them set off for the drive, Olly jogging to catch them up.

Amanda was still hiccupping. 'Would you like me to put a key down your back?' Sophie offered solicitously, 'or an ice cube?'

'I think that's for stopping nosebleeds, Soph,' I told her. 'Not for hiccups.'

'It's all the same,' she responded, as Amanda, her pale blue eyes watering, was firmly shaking her head. 'It's just the shock of something cold.'

'I don't think we need to go that far,' Elizabeth guided Amanda to a chair. 'Just hold your breath,' she advised her.

The hiccups had been stopped for a full twenty minutes before the men returned. In fact, we were thinking of going outside to see if they needed rescuing, when they came back in through the French windows.

'Anything?' I asked.

Ricky shook his head. 'We had a good look around, but there was no one about.'

'No sign of a car either.' Digby pulled a face.

'But someone had definitely been there,' Morris insisted.

'Well, we all saw the torchlight,' Tom agreed.

'We had a good poke around under the rhododendrons,' Ricky added, pulling something from his pocket, 'and we found this.' It was a black woollen glove.

'You think he just dropped it?' I asked.

'Well, we don't often get people hiding in the rhododendrons.'

'Perhaps it was just kids messing about,' Sophie suggested.

'I think we should call the police,' Elizabeth said calmly.

'Oh, I don't think there's any need to worry them,' Digby assured her. 'I think we've scared them off.'

'That's not the point.'

'No, it's not,' I agreed. 'Someone comes here at night, with a torch, lurking in the shrubbery just a few yards from where Bob Millard was murdered . . .'

'You think the murderer might have returned?' Digby asked.

'It's possible,' I said. 'And if it was him, perhaps he was searching for the murder weapon.'

Whatever it was the murderer had been searching for, if indeed it was the murderer returned, the police didn't find it. But they didn't really expect to. They'd been over the entire shrubbery with a fine-toothed comb on the day following Bob's murder. We never got to hear the end of the ghost story, either. The party broke up and we all went home. Perhaps it was just kids messing about, and one had dropped his glove, a small insignificant event that had no meaning, but for me it had a strange effect. There might be days of festivities left to go, but I felt as if Christmas was over.

CHAPTER THIRTEEN

New Year's Day bank holiday and the first giant boot sale of the year; Newton Abbot racecourse was packed. I was suffering just slightly from the effects of the night before. There had been a New Year's Eve party at the house of one of Sophie's friends, followed by a firework display in their garden. I must have drunk more than I realised because this morning I couldn't remember much about it and I felt fragile, the daylight too bright, Bill's purring painfully loud. I decided that a morning spent in the fresh air would do me good.

There had been no more snow since Boxing Day, and it was another cold, bright day and not too windy, perfect boot sale weather. Fortunately, I'd wrapped up well and remembered my sunglasses. I had devoted most of the last two days to driving Chloe everywhere she wanted to go but today I was dedicating to the hunt for stock. Nothing major, just a few nice items to fill in the spaces left on my shelves by Christmas. Chloe had been right about the Plymouth One, as it turned out. He'd lost money through what turned out to be a disastrous investment and was looking to her to dig him out of the hole he was in. How deep she was prepared to dig she didn't say. 'He has lost a horrible sum of money,' she told me with a shudder. 'I suppose I shall have to help him out. The problem is, I can't ignore the Other One then, if he wants anything.'

There might have been some unwanted Christmas presents being sold off at that morning's boot sale, but there were also some tasty collectibles. I picked up a chunky orange vase, dating from the 1970s and, frankly, pretty hideous, but I recognised it as a brand of Scandinavian pottery that's quite fashionable at the moment. It cost me a bit but there should still be a profit in it. I won't pay silly money to people who are being greedy, though. I passed over two Rupert Bear annuals, opting instead for a stoneware ginger beer bottle and two Royal Doulton plates, carrying my swag around in a big tote bag I'd bought for the purpose.

I came to a stall selling old tools, everything from ancient gardening trowels to farm implements and saddlery. There was unlikely to be anything of interest to me here, although occasionally I came across decorative plant labels that were worth buying. But there's something wonderful about picking up a tool that's been used for over a hundred years, holding a handle worn smooth from use and wondering how many generations of hands have held it before you. A good tool is well-crafted and beautifully weighted, sits well in the hand, is tactile. And, sometimes, people come into the shop looking for them.

I ignored large items like garden rakes and hoes, and the Victorian planters because the seller wanted too much for them. I wasn't interested in spokeshaves or vintage micrometers but I picked up a baffling metal thingy a few inches long with a wheel on one end. I couldn't work out what it was for. 'That, my beauty,' the stallholder told me when I asked, 'is a wimble, or scud winder, used to make string from straw and such. Dates from about 1910.'

I put it down and picked up an interesting wooden tool with a sliding metal bit in the middle. 'And what's this?'

'That's a sliding bevel, my love, for marking angles in woodwork. It's rosewood and brass, late nineteenth century.'

I liked it. It was a nice *thing*. 'How much?'

We haggled over the price. For an extra pound, he offered to throw in the scud winder. We struck a deal. Then my eye was caught by another tool, lying amongst a heap of others. I drew it out by the handle and studied it.

'Now that thing,' the stallholder told me, 'is a blacksmith's—'

'Oh, I know what it is,' I cut him off, my eyes still glued to the implement resting in my hand. 'It's a pritchel.' How likely is it, I asked myself, that this is the pritchel used to attack Bob Millard? 'Where did it come from, do you know?' I asked.

He shrugged.

'Well, do you know how long you've had it?' If he'd had it for a long time, that would eliminate it as a likely weapon straight away. If the stallholder considered it an odd question, he didn't say so. He turned to his mate, selling a wheelbarrow to a couple a few feet away. 'Jack! Do you know where this 'un came from?'

Jack turned his head and looked at the pritchel I was holding. He shook his head.

'I don't remember seeing it before,' he admitted, 'to be honest.'

Should I buy it? If I were the person who had attacked Bob with it, what would I do? Would I throw it away up on the moor somewhere, hoping it would never be found? Would I keep it, clean it off, knowing even a microscopic drop of blood would incriminate me if it was found in my possession? Or would I slip it surreptitiously into a lot of other tools where it could be handled by dozens of people, all leaving their prints on it; where if my prints were identified, I could say I must have touched it at a boot sale, and no one could prove any different. I could just imagine the reaction if I took it to the police, especially to Cruella. 'Do you imagine we have the financial resources to get every pritchel in Devon forensically investigated?' she would say, her little mouth twitching. 'Please don't bring us any more, Miss Browne.'

I decided to buy it in the end. The very least the police could do is find out whether Jackie Millard recognised it.

Penny popped into the shop the day after next, to remind me about her get-together. This was annoying as I couldn't now stay at home and pretend that I had forgotten about it. When I arrived, she was deep in conversation with

Sophie, who having discovered she was an astrologer, was staring at her from huge, dark eyes and drinking in every word she said.

'So, if you cast my birth chart for me,' she asked naively, 'would you be able to tell when I might start earning some proper money? Or if anyone . . . I mean, can you tell about relationships and that sort of thing?'

'She wants to know when she's going to get a man,' I said, leaning over her shoulder.

'I do not!' she cried hotly. 'I just—'

Penny laughed. 'Of course you do! Love and money are the two things everyone wants to know about. They make the world go round.'

'I don't know how much you charge,' Sophie went on in a slightly wheedling voice.

Penny told her and her face fell. 'Oh, I see.'

'You won't forget the meeting at my place tomorrow night, will you, Juno?' Penny asked.

'I'm looking forward to it,' I lied.

She turned back to Sophie. 'If you want your chart done, perhaps we could do a deal,' she said kindly. 'If I find a painting I like . . .'

I decided to leave them to it. They could wrangle without any help from me.

The living room of Penny's Loft Cottage was packed when I walked in the following evening. I was a little late arriving and all the seats were taken, the screen for tonight's PowerPoint presentation already set up. My entrance caused quite a stir. Perhaps it was the green cape I was wearing. Several surprised voices called out my name and I gave a general wave in the direction of people I didn't really recognise. I hadn't seen them in at least twelve years.

'Juno!' said a deep voice. A man got to his feet and gripped my hand. David Fairweather was the author of several famous books on the links between astrology and personality. He and Cordelia had been an item at one time. At least as a child, over one long summer holiday, I'd got used to seeing him at breakfast. Before he moved on. His thick, golden hair had turned more silver now, and been cropped to a shorter, modern style, the professorial beard trimmed to designer stubble, but his blue eyes twinkled just as brightly, and there was genuine warmth in his voice. 'You're so like her,' he whispered, continuing to grip my hand.

'Not really,' I told him, slightly embarrassed by the intensity of his gaze.

'I always knew you'd grow up to be beautiful.'

Then he'd had more confidence in that gangly ginger teenager than I had.

After another lingering moment a woman also stood, long and thin with straight, dark hair. 'We haven't been introduced,' she said, giving me a frigid smile, and then added pointedly, 'I'm David's partner.'

David grinned. 'Juno, allow me to introduce Aurora.'

Aurora? The Sleeping Beauty? We were obviously in Disneyland. I shook a hand heavy with silver rings, the

166

tanned wrist encircled with knotted and corded friendship bracelets from a hundred hippy festivals, and stared into light blue eyes ringed with black kohl. She wouldn't have looked out of place at one of Cordelia's gatherings all those years ago. She was, it turned out, also a professional astrologer. 'I specialise in karmic astrology,' she told me, 'and in past-life regression.'

Nice to know the fairies still visited. 'Ah!' was all I could think of to say. Fortunately, Penny rescued me at this moment. 'Juno!' She grabbed my arm and steered me to the other end of the room where an individual seated in the corner was flapping a hand at me trying to catch my attention. 'You remember Reggie!'

I did remember Reggie. I remembered him as a scruffy young man with a wealth of dark curls. Now he was bald on top, what remained of those luxuriant curls turning grey. His head looked awful. He would have looked better if he'd shaved the lot off.

'Hello, Reggie.' I remembered he'd been a keen, almost obsessive cyclist, constantly doing road trials and going for long rides across the moor. 'Still on the bike?' I asked.

'I cycled here this evening,' he told me. 'It's a flat run between here and Totnes, along by the river and then on the Buckfast road. I can do it in twenty minutes, easy.'

'Good for you.'

'I had a brush with cancer a few years ago, you know.'

'Oh? I'm sorry to hear that.'

'I'm very careful now. I watch my diet. Cycling keeps me fit.'

The meeting seemed about to begin, so I sat on the floor near his feet, there being no chairs left, and Penny gave me a cushion, so I could park my derrière in comfort.

Reggie leant forward over my shoulder and whispered in a voice like the rustling of dry leaves, 'I haven't been as fortunate as our friend David over there.' Then he added, with a wicked smile, 'I'm not as photogenic as he is.'

I bit back a laugh. Reggie was right in a way. It was David's good looks and charisma, as much as his abilities as an astrologer, that had led to his appearances on television and played a part in his success.

It was our friend David who was in charge of tonight's presentation. 'Welcome, everyone,' he smiled. 'I think we should begin this evening with a short meditation. If everyone is sitting comfortably, can we all close our eyes? Let's focus on cleansing ourselves of any negative thoughts or vibrations we may have brought in with us this evening from our external lives. For a few moments, let's just give ourselves over to Spirit.'

Gin would be good, I thought, closing my eyes obediently. I could give myself over to that spirit, no problem.

'Let's all just take one deep breath in . . .' David's voice continued calmly, 'And out.'

There was a soft whooshing noise around the room as fifteen people exhaled simultaneously. I already wished I hadn't come. I sat there, eyes closed, for what seemed an interminable time. Everyone else might have been cleansing their negative vibrations, I was just wishing I'd had time for supper before I'd come out. I'd been busy helping the Brownlows clear up after one lot of new year guests and get rooms ready for the next lot. I'd also had to take Chloe to see her doctor in Exeter and let Malcolm into Maisie's cottage to put in her new boiler. A quick shower was all I'd had time for. Thank God, Adam and Kate would be back home tomorrow. Bill was still okay for cat food, but I'd run out of leftovers.

At last David asked us to open our eyes. He beamed genially at everyone, his eyes resting for a moment on me before he stood up, ready to begin his presentation. Tonight, he announced, he would be talking about the famous French astrologer, Michel Gauquelin. That was a name that prodded the memory. I'd heard of him before.

'Michel Gauquelin,' David began, as a photograph of the man came up on the screen 'was a psychologist and statistician. His most famous works are probably *The Scientific Basis of Astrology*, and *Cosmic Influences on Human Behaviour*. He is credited as one of the founding fathers of astrology as we study it today.'

Unfortunately, I missed whatever David had to say next, because Reggie was hissing in my ear. 'I wrote my own book on Gauquelin's discoveries, years ago. But I couldn't get it published,' he added sadly. 'I had to publish it myself in the end. I remember, I sent a copy of the original draft to Cordelia, but tragically . . .'

Someone near to him nudged him to be quiet and he gave an apologetic little wave as David went on to discuss Gauquelin's career and his tragic death in 1991.

It was all very fascinating. I couldn't help feeling sorry for poor old Gauquelin, unable to get his work accepted by the scientific community. I accepted a glass of wine from a girl going around with a tray and lurked near Penny, listening in on her conversation with David.

He was laughing. 'Penny, you can't possibly still calculate charts by hand! It must take you hours. Use your computer, that's what it's for.'

'It seems like cheating to me.'

'It saves time and, with the greatest of respect, the calculations are far more likely to be accurate.'

'Back in my day you had to calculate charts by hand or you couldn't get your diploma,' Reggie put in.

'Times change,' David reminded him.

'But it's still the case,' Reggie's voice was scratchy with irritation, 'despite Gauquelin, and all the work done on chart interpretation in the years since, astrology is still not taken as a serious subject for scientific study.'

Someone touched me lightly on the elbow. 'Do you remember us, Juno?' I turned to find two elderly women standing behind me. 'We used to come to Cordelia's every week.'

I gazed at the first one, long silver plaits hanging down from under a knitted beret and earrings the size of dreamcatchers, then the other, her bobbed hair dyed a deep aubergine that made her skin look sallow, a silver nose-stud glinting on one nostril.

'Clemmie,' she said, pointing at herself.

'And Maya,' added her silver-haired friend.

I remembered. One of them had been into tarot and the other into crystals, I couldn't remember which. They lived together and used to stink of cats and cannabis. They still did. 'I run circle-dancing workshops now,' Clemmie told me enthusiastically, 'and Maya does inspirational Native American art.'

'My paintings are channelled through my spirit guide,' Maya explained in perfect seriousness. 'Moon Wolf.'

Moon Wolf? I'm sure I've seen pictures of him on a T-shirt. 'I'd love to see them sometime,' I lied.

'You must come over to Totnes. We have a stall at the market.'

'And what do you do with yourself these days, Juno?' I turned to find David at my elbow again.

'I have an antique shop here in Ashburton,' I told him, 'and a domestic help business.'

He smiled, blue eyes crinkling at the corners. 'Busy girl.'

Oh, you don't know the half. I didn't mention sleuthing.

'You didn't think about following in Cordelia's footsteps?' he asked. 'As an astrologer?'

'She advised against it,' I told him, which was true. 'She was always broke.'

He gave a soft laugh. 'Big money in it these days, especially on social media.'

I remembered what Cordelia had told me about David: intelligent, dangerously charming, terrific in bed, but emotionally, a lightweight. I wondered if Aurora was finding the same. Perhaps the sleeping beauty hadn't woken up yet. Whatever, she appeared at that moment to claim her prince. He squeezed my elbow as he took his leave. 'Lovely to see you again.'

Reggie was trying to catch my eye, something I was anxious to avoid. Penny had warned me if I stood still long enough, he'd try to sell me a copy of his book. But there was a man standing with him, who was too young to have been a member of Cordelia's original group, I suspected, a little younger than me. He smiled a warm smile, impossible to resist. 'Seth,' he said, extending his hand. He was nice-looking, actually, although a bit on the short side.

'Juno,' I told him. 'Have you joined the group recently?'

'Not really. I'm just here for the holidays. My family live in Buckfastleigh. David invited me along this evening.'

'You're interested in astrology, then?'

'I'm doing an MA at the University of Wales. It's actually part of a psychology course.'

'Marvellous, isn't it?' Reggie complained bitterly. 'When I was Seth's age you couldn't study astrology at university level anywhere outside of India.'

'Things have moved on a bit since then,' he told him. I sensed he'd already had enough of Reggie moaning on, and was looking for a way to excuse himself. He nodded at me. 'Nice to meet you, Juno.' And I was left once again with Reggie.

'So, what do you do with yourself these days?' I asked. 'When you're not cycling.'

Before he could answer there was a tinkling noise as Penny tapped a wine glass with a teaspoon, to catch everyone's attention. 'Before you all go, can I just tell you about our next meeting?' She pointed at a slim young woman with straight hair, who I hadn't been introduced to, or taken much notice of. For a start, I hadn't noticed until that moment she was wearing a dog collar.

'This is Mary, from the Society of Christian Astrologers, who will be giving our talk next week, and has some fascinating insights to offer us about Christian attitudes towards astrology and how they have changed over the ages, as well as discussing what the Bible has to say about it. Mary?'

'Yes, that's right,' Mary smiled benignly. 'That's all for next week. I just wanted to say, because I know that some of you here, like me, are keen on finding examples of zodiac signs in churches, there aren't many examples in Devon, but I've just discovered some quite close to home, at the church of St Mary's in Upton Hellions, near Crediton. Apparently,' she went on enthusiastically, 'there are some tiles in the chancel that are well worth looking at. So, if anyone is interested and wants to come with me,' she offered, looking around expectantly, 'do come and say hello.'

I noticed Reggie did, before he took his leave. After a while, everyone drifted away, including David and Aurora, leaving Penny and me with the washing-up.

I carried coffee cups and wine glasses to the sink. 'Tell me,' I asked Penny, as I looked about for a tea towel. 'Have you ever discussed your theory with any of the people here tonight?'

'What theory is that?' she asked.

I looked at her in surprise. 'You know, what we were talking about before Christmas, the astrological murders?'

She shook her head.

'Wouldn't they be the ideal people to talk to?' I asked. I glanced at her profile. She had become very still, letting the water run into the sink. 'Perhaps you don't feel you could trust them to be discreet?' I added as she remained silent.

'No, I couldn't. It would be awful if those murders became the subject of gossip.'

Something in those downcast eyes and folded lips alerted me. 'You don't think it's one of them, do you?' I breathed, astonished. 'You don't believe your murderer was here tonight?'

She gave a slightly forced laugh. 'No, of course I don't.'

I knew she was lying. 'Well, who?' I persisted. 'Who do you think it is?'

'I don't think . . .' She raised her hands in a helpless gesture.

'You must tell me,' I insisted.

'I don't think it's anyone.'

'Is that why you told me about it?' I carried on, thinking aloud. 'You want me to be the one to find out who the murderer is, because you're afraid to.' I could understand that. If she suspected a friend, it would be awful to be proved right.

She shook her head. 'I should never have mentioned it to you. Please, Juno!' she begged. 'Just forget the whole thing! I'm probably mistaken, and anyway, it was all a long time ago . . .'

'Bob's murder wasn't a long time ago. It was just before Christmas.' I could see she was growing more agitated, so I decided to let the subject drop. I was intrigued to know who she suspected, though, as I told Bill when we were curled up on the sofa later that night. Frankly, I wouldn't have thought any of the crowd I'd been with this evening would have the common sense to murder anyone.

Exeter Cathedral, where Lily Marwood's friends had celebrated their nuptials, is considered by many to be one of the finest architectural gems in medieval England. It has the longest unbroken stretch of Gothic stone vaulting in the world. I found out this from the guidebook. It's certainly a beautiful building, its carved west front standing on a green surrounded by the cobbles of the Cathedral Yard, a walled enclosure pierced by seven gates. Inside the Yard are fine buildings ranging from gorgeous Georgian to black-and-white timbered Tudor, most of which have been turned into smart shops and expensive restaurants.

I lurked outside one of these shops for several minutes, trying to peer through the window and get a good look at the woman arranging exorbitantly expensive handbags and accessories inside. I hadn't seen her for about fifteen years, since I left boarding school, and I wanted to be sure this was the right woman. I felt a little guilty about looking her up now, when I hadn't kept in touch, but decided there's no point in having connections and not making use of them. I'd dressed the part, in my green velvet cape, jeans and ankle boots, an imitation Louis Vuitton bag I'd picked up in a charity shop, slung over my shoulder. I wanted to look casual, but I didn't want to look as if I'd spent the morning scrubbing scabs of congealed gravy from between the tiles of the Brownlows' kitchen floor, which I had.

I wandered inside, looking about me with what I hoped appeared to be indifferent interest. From the corner of my eye, I saw my old school chum Charlotte clock the fact she had a potential customer. 'Good afternoon. Can I help . . . Oh my God! Juno?'

I suppose I am easily recognisable. I turned, raised my eyebrows in a vaguely enquiring look, and her sweet little face broke into a broad smile. 'It is you! Juno Browne!' She laughed in delight. 'It's me!' she went on, pointing to herself. 'Charlotte! We were at St Bridget's together. I was two years below you when you were house captain. Charlotte Webb. Don't you remember? Everyone used to call me Spider.'

'Of course I remember you, Charlotte,' I smiled, reaching out to take her hands. 'I'm just so surprised to see you. How are you?' We gave each other a rather polite embrace.

'This is gorgeous!' Charlotte exclaimed, her face emerging from the velvet folds of my cape. 'Where on earth did you get it?'

'Oh, I had it made for me,' I responded airily. I made a pretence of looking around. 'But, is this place yours?'

'Yes.' She giggled. 'I was too dense for university, so I decided to go into retail. If I say so myself, I've done rather well.'

Charlotte had always been a little dumpling at school, with flaxen hair and blue eyes. Anyone less like a spider it was difficult to imagine. Now she was taller and slimmer, and the long blonde hair had been cropped into a fashionably flyaway style. But her face was unmistakeable; the same round blue eyes and engaging smile. She'd stopped biting her nails, I noticed, and they gleamed with pale pink polish. I was glad I'd hidden mine inside gloves.

'But what are you doing in Exeter?' she asked. 'You don't live here?'

'No, I'm just shopping,' I responded. 'I have a little antique shop in Ashburton.'

'How delightful!' Her round eyes widened. 'I don't suppose you've got time for a coffee? The machine is always on.'

'Well . . .' I looked undecidedly at my watch.

But Charlotte was already calling into the storeroom for someone called Josie to come and mind the shop, and more or less bundled me up a flight of stairs that led on to a wide landing with a view across the green to the cathedral. It was occupied by two chairs and a low table, and a station in the corner with aforesaid coffee machine and accoutrements. 'Do sit down,' she invited, 'and we can a lovely long chat.'

This was precisely what I was hoping we would have. Charlotte, I remembered, was a great chatterbox. I sat down with pleasure. 'You know, Charlotte,' I told her, 'this is really quite spooky.'

'It is?' She turned to blink at me in surprise. 'Why?'

'I saw a picture of someone who looked just like you the other day, in a newspaper. There were photos from a wedding at the cathedral here, and I remember thinking it looked like you, but of course, it couldn't have been.'

'It was me!' she squeaked excitedly as the coffee machine gurgled behind her. 'It was my cousin Tamsin's wedding, just before Christmas.'

'That's amazing! We haven't seen each other for years and then I see a picture of you, and then a few days later I walk into your shop. What an astonishing coincidence!' I didn't mention the part our old school website, The Friends of St Bridget's, had played in it. I'd never have tracked her down without it.

She sat down with our coffees and we reminisced about various old schoolfriends, assassinating their characters and updating each other on what had happened since to those we'd kept in touch with. We moved on to Charlotte's brief and disastrous engagement. Eventually, I managed to steer the conversation back to the wedding. 'There was another face I thought I recognised,' I told Charlotte. 'The maid of honour. Lily someone?'

'Oh, Lily Marwood.' Charlotte shook her head. 'No, she didn't go to St Bridget's. She's Tamsin's best friend. Do you know, Tamsin's mother didn't want Lily to be maid of honour because she's a single mum? I mean, really, in this day and age! And Oscar's such a dear little boy.'

'Oh?' I raised my eyebrows. 'The child's father not . . . um . . . ?' I left the question hanging, knowing I could rely on Charlotte to fill the breach.

She leant towards me confidentially, 'Oscar's father was actually murdered, not long before Christmas?'

I let my jaw drop in dismay. 'No!'

Charlotte was nodding. 'They haven't found out who did it yet. He was a blacksmith. I know!' she added, before I had the chance to make any comment on his status. 'Lily always was a bit wild. She'd already had an affair with one of her college tutors. Apparently, she met this blacksmith at her father's stables, and they well . . . hit it off! She said he was fun. Different from the sort of men she usually met.' Charlotte giggled. 'But when she found out Oscar was on the way, he tried to deny he was the father. Lily didn't want any more to do with him after that, especially when Oscar turned out to be . . . well, you know . . .' she hesitated and made air quotes around the next two words '*special needs* . . .'

'Oh dear,' I said. 'What's the matter with him?'

'He's profoundly deaf, poor little thing. But as I say, Lily didn't want any more involvement with his father, but her parents kept arguing that just because she's got a lot more money than he has, is no reason for him not to contribute to his son's upkeep.'

'So, they were the ones who were pushing?'

'Oh, yes.'

'Well, they're not going to get anything out of him now, sadly.'

'Anyway, Lily's engaged now, and Harvey absolutely adores Oscar, so it's all worked out all right.'

'Hmm. And Lily doesn't have any theories about who might have murdered Oscar's father?'

Charlotte shook her head. 'Well, no. But she hasn't had any contact with him for years.'

'Except suing him for money.'

She pulled a face. 'Well, as I say, it was really her parents who were behind that, and anyway, it was all done through her solicitor.'

We chattered on for a while longer before I made my escape. We promised we'd meet again.

I had genuinely enjoyed seeing sweet, silly Charlotte again.

'Just out of interest,' I said to her as I left. 'Where is Lily living now?'

'She's got a place near Crediton,' she volunteered, without questioning why I wanted to know. 'A tiny village called Upton Hellions.'

Now, that name rang a bell. I thought for a moment. Of course, this was where the lady vicar was organising a trip to look at astrological tiles in a church. I decided I might join the party after all.

CHAPTER FOURTEEN

'Definitely not Bob's pritchel.' Dean placed it down in front of me on the counter in *Old Nick's*.

'Jackie's sure?' I asked.

'Certain. Bob had several of them apparently, all identical. He'd forged them himself. This is not one of them.'

I picked it up. Would the man on the tool stall at the car boot sale like to buy it back? Unlikely. I was stuck with it, unless I could find another blacksmith to sell it to. A good job it hadn't cost much.

'Anyway,' Dean grinned, 'nice try, Juno.'

I heaved a martyred sigh. 'As long as the police appreciate my efforts on their behalf. Any news on . . . anything?' I asked casually.

He turned his head to look at Sophie painting at her table nearby and Pat, busy with her knitting. They were both trying so hard to look intent on what they were doing it was obvious their ears were on stalks.

'Like what?' he asked, lowering his voice.

'Well, this fella for a start.' I tapped the page of the latest copy of the *Dartmoor Gazette* I had spread out on the counter before Dean had arrived. There was a photograph of Don Drummond grinning up from it, probably the only time I'd ever seen him smile. He was with Carol from Cold East Farm and between them they were holding the cup he had made for her wassail. *Local Craftsman Creates New Wassailing Cup for Ancient Tradition* the headline read. The article went on to say that Don had made the cup from maple wood, although in more ancient times it would have been made from ironwood, or lignum vitae, the Tree of Life, known for its medicinal properties. It added that because of lack of conservation in the Caribbean countries where it grew, lignum vitae is now a diminishing resource. I'd been reading up on it myself. A seventeenth-century wassailing cup made from this rare wood had recently fetched thirteen thousand pounds at auction. The article then went on to list the dates when wassails were being held around Devon throughout the month. It seemed there was one happening in a different town or village almost every night.

'Why are there so many?' Dean asked.

'Because everyone who owns an orchard wants one.'

'Can't they all do it on the same night?'

One has to make allowances and remember Dean's a northerner. 'Not if you want musicians and Morris dancers. They get booked up really early, especially if you want the Border Morris. You have to wait your turn.'

'What's it all about anyway?'

'It's a ceremony for blessing the apple trees,' I told him. 'It ensures a good crop.'

'You have to frighten away the evil spirits,' Pat added. 'That's why you want the Morris men.'

'Those blokes who skip about waving hankies?'

Pat tutted at his ignorance. 'This is the *Border* Morris.'

'They're different, are they?'

'They hit the ground with sticks. And wear black.'

'And they black their faces.'

'And fire rifles,' Sophie added, 'into the trees.'

'They do *what?*' he asked, scandalised.

'They only use blanks.'

Dean shook his head at yet another weird West Country custom he didn't understand. He cleared his throat. 'Any road, the answer to your question is no, there is no further news.'

He went to the door and peered outside, up at a gloomy grey sky. 'There's snow in that,' he prophesied bleakly, and left.

It wasn't long before the shop bell tinkled again, this time letting in Penny, arm in arm with Reggie Ryecart. 'Look who I found lurking outside your shop!' Penny declared, laughing.

'I was not lurking,' Reggie said indignantly, 'I was on my way to see you, Penny, and thought I'd try and find Juno's shop whilst I was here. Someone directed me down this alleyway.'

'Well, it's nice to see you,' I told him. 'Feel free to look around. You might see something that takes your fancy.'

Although, frankly, the idea of getting any money out of Reggie was a long shot to say the least. He was always broke.

But he wasn't listening. 'I don't like leaving my bike outside. Is it safe out there?'

'Bring it in the side door, if you're worried,' I told him. 'There's room for it in the hall.'

'Stop fussing, Reggie. We'll only be a moment.' Penny explained, 'You phoned me earlier and asked if there was room for you on the Upton Hellions trip?'

'That's right, I did.'

'Yes, there is. Apparently, Reggie and I are the only other takers, so it'll just be the four of us going in Mary's car.'

'I knew the old astrology bug would bite you,' Reggie smirked.

I groaned inwardly. 'It's not that at all,' I responded. 'I just love old churches.' At least that part was true.

'Mary says there's an Elizabethan manor house nearby,' Penny put in. 'We might get a chance to look at it whilst we're there.'

'I'm sure the trip will be interesting,' I smiled, thinking this might be an exaggeration of the truth. The two of them left then, Reggie still fretting about his bike.

They were barely out of the door, when Seth, the astrology student, walked in. Astrologers must be like buses, I decided. You don't see one for years and then three of them arrive at the same time.

'This is where you are,' he said, seeing me.

I hesitated, a little taken aback. Had he come here to see me? He was a nice fella, but I hoped he wasn't about to get keen. My heart is taken. 'Back in Ashburton so soon?'

'I go back to Wales tomorrow and I need some new guitar strings. We don't have a music shop in Buckfastleigh. Okay if I look around?'

'Be my guest.'

'Wow! That's amazing.' He was standing in front of one of Sophie's paintings, a stunning study of a barn owl perched on a fence post. 'It's really beautiful,' he breathed, nodding to himself.

I introduced him to the artist, who accepted his compliments demurely, if giving him the full treatment from her orphaned-seal eyes and fluttering her long black eyelashes could be described as demure. He smiled at her and turned his head so he could look at the painting she was currently working on. 'You are really talented,' he told her.

'Thanks.' Her paintbrush hovered above her work, her lips in a coy smile.

He glanced around at the display of artwork on the walls. 'Are these all yours?'

'Oh, yes,' she answered modestly.

He hesitated for a moment, his hands in his pockets. Then he turned to me, and smiled. 'I wondered if you fancied a cup of tea?'

I glanced at Sophie, who was studying her work with sudden intensity, then at Pat, who was frowning at her knitting.

'I'd love one,' I said deliberately. 'But not here.' I grabbed my coat and bag. 'I won't be long,' I promised the girls sunnily, and we made our exit.

Outside I shivered. Dean had been right about the sky. It had a strange ghostly whiteness about it that often heralds snow.

Seth and I hurried along to the welcoming glow of Taylors Tea Room. He gazed longingly at the array of cakes displayed on the table in the window. 'I'll have to have one of those.'

A man after my own heart. There was a brief discussion about tea. I'm always in favour of English Breakfast myself. But the tea menu at Taylors is extensive, and as it was still technically Christmas we settled on cranberry and orange, and slices of mincemeat tart to go with.

'The young girl in your shop, the artist,' Seth smiled once we'd placed our order, 'she's very talented.'

'Well, strictly speaking,' I told him, 'she's not a young girl. She often gets mistaken for a teenager but she's actually twenty-five.' I grinned. 'She gets really fed up of having to prove her age in pubs.'

He was quiet for a moment, seemingly absorbing this information. I felt it was time to change the subject. 'I know I'm very ignorant, but where exactly is the University of Wales?'

'Trinity St David's,' he told me. I wasn't sure I was any the wiser. 'It's the only university in the UK that offers the course I'm on.'

'Astrology?'

'Among other things. The course I'm studying is really about how human beings attribute meaning to things like planets and stars, and construct belief systems around them.'

'Sounds fascinating.'

'There's a lot of psychology involved as well.'

'Is that how you and David met?' I asked.

'No, I wrote to congratulate him on his books.' Seth smiled. 'When I discovered he lived so close, I asked if I could call on him at home, and he invited me to come along last night.'

'I haven't seen any of Cordelia's friends for years,' I confessed. 'I used to think they were an odd lot.' I couldn't help smiling at the thought of them. 'I still do.'

'Reggie is a funny guy. Do you know what he does?'

I realised I'd never known how Reggie kept body and soul together. 'He spent years writing a book and then couldn't get it published. He had to publish it himself in the end. He didn't try to sell you one last night, did he?'

Seth laughed. 'No.'

The only thing I remembered about Reggie, apart from his cycling, was that he was always down on his luck. And judging by what he had to say last night, it hadn't improved. Poor Reggie.

'David has done well for himself. Do you listen to his podcast at all, or follow his blog?'

I didn't like to say I wasn't interested. 'No, I'm afraid I don't. Cordelia was the astrologer and after she died, I lost touch with all that kind of thing. Well, that's not quite true,' I admitted. 'Astrology is a bit like religion. You can never entirely shake it off.'

Our tea and mince tart arrived and I waited until our waitress had placed everything on our table, including a dish of clotted cream. I wondered what Seth would think about Penny's murder theory. 'Wasn't there once a famous case of an astrologer-murderer?' I asked, trying to appear casual. I picked up the clotted cream, watching as a goodly blob slowly oozed down the spoon and dropped onto my tart.

'The Zodiac Killer,' Seth responded, taking the dish of cream I handed him, 'in America. San Francisco, I believe, back in the sixties. He killed several people. They made a film about him.'

'Did they ever catch him?'

'No.' He studied me a moment. 'I hear you're quite the sleuth.'

I sighed. 'Not really.'

'Hmmm.' He folded his arms. 'I bet if we looked on your birth chart, we'd find good sleuthing qualities. Scorpios are traditionally the detectives of the zodiac, you can't pull the wool over their eyes.' He frowned thoughtfully. 'Virgos are forensically analytical, but sometimes they get bogged down in minor details, can't see the wood for the trees.' He grinned. 'No. Capricorn – fearless, determined, cautious but prepared to take calculated risks.'

I laughed out loud. 'I don't know about the cautious and calculated bit. I'm always being accused of being irresponsible.' At least, I added privately, it was what

Daniel had called me. But to me, it had never seemed I was being reckless. I just did what I had to do.

'I was surprised to see the lady vicar there at the meeting,' I admitted, trying to take the focus away from me. 'I thought Christians considered astrology to be the work of the devil.'

He laughed. 'Some Christians might. But there's nothing in the Bible that condemns astrology. For centuries the church accepted it as part of the natural order of things. The signs of the zodiac were just a reminder of the agricultural calendar.'

'You mean, like Virgo being associated with the harvest?'

'That's right. It was impossible to shift people from their old pagan beliefs, so the early church incorporated them. That's why we see so many carvings in churches of the Green Man – you know, the guy with the leaves sprouting out of his mouth? He's essentially the pagan symbol of spring and renewal . . .' Suddenly he looked up, eyebrows raised in surprise. I was sitting with my back to the window and had to turn to see what he was staring at. Snow was falling. Not the big feathery flakes of Boxing Day, but tiny white flecks, driven by the prevailing wind. And it was settling. It could only have been falling for a minute or two but already the pavement and window ledges outside were covered in a white dusting like icing sugar.

It continued to fall as we drank our tea and munched our mincemeat tart. By the time we'd finished and paid up, it was going strong, and our feet left dark footprints in the fine white crust as we walked along the pavement.

Seth turned up his coat collar. 'I hope this isn't going to keep up all night. It could make the drive back to Wales interesting tomorrow.'

I ran my gloved finger through the snow collecting on the roof of a parked car. Much as I love snow, I didn't want it to keep snowing all night either, blocking the roads. Tomorrow night I'd be driving to Widecombe for the wassail.

CHAPTER FIFTEEN

'I'm not blacking my face up,' Olly insisted indignantly. 'I think it's wrong.'

'Keep still, you horrible little squirt,' Ricky recommended, trying to pin a ragged patch onto the shoulder of the black coat Olly was wearing.

We were on an emergency visit to Druid Lodge for a costume for him to wear to the wassail. He'd received a call at school from Benny, one of the musicians he played with at the Victorian fair, asking if he could play for the Border Morris that night at Cold East Farm. Their usual flute player had fallen victim to the flu, so could Olly fill in on his penny whistle? He was so excited to be asked. But he needed a costume in double-quick time, so Ricky and Morris were adapting the one he'd worn at the fair.

The members of the Border Morris do not wear flowers on their hats or skip about with hankies. They wear black coats, traditionally rag jackets hanging in strips and patches, and black top hats with fans of crow or pheasant feathers stuck in the hatband. The overall look is sinister, like giant crows. Traditionally, they also black their faces.

'They don't still do that, do they?' Morris asked, sticking feathers on to the band of a battered top hat with a hot glue gun.

'They used to rub charcoal onto their faces as a disguise,' I told him. 'Morris dancers were often farm labourers who'd dance for money when times were hard. But begging was illegal and they didn't want their employers to recognise them.'

'That's what I told Miss Clarke in my class,' Olly nodded, earning a tut and a buffet on the shoulder from Ricky. 'But she said Morris is a corruption of *Moorish* and Morris dancing was brought over to this country by black people, and that blacking your face is insulting to people of other . . .' he sought for the word, 'Ethnics.'

'Whatever its origins,' Elizabeth observed calmly from her seat in the corner, 'it's certainly not necessary for people to black their faces these days.'

'Except it's traditional,' Ricky pointed out, snipping off his sewing thread with his teeth, 'and for some people that justifies anything.' He grinned. 'Including human sacrifice.'

'If you want a disguise . . .' Morris started rooting about in a box on one of the workroom shelves and came out with a strip of black silk, which he flung at Olly, 'have a highwayman's mask.'

Olly caught it and put the mask on, his pale blue eyes shining through the slits, then donned the top hat Morris passed him. He grinned at his reflection in the mirror. 'I look cool!'

'You're scaring the hell out of me,' Ricky told him. 'Now, you'd better get going, hadn't you, you lot? Are you going to be all right in that crappy old van?'

'If you're referring to Van Blanc,' I told him loftily, 'she is more than capable of dealing with a few inches of snow.' But I had my fingers crossed.

'They've gritted the A38.' Morris looked worried, polishing his specs, 'but I doubt if they've touched the road to Widecombe.'

'Then the hills could be interesting.'

'If you get stuck, give us a call,' Ricky told me. 'We can always come and rescue you in the Saab.'

'That old thing!' I scoffed, although it was built like a tank and far more suited to the snowy conditions than my poor little van.

'The snow stopped falling hours ago. I'm sure we'll be fine,' Elizabeth picked up Olly's school coat from the floor where he'd dumped it on coming in. 'Thank you very much, both of you,' she added as Ricky and Morris showed us to the door.

We promised them a full account of the event, and clambered into the van, Elizabeth in the front seat, Olly, refusing to take off his top hat, riding in the back where the dogs usually go.

The hills *were* interesting, although the snow was only a few inches deep and had stopped early enough in the day to turn to slush on the road. The temperature was falling again now, though, freezing what snow remained and on the steep road up to Buckland we encountered a patch of ice that had Van Blanc sailing across the tarmac like a skater, ending in a graceful turn and finishing with us facing downhill again. It took Elizabeth at the wheel, with Olly and me lending our grunting muscle power to the van's rear end, to persuade her back into an uphill direction.

'Well, this is fun,' Elizabeth declared as we swopped over and I got back behind the steering wheel, puffing a little with the exertion. 'If this keeps happening, we'll never get there.'

But we carried on without further upset, our wheels hissing through the slush, the dark boughs of the trees above our heads clumpy with their loads of snow. In the back, Olly was in a world of his own, whistling soundlessly to himself as his fingers played the stops of an imaginary flute. Elizabeth slid a sly glance at me. 'I hear you had a visitor yesterday.'

My God, the jungle drums have been busy. She had been on duty in the shop this morning and would have got the low-down on Seth from Sophie or Pat. 'I hear he was rather nice.'

I heaved a sigh. Did I really need to explain to Elizabeth of all people, that however nice he might be, I'm not interested in anyone at the moment? All I want is to know when Daniel is coming home. 'I met him the night before at Penny's. He was just being friendly. He's heard things about me . . . about sleuthing,' I added reluctantly, 'and I think he was curious.' After our tea together he certainly hadn't indicated he wanted to keep in touch, or that he wanted to see me again, beyond a vague *maybe we'll have a coffee when I'm next back from Wales* kind of thing. Although he had mentioned he would be back very soon, something to do with a big family birthday. I glanced in the rear-view mirror at Olly, still lost in a world of his own, and lowered my voice slightly. 'You haven't heard anything from Daniel, have you?' If there was one person in Ashburton outside of myself who Daniel might communicate with, it would be Elizabeth. 'I mean, you would tell me, wouldn't you?'

'Of course, I would.' She sounded cross at the suggestion she might withhold information from me. 'But no, Juno, I haven't.'

I had to be satisfied with that, even though I knew she would also never break her promise to him, if Daniel had been in touch but asked her to keep silent.

We reached the top of a hill and suddenly the Vale of Widecombe was spread out before us, snowy fields glowing white under a silver moon, the shadows faintly blue, the distant spire of the Cathedral of the Moor standing up like a dark, pointing finger. I braked so that we could take the scene in for a moment, white fields edged by dark lines of hedgerow, their tops dusted with white, scattered buildings roofed in snow. It was perfect, like the scene inside a child's snow globe. I wanted to pick it up and give it a shake, set the snowflakes whirling. Except whirling snowflakes would be a bit of a nuisance just now, as I edged the van cautiously down the steep hill towards Cold East Farm.

'I'll tell you what was interesting, though,' I added to Elizabeth. 'When I asked Penny if she'd discussed her murder theory with any of her old friends, she reacted really oddly.'

Elizabeth slanted me a glance. 'In what way?'

'She backed right off. And when I asked her if she suspected anyone in the group, she told me to forget she'd ever spoken, as if she'd decided her whole theory was rubbish. And I don't believe she thinks so for a moment.'

'So, you think she suspects one of her friends?'

I shrugged. 'I don't know.' What I did know was that if I had any sense, I'd forget all about it. Except now I was curious.

But I couldn't think about it just then. The snow-covered thatch of Cold East Farm, smooth and white as the icing on a cake, loomed on our right. Outside, parked vehicles cluttered the road, and I could see knots of people gathered outside the farm door, lighted torches glowing gold in the dark. The wassail was about to begin.

CHAPTER SIXTEEN

I parked the van on the verge and we trudged up the path towards the noisy, chattering crowd outside of Neil and Carol's farmhouse. It seemed the snow was deeper on this side of the valley. Neil had cleared the path, heaping it up in piles on either side. About fifty people were gathered: the members of the Border Morris, a family of holidaymakers spending New Year at the farm, the rest were locals. Everyone wore scarves, hats and gloves, but the air was icy, cold enough to sting bare cheeks and noses.

Evie from the *Dartmoor Gazette* was among the crowd, and, standing by himself, Don Drummond. I couldn't see Fizz, she didn't seem to be there. Just as well, it would have been awkward trying to chat to his wife with him present.

The Morris team were dressed in their traditional garb, a few with blackened faces, but most had only a bit of extended smudging around the eyes. Olly's highwayman's mask fitted in with their look very well.

Several of the team were women, who wore the same top hats, rag coats and clumpy boots as the men, but instead of trousers, wore them with fishnet tights. I wondered when that had crept into the tradition. Bit chilly for a night like tonight, I would have thought. I was certainly glad of all my layers. The fishnets, and the extravagant black eye make-up they wore gave them an oddly Goth appearance. There was no sign of Jackie Millard, although there was a girl fiddler, and Benny from the fair was on the squeeze box. Olly, whistle in hand, rushed over to join them.

'Hey, lad!' One of the Morris men cried out as soon as he saw him. 'How old are you?'

'Nearly sixteen,' Olly responded. 'Why?'

'We can't persuade any of these young ladies to be our wassail queen.' He swept an arm around the assembled onlookers and there was shy giggling and headshaking from a group of teenage girls. 'Then it falls to the youngest man present to be Tom Tit. And if you're only fifteen,' he added with a laugh, 'that means you.'

'What's Tom Tit?' Olly's cool highwayman's mask couldn't disguise his alarm.

'Don't worry, Ol!' Benny clapped him on the shoulder. 'We only burn you on the bonfire at the end.' This brought a roar of laughter from the crowd. 'Just joking! All you have to do is climb up in the apple tree and put toast on the branches.'

'Oh.' Olly straightened his shoulders, obviously relieved. 'I can do that.'

'Good lad. I'll tell 'ee what to say.'

One of the teenagers in the crowd raised her hand as if she was at school. 'Why do you put toast in the tree?'

The man who had spoken before, raised a finger. ''Tis toast soaked in our wassail bowl – soaked in cider. And we put it in the tree to encourage the robins, because they are the guardian spirits of the orchard and ensure a good crop.' Just then, the door of the farmhouse opened. Carol came out, carrying her little daughter Amy in her arms. She stood aside and a cheer went up as Neil came through, bearing the steaming wassail bowl in both hands, full of warm, spicy cider.

There was a round of applause, which everyone joined in, except Evie who was too busy snapping away on her camera. One of the Morris men, standing in front of me, leant in close to his neighbour. 'Is that him?' he murmured, pointing. 'Is that Don Drummond?'

'That's him.' His neighbour's voice was a low growl. 'Murdering bastard.'

I tried to draw closer, to catch what else they might say, but I couldn't hear. Neil's appearance with the wassail bowl was the cue for carousing to begin. The musicians struck up and singers started, '*Apple tree prosper, bud, bloom and bear, that we may have plenty of cider next year . . .*' and the members of the Morris flung themselves into a dance, their big boots stamping like carthorses as they dodged around each other, arms swinging vigorously, clashing together their lighted torches each time they passed, with a contemptuous disregard for health and safety.

I kept half an eye on Don during all this. Did he feel vulnerable here alone, amongst people who had called Bob Millard and his widow their friend?

The clashing of the torches was meant to wake up the ground and frighten away evil spirits. Just in case the ground wasn't sufficiently woken, or there were spirits who still hadn't got the message yet, the Morris team launched into another dance, abandoning their blazing torches and taking up hefty sticks, which they alternately clashed with their partner's, or used to beat the ground. They did this with great enthusiasm, shouting and sending clods of snow flying up into the air. It was all very boisterous and folksy with touches of Robin Hood, or Little John, or whoever it was who used to fight with staves.

At the very edge of the crowd, hanging back behind everyone else, I glimpsed another figure, barely lit by the flickering torches. He was dressed like the other Morris men, in black jacket and top hat. But there was green foliage twisted around his hatband and his face was painted green, the lower half obscured by a false beard made of leaves. I smiled. This was the Green Man, meant to represent the spirit of fertility and new life. I didn't know what part he played in the ceremony. I leant over to nudge Elizabeth, to point him out to her, but when I looked back a moment later, he had disappeared into the shadows.

The Morris ended their second dance, and after a moment for them to catch their breath, it was time to make the torchlit procession to the orchard, everyone singing the traditional Wassailing Carol. Our voices sounded loud and raucous, our breath making clouds in the cold, clear air.

Here we come a-wassailing among the leaves so green,
Here we come a-wandering, so fair to be seen . . .

Something hit me hard on the sleeve. A snowball. I turned, but couldn't spot the culprit. It couldn't be Olly, he was playing his whistle, and anyway, he was in front of me. It was unlikely to be Elizabeth, who'd joined the group of singers. I scooped up my ammunition, ready, balling snow between my woollen gloves. If someone wanted a snowball fight, bring it on.

'*. . . Love and joy come to you,*' we sang on, '*And to your wassail too,*
And God bless you and send you a Happy New Year . . .'

We gathered together around one gnarled apple tree, the oldest in the orchard, its twisted goblet of branches laden with snow. We circled it three times, and then stopped to pass around the cider. As I waited for the wassail cup to come my way, trying to stifle any thought of contagious disease, I looked around for Don Drummond. Wasn't this his big moment?

But he was standing a little way apart, talking

to someone I couldn't see, someone whose face was hidden by the trunk of a nearby tree. I could just see the ragged edge of a coat and a top hat, so it must have been a member of the Morris. It seemed to be a lively conversation. Even in the flickering light of the torches I could see Don's angry snarl and belligerent, clenched fists. I edged back a little, dropping the snowball that was freezing my fingers and making my glove wet, until I could just catch his voice. 'So maybe Bob let Gary sleep on his sofa a few times? So what? You think that gives him the right to have a go at me? He didn't know my brother. How many times did he bail him out, give him money for his rent only to find he'd blown it on drugs? Or persuade a friend to give him a job, then find Gary never turned up? Or take him in because he's homeless, only to find he'd stolen from you?' He gave a bitter laugh. 'How would you like to find your wife in tears because Gary's broken in and stolen her laptop, or another piece of her mother's jewellery is missing? How many chances do you think I gave him? How many chances would you give him, eh?'

I didn't hear the muttered reply because at that moment the crowd around the tree roared for Tom Tit. As I turned my head, Don noticed me standing close by and glowered. I quickly moved away.

It seems I had missed the passing of the wassail cup. By now Olly was being lifted up into the apple tree's gnarly embrace and trying to find a foothold on its slippery branches. He kicked clumps of snow away with his boots, sending down a pebbly shower of white, until he found a position where he could squat securely. Neil passed him up a piece of toast, soggy with cider. Olly pierced it on a twig, where it hung limply, and then repeated the procedure several times over, as he recited the words Benny had given him.

> *'Wassail! Wassail! All over the town,*
> *Our toast it is white and our ale it is brown.*
> *Our bowl it is made of the . . .'*

his little face crumpled for a moment, hesitating,

> *'white maple tree,'*

he went on, grinning.

> *'With wassailing bowl, we drink unto thee.'*

Then Neil stepped forward and poured cider into the roots of the tree. It was all good fun, but how anyone ever thought this nonsense would help to secure a good apple harvest is beyond me. You've got to give them credit for trying, I suppose. But there was more to come. Once Olly had climbed safely down from its branches, there was more singing and another go-round of the wassail bowl. Then would come the firing of shotguns up into the branches, using saluting blanks these days, instead of lead shot. This was supposed to strengthen the poor old tree. After that, it would be a ceremonial walk back to the farmhouse for more cider and slices of warm apple cake.

There were four men pointing shotguns. Neil was one, his neighbour another, and two members of the Border Morris. Everyone was watching, their attention fixed on what must be the strangest part of the ceremony. They pulled their triggers on the count of three, loud shots echoing around the orchard. But there was another noise at the same time, a high-pitched crack. I saw Elizabeth's head turn sharply. She had heard it too, and recognised the sound. A pistol shot. Elizabeth knows about pistols. She used to carry one in her handbag and I suspect she's fired a few, back in another life.

Yards away, beneath another tree, I saw something on the ground, a dark shape lying on white snow. Not something but someone, still as stone. My heart gave a sickening thump and I ran towards the body.

'What's happened?' Neil shouted, a laugh in his voice. 'Someone fainted from the shock?'

'I think someone's hurt,' I called back.

I could hear footsteps then, pounding behind me, a hubbub of slowly dawning questions. I sank to my knees and looked at the body lying on its front, arms flung out, face half turned towards me. Even in the shadowy darkness I could see who it was. Don Drummond. Looking very dead.

But he wasn't. I could feel a pulse in his neck. And

as I leant in close to his face to speak his name, I felt the whisper of his breath. I thought he moaned softly. By now Elizabeth was on her knees beside me, and slid her hand up under Don's jacket. She drew it out and her fingers were dark with something sticky and wet. 'He's been shot,' she said calmly. 'Someone, call an ambulance.'

'Shot!' Neil's voice repeated. 'But we were firing blanks!'

'Not with a shotgun.' Elizabeth slid her hand under Don's body, as if checking for an exit wound. Her hand came away clean. 'He's been shot with a pistol.' She nodded towards the trees, 'from somewhere over there.'

People surged in around his body, asking questions. Should he be moved, would it be safe? Would it be more dangerous to leave him lying on the cold ground? Had someone phoned for an ambulance? Yes, someone was doing it now, and calling the police. Was he breathing? Did he need CPR? I stood up, backed off, leaving him in the calm, capable hands of Elizabeth and a girl from the Morris who said she was a nurse.

I stared up towards the end of the orchard. If it had not been for the moonlight, for the brightness of the snowy ground, I could not have seen him, the dark figure standing just beyond the orchard's edge, watching. I would not have made out the shape of his coat and top hat and the pointed leaves that made up his beard, seen his breath curling away from him like smoke. The Green Man. My feet seemed to start moving of their own accord. I began walking towards him, and then stumbled into a run. 'Hey!' I called out, as he turned and began to stride away from me across a snowy field. 'Hey! Stop!'

A couple of the Morris men at the back of the gathering heard me and began to follow. 'Who is it, love?' one of them asked as they caught up with me.

'Him,' I pointed, 'the Green Man, he's the one who shot Don.'

The man nearest me held up a flaming torch. 'C'mon!' he called to the others. 'Let's get after the bastard!'

Four of them raced off in pursuit, me following behind, rushing through the shadows beneath the trees, through the changing kaleidoscope of blue, grey and white as we passed beneath the branches, trying not to trip on roots hidden under the snow. Ahead of me the first runner was way in front, moving fast, his top hat flying off and landing in the snow. 'Be careful!' I shouted after him. 'He's got a gun!'

As if to confirm it, the distant figure stopped and turned calmly to face his pursuers, slowly raising his arm to aim, like a man in a duel. There was a glint of moonlight on metal and the sharp crack of the pistol as he fired. The Morris men all stopped in their tracks, the foremost backing away out of range.

'Leave him!' I was breathing hard, the icy air hurting my chest as I gulped it in. 'The police will be here soon.'

'Watch where he goes!' The foremost runner stooped to pick up his top hat, brushing off the snow as the Green Man turned and walked away, cool and unhurried. After a few moments, he disappeared into the darkness of the trees at the far edge of the field. His footprints left a clear trail in front of us. And there was something else lying there, something small and dark against the crisp white surface, like a shrivelled leather purse. I picked it up. The breathless Morris men came lumbering back towards me.

'He can't get far,' one said. 'Not on foot. What's that?'

He held the flaming light close, so that we could see the object in my hand, a bundle of dry leaves, wrapped around with red ribbon.

'Our friend must have dropped it.' I fingered the leaves; dry and brittle, their green colour faded, they were rough triangles with sharp, serrated edges. Birch, I thought.

'It's just a bundle of leaves,' a voice said. 'What's it supposed to mean?'

I shook my head. I didn't know its significance either. But what I suspected was that if our Green Man had had his chance, this bundle of dry birch leaves would be lying on Don Drummond's dead body.

CHAPTER SEVENTEEN

'What exactly makes you think that, Miss Browne?' Cruella demanded, as we both stared at the leaves on the table between us.

'Remember the sprig of elder left on Bob Millard's body?'

Her little mouth twisted in a smirk. 'I don't think we should leap to conclusions and assume this is the same perpetrator. The crimes may not be connected.'

I sat back and stared at her. How had I managed to draw the short straw and get interviewed by Cruella? Where were Inspector Ford or Dean Collins when I needed them? Simple answer, they were outside examining the scene of the crime whilst a dozen uniforms were combing the surroundings for traces of Green Man, whose trail of footsteps had ended very suddenly in the lane beyond the field, as if he'd disappeared in a puff of smoke. Detective Sergeant deVille had been given the job of interviewing witnesses and she'd decided to start with me. I folded my arms.

'You think not? Two men who knew each other, fought each other? One's dead and the other's been shot, and you don't think the crimes are connected?'

I got the violet glare of loathing. 'I'm certainly not going to speculate about the crime with you,' she snapped, picking up her pen. 'All I want from you is your witness statement. Stick to what you saw and what you heard.'

'Okay.' I gave her the full story: seeing the Green Man before the wassail started, hearing Don Drummond's argument with someone I couldn't see, hearing two men calling him a murdering bastard, hearing the pistol shot as the blanks were fired, seeing the Green Man again after Don had been shot, then finding the bunch of leaves.

'This bunch of leaves could have been part of the Green Man's costume, couldn't it?' Cruella, it seemed, was prepared to speculate after all.

I shrugged. 'I couldn't say.'

'You assumed he was part of the Border Morris,' she went on, 'but, speaking to some of them outside just now, they say he definitely wasn't one of their team. None of them seem to know who he was. Most said they hadn't noticed him at all until the shot was fired.' She frowned, a little pucker between her finely arched brows. 'You can't describe him?'

'No more than I already have. He was dressed like the other men in the Morris, except there was greenery around his hat, his face was painted and he wore this leafy beard.'

'Height?'

'Average. It's difficult to tell when someone's wearing a top hat.'

'What about his hair? Long or short?'

I puffed out my cheeks in a sigh. I couldn't really see it under the hat. 'Now you mention it, it was hanging down a bit, quite straggly, so it must have been longish. It could have been a wig, I suppose.'

'You're sure you've never seen this person before?'

I'd given that question some thought myself as I hung around in the crowd, waiting for the ambulance to take Don Drummond off to hospital. Could the person disguised in the false beard have been Jackie Millard, taking a potshot at the man she believed had killed her husband? Could it have been a woman? It was possible, I suppose. 'No,' I said. 'I didn't recognise him at all.'

'And you can't identify the man you say the victim was arguing with?'

'Sorry, no. I didn't see his face. But he was dressed in a rag coat and top hat, so I suppose he was one of the Morris team.'

'And the two men you heard talking, who you say pointed Mr Drummond out?'

'I was standing behind them. I don't think I could pick them out.'

Cruella favoured me with a patronising smile and a slight shake of the head as if I was a hopeless witness. I wanted to thump her. 'In that case, Miss Browne,' she said, 'I think we've finished with you for now.'

'Do you think you could interview Elizabeth Knollys

next?' I asked. 'Then we could take Olly home. He's got school in the morning.'

She arched an eyebrow, considering my request.

'I can't go without them,' I added, as I stood up. 'And I'm sure you don't want me hanging around here, making a nuisance of myself.' I laid heavy emphasis on the last few words.

The last thing she'd want was to give me the chance to compare notes with other witnesses.

She gave a faint snort of annoyance at having to comply with my request, then snapped at the constable standing at the door. 'Send Ms Knollys in next.'

'Thank you,' I said, and gave her my most angelic smile.

Cruella wasn't there to stop me speculating with Elizabeth and Olly on the drive home, despite the fact we'd all been warned to keep our mouths shut. The usually sharp-eyed Elizabeth admitted she hadn't spotted the Green Man, but Olly was convinced he had seen him. 'Just hanging about at the edge of the crowd, like. He had all green stuff around his face.'

'That was him,' I nodded.

'It's odd,' Elizabeth said thoughtfully. 'If he wanted to mingle, to pass as one of the Morris men, why didn't he just black his face, like the others? He could have got much closer to Don Drummond then, stood far more chance of killing him with that pistol shot. Whereas he fired from too far away, luckily for Don.'

Don had been shot in the back of the shoulder, no more than a flesh wound, and returned to consciousness before the ambulance arrived. We decided someone he knew ought to travel in it with him, for emotional support. As the very sight of me was likely to send his blood pressure sky-high, Carol had volunteered to go.

Elizabeth gave a smile. 'No, I think we can safely assume our perpetrator is an amateur, at least where guns are concerned.'

'And why didn't he use a shotgun?' I asked. 'It would have confused the issue, cast suspicion on some of the other shooters, at least at first.'

'Perhaps he didn't have one,' Olly pointed out practically.

'It's easy enough to get hold of one around here,' Elizabeth answered, 'easier than a pistol, I'd have thought.'

A sleety rain had begun to fall and I set the windscreen wipers swooshing across the glass. 'It's almost as if he wants to stand out,' I said, as the wiper blades squeaked in accompaniment, 'as if he wanted to be noticed.' I didn't mention the bundle of leaves, my theory that it had been intended to be left on the body as a trophy, as if the would-be killer had some point to make.

'D'you think it was one of the Morris men,' Olly asked, 'trying to avenge Bob 'cos they think Don killed him?'

'All the more reason to dress just like the others,' Elizabeth responded, 'not to stand out.' She shivered, pulling her scarf tighter around her neck. 'Can't you get any more out of this heater, Juno?'

'No, sorry. It's on full now.'

'It's pathetic,' she complained. The windscreen wipers squeaked mournfully in agreement like some tragic Greek chorus. Olly leant forward in the back, still sporting the highwayman's mask, his face up close against the security grille. 'How did whoever tried to kill him,' he asked in tones of serious sleuthiness, 'know he was going to be there tonight?'

'Oh, that's an easy one,' I told him. 'His picture's been in the *Gazette*. They wrote an article about tonight and Don making the wassail bowl. In fact, I think it's been in more than once.'

'Oh yeah.' Olly sank back, deflated.

We passed Buckland church, just visible through the falling sleet, and began our long, slippery descent towards Ashburton. At least we had gravity on our side.

'So, do we assume someone has a grudge against both of them, Bob and Don?' Elizabeth asked, 'and that whoever murdered Bob was the same person who tried to kill Don this evening?'

'But who?' I asked. 'And why?'

She sighed. 'I suppose we'll have to leave that to the police to work out.'

After I'd dropped Olly and Elizabeth back at their cottage, I went home. Noah's buggy was standing in the hall, a comforting reminder of Kate and Adam's return.

The cafe would be open again in a day or two, starting off a new supply of leftovers. Kate wouldn't be able to help so much at the cafe with baby Noah to look after. I wondered if Chris Brownlow might help Adam out for the rest of his holidays, as he had back in the summer.

I didn't go to bed. I made myself a mug of hot chocolate and then set about pulling the boxes out from under my bed, emptying them, much to the delight of Bill who loves nothing better than an empty cardboard box to sit in. They contained all I had left of Cordelia's belongings. A question was niggling in the back of my brain, and I was pretty certain that among her possessions I would find the answer. Whilst Bill sniffed the boxes, finally selecting one to curl up in, I leafed through all her old astrology books, checking for any odd pieces of paper she might have slipped between the pages. I found a book by David Fairweather, his photo on the back cover, taken during his bearded professor phase, looking handsome and rather smug. I sifted through piles of old birth charts Cordelia had cast, all drawn by hand. She never owned a computer to do the work for her. The sight of her bold, black writing caught at my heart, made me remember how much I miss her. I sorted through tattered envelopes chunky with correspondence. Finally, I found what I was looking for, a simple piece of paper, edges dog-eared and torn, with an illustrated list printed on it, decorated with leaves. For many years, it had hung up on Cordelia's kitchen wall. I studied it and smiled.

'Gotcha!' I said, and reached for my hot chocolate.

CHAPTER EIGHTEEN

'Tree calendar,' Dean repeated flatly, staring at me in mystification across *Old Nick's* kitchen table. I'd rung him as soon as I'd got back from walking the Tribe next morning, and asked if he could pop in the shop to see me that afternoon. I'd also called Fizz, who'd spent the night at the hospital, to see how Don was coming along.

'He's been incredibly lucky,' she told me, her voice quivery and tearful. 'He's going to be all right. He'll probably be coming home in a few days.'

'That's wonderful,' I said dutifully, wondering if a near-death experience might have sweetened his temper any. I went to Chloe Berkeley-Smythe's place next; I'd promised to take her shopping for clothes for her next cruise. I checked in on Malcolm, still installing the new heating system at Maisie's cottage. She'd be back soon, and I wanted to be sure the work would be finished. Then I called on Penny to talk about the tree calendar I had found in Cordelia's things, and check I had my facts right before I talked to Dean.

'It's the ancient Celtic system,' I explained to him, pointing to the calendar I'd spread out on the table. 'The Celtic year was divided into the thirteen lunar months, and each month was named after a particular tree.'

Dean nodded to show he was keeping up. 'Right.'

'This month we're in at the moment,' I said, pointing to the relevant picture on the calendar, 'is called the Birch Moon. The Celts used to a hang a bunch of birch leaves tied in red ribbon over a newborn baby's cradle for protection, to ward off evil spirits. Last month,' I went on deliberately slowly, 'back before Christmas, when Bob was killed, was the Elder Moon. Elder was the symbol of birth and death. They used it to protect against demons.'

'Oh, bloody hell,' Dean groaned as realisation dawned. 'Birch and elder. We're looking at the same person – Bob's killer, and Drummond's would-be assassin – and you're saying he's the follower of some ancient Celtic religion?'

'Possibly a Druid,' I nodded. 'And if that's true, there might not be just one killer. It could be the followers of a cult.'

'Oh, bloody hell!' he repeated, sinking his chin in his hands. 'I can just imagine the boss's reaction when I tell him that.'

It was just as well I'd never bothered him with Penny's astrological murder theory. He'd think I was even further round the bend. 'We could wait for the Rowan Moon in February, wait for a body to turn up with rowan berries on it,' I suggested flippantly, 'just to prove the point.' I got up and flicked on the kettle.

Dean sat frowning as I busied myself making tea. 'But why choose Bob Millard and Don Drummond as victims? They're not exactly sacrificial virgins, are they?'

'I think your view of the Druids might be coloured by popular fiction,' I told him loftily. 'They didn't indulge in human sacrifice.'

'What?' He looked disappointed. 'Not at Stonehenge?'

'No. Nor anywhere else. In fact, Druids were probably rather dull.'

'But what's the point of leaving this stuff on the bodies, these Celtic symbols or whatever they are?'

I shrugged. 'Over to you, Constable.' I slid him his mug of tea. 'Any sign of the Green Man?'

He shook his head. 'Not a trace of him. No one saw him arrive and the none of the Morris lot knew who he was. He was nothing to do with the wassail. They say the Green Man doesn't usually pop up in their celebrations until May. And we don't know how he got away. Is he part of this Celtic stuff?'

'He's pagan, a sort of spirit of the green wood. He's meant to symbolise spring and rebirth. I was asking Penny about it. She says that in some celebrations the Green Man is slaughtered – sacrificed, to give birth to the summer.'

'I thought you just said they didn't do human sacrifice?'

'Not literally. It's just part of the celebrations.'

Dean sighed and rubbed the back of his head. 'There used to be a Green Man pub near where I lived. I remember the inn sign.'

'They're everywhere. And in churches. There's a carving of the Green Man on one of the roof bosses in Widecombe Church. He's horrible.'

'Why is he horrible?'

'Well, he has leaves coming out of his mouth – just like all the others. But his mouth is open so wide, you can see all his teeth. He looks as if he's screaming.'

Dean grunted and sipped his tea.

'One thing does occur to me,' I went on. 'If this – God forbid – is the work of a serial killer, it might be wrong to assume these are his first victims. It could be worth checking out old murder cases to see if any other bodies had bits of foliage attached.'

Dean frowned over the calendar. 'Can I borrow this?'

'You can,' I told him. 'But I want it back. It's got sentimental value.' For a start there was writing on the back. *This, instead of a card. Merry Christmas Cordelia. Love from R.R. xx*

Reggie Ryecart had sent this to Cordelia. She'd always had a soft spot for Reggie, and I suspect he'd had a soft spot for her.

'I'll get it copied and return it to you,' he promised, folding it up.

'Just suppose for a moment these Celtic symbols are nothing more than a smokescreen, a trick by the killer to get the police barking up the wrong tree.' I opened my sacrificial tin of biscuits and pushed it in his direction. 'Have you got no real clues about Bob's murder? No suspects at all?'

He shrugged, dipping into the tin and pulling out a chunky choc cookie. 'Jackie, obviously,' he said, munching. 'But so far, we can't link her to the murder. We've also checked out last night and she has a great alibi. She was at a friend's house with several other people, so we can forget the vengeful widow trying to shoot Don Drummond.'

I watched another chunky chocolate cookie being sacrificed.

'Unless she got someone to do it for her,' I suggested.

Dean almost choked. 'Evidence, Miss Marple?' he spluttered.

'I've told you not to call me that.' I do not wish to be compared with some shrivelled up, prying old maid, but he does it because he knows it annoys me. 'There are women in the Morris now. Perhaps Bob had a new girlfriend.'

Dean patted his chest, wheezing as he struggled to get his breath back. 'We are currently investigating all the members of this Border Morris,' he informed me.

It just sounded like police-speak as far as I was concerned. 'What about Don Drummond. Any suspects?'

'He's been under sedation. We've hardly had a chance to speak to him yet.'

'Well, I was talking to one of my clients this morning, Mrs Berkeley-Smythe. Her son, the Plymouth One, is currently trying to sue the firm Don works for in Exeter.'

Dean looked interested. 'Why?'

'He's lost a lot of money and he holds the firm responsible for giving him bad financial advice.'

'What's the name of this firm?'

'Aigler Wealth Management, in Exeter.'

He wrote it down. 'Does he hold Drummond personally responsible?'

'I don't know, but someone might. I was just thinking, someone with a similar grudge . . .'

Dean swallowed his tea and grinned. 'You keep thinking, Juno. That's what you're good at.'

'There's also the possibility,' I carried on, ignoring this provocation, 'someone connected to Don's brother might have wanted him dead. He was arguing with one of the Morris team about Gary last night.'

Dean nodded. 'We interviewed that bloke. He came forward and admitted he and Don had a few words. He said he didn't know the full story about Gary, and he regretted opening his mouth. But crucially, he was one of the four men firing a shotgun. He couldn't have been standing in front of Drummond, firing a shotgun into the tree *and* behind him firing a pistol at his back.'

'What if the Morris team are all in it together?' I suggested. 'What if the Green Man is really one of them and they're covering for him? All that chasing after him could have been pretence.'

Dean eyed me uneasily. 'You know I just told you to keep thinking? Well, I've changed my mind now. I want you to stop.'

CHAPTER NINETEEN

Penny came to the window of Loft Cottage as soon as I started tapping on the glass.

'How is the poor man who was shot?' she asked, stepping aside to let me in.

'He's going to be fine,' I told her. 'I talked to his wife this morning. Thanks for the help with the Celtic calendar, by the way.'

'Do you think the police will take it seriously?' She gestured for me to sit down.

'I don't suppose they'll be rounding up Druids any time soon, but it must make them think about the kind of person who's doing this.' I smiled. 'At least we don't have to worry that there's any astrological connection this time.'

'How so?' she asked.

'Well, Fizz mentioned this morning she hoped Don would be well enough for them to take their holiday. He's got a big birthday coming up at the beginning of April, and they are going away to celebrate.'

'So, he's an Aries?'

'Yes, not a Capricorn, which he would have to be, to fit in with your theory.'

Penny sat frowning and chewing her lip. 'Oh dear,' she murmured. Then she looked up at me, clearly agitated, her hands tightening into fists. 'But there is, you see, Juno! There is a connection. Aries is ruled by Mars, the god of war, and so it's associated with all metal tools, especially weapons.' I stared for a moment, not understanding. 'Guns!' she said, seeing my confusion. 'Guns, Juno!'

Oh, why did I open my stupid mouth? 'But Penny, all of the previous murders took place during the sun sign of the victim. It's one of the things that links them.'

'Yes,' she agreed, nodding, 'but whoever shot this Don must have had a motive. Somehow, he knows he's going to be at the wassail, and here is an opportunity to kill him, with a weapon of war. Or he has to wait another three months, when he can't be sure he'll have an opportunity.'

'It's a bit of a stretch, Penny,' I told her frankly. 'You're making our killer sound desperate.'

She gave a little shrug. 'Perhaps he is.'

'Okay. Let's just suppose for a moment that the person who murdered your university colleagues, and Bob Millard, and whoever tried to shoot Don, are all the same person,' I said. 'Why, suddenly, does he start bringing Celtic symbolism into it? There was nothing found on any of the previous victims, was there?'

'I don't know.' She shook her head miserably. 'I just have this terrible feeling that whoever is doing all this isn't

222

a believer at all. That it's all cynical, just playing a game.'

'And there's motive, Penny. I can see the same person might have had a motive for killing Bob and Don, because they knew each other, but they can't be linked to those earlier murders at the university, unless there's some connection between the victims we don't know about.'

'Perhaps there is.' She stared at me anxiously. 'Perhaps it's just a case of finding it.'

Oh, buggeration, I cursed silently.

Don Drummond did not look pleased to see me. It was three days now since he'd been shot so I didn't think my visit would cause him to have a serious relapse but, on the other hand, he had ordered me to stay away from him. I tapped tentatively on the open door of the room he was occupying in a small, private hospital. He was there for a few days' rest and rehabilitation. Fizz told me his firm were paying for it. Private health care was one of the perks. He didn't look as if he was resting much, propped up against the pillows, a mobile phone, an open laptop and a copy of the *Financial Times* on the table across his bed.

I'd decided to forget about Penny and her theories and follow Cruella's advice: stick to what I'd seen and what I'd heard, and follow up on that. Except she hadn't actually mentioned the following up bit. 'May I come in?'

He glared at me for a long moment before he spoke. 'On one condition.'

'What's that?'

'You don't tell me how lucky I am. If one more person says it . . .'

'I promise I won't.'

He nodded towards the chair placed by the bedside. 'Come in, then. Anyone who thinks it's lucky to get away with a flesh wound wants to get one of their own.'

'Painful?'

'Not a lot of fun.'

I tried to resist fidgeting under his gaze. Even confined in a hospital bed I found him unnerving.

'I thought you might turn up,' he said at last.

'I want to find out who tried to kill you.'

'So do I. It's the only reason I'm letting you sit there.'

'Oh?'

'You may be a nosy, interfering, dangerous sort of woman, Juno Browne, but you're not stupid.'

I laughed, taken aback. 'I'll take that as a compliment.'

'Take it how you like.'

We weren't bothering with niceties, obviously. 'Okay. I'm assuming you didn't kill Bob Millard?'

He groaned. 'I didn't go near Bob Millard! Not on the day of the fair or any other time. I can't help it if those lunatics dancing the other night blame me for his death, or some nutcase dressed as a green man, I had nothing to do with it.'

'Do you know Jackie Millard?'

'No, never met her! And I've steered clear of Bob since we had our little disagreement back in the summer.'

'When you fought about your brother?'

He didn't seem surprised I knew. 'He started it, had a go at me about Gary, although he doesn't know half of what's gone on over the years.' He shrugged his shoulders and then winced as if he regretted it. 'Maybe I threw the first punch.'

'Can I ask you about Gary?'

'Didn't you overhear enough the other night?'

I could feel myself blushing, but I ploughed on. 'I gather he's been a problem over the years.'

He gave a bitter laugh. 'I spent thousands getting him into a rehab clinic. He was there six months. We thought he was clean, cured. But within a few weeks of getting out, he was back in there again. Trouble is,' he added, his voice softening, a note of regret creeping into it, 'when someone gets into drugs, if they can't kick the habit, there's only one way it can end.'

'I know.'

He looked sceptical. 'Do you?'

I held his gaze. 'I do as a matter of fact.' But I didn't intend to tell this man about my mother. I took a breath. 'You can't think of anyone who might have a motive for trying to kill you? Someone connected with Gary, for instance?'

'No, I can't.'

'What about your work?'

His brows snapped together, immediately suspicious. 'What about it?' he demanded.

'I know the firm you work for is being sued by one of its clients, Jonathan Berkeley-Smythe.'

'I can't talk about that.'

'Is he your personal client?'

'Client relationships are confidential.'

I ignored him and pressed on. 'Whether he is or not, is it possible that he, or someone like him, might hold a grudge against you, if they'd lost money?'

He sighed. 'Look, any form of financial speculation – stocks and shares, hedge funds, crypto-currency, any of it – it's all a form of gambling. You can win but you can lose. Our firm has made millions for some of our clients, but occasionally things don't turn out as expected. And sometimes,' he hesitated a moment, 'there are consequences. But if you can't afford to lose, you shouldn't gamble in the first place.'

'That doesn't really answer my question, does it?'

'Look,' he went on impatiently, 'in the case of the client you referred to, it was nothing to do with me personally. There was a screw-up by a younger colleague. But we can all make a mistake.' He smiled reluctantly. 'Not too many, though, or you're out of a job.'

'Could there be someone, in your past perhaps, who might hold it against you if you'd made a mistake?'

He rubbed his face with his hands as if he was suddenly tired. 'I don't think so.'

I wasn't sure he was telling the truth. 'Well, think about it.' I stood up. 'I'll let you get some rest. Just one more question,' I added as I turned to go, 'and this might seem like a strange one. Do you know anyone who's into Celtic mythology?'

He raised an eyebrow. 'Why?'

'Just something I need to find out.'

'Fizz uses Celtic designs on some of her silk scarves.'

I remembered them, patterns weaving themselves into intricate, sinuous, knots.

'And a lot of jewellery makers use them,' he went on.

A sudden vision of Jackie flashed into my mind, her Celtic cross dangling from one ear.

'But I don't know anyone . . . oh, hold on,' he said, clicking his fingers. 'There's a guy who works out of a craft collective near South Brent, a woodcarver, he's very into Celtic stuff. He—' Don's mobile played a tune at that moment. He picked it up and stared at the screen. 'I'm going to have to take this,' he said. 'It's work. Bye.'

Summarily dismissed, I gave him a wave and left him to his business.

'I'm getting out of here tomorrow,' I heard him tell his caller as I left the room.

I made my way back towards the hospital reception. Visitors had to sign out as well as in. I sauntered down the long corridor with its shiny, polished floor, and saw a familiar figure come bustling through the swing doors in front of me. She stopped sharp, her dark brows raised in suspicion. She must be on her way to see Don Drummond too.

'What are you doing here?' Cruella demanded.

'Just visiting,' I smiled and walked on by.

* * *

Old Nick's seemed crowded when I got back. Apart from Sophie, who was painting, Pat, who was busy making bead earrings, and Elizabeth, who was sorting books, Olly was lounging against the counter in lively conversation with Reggie Ryecart of all people, a large-scale map of Dartmoor spread out over its surface.

Sophie rolled her eyes at me. 'Their bikes are in the hall.'

Reggie was jabbing at the map with a finger. 'There's quite a difficult descent down here towards the river,' he was saying. 'Just a single track, and then the only way across the water are these stepping stones. You'll have to carry your bike.'

'I'm sorry about this, Juno,' Elizabeth said.

'Hi, Juno!' Olly called out, without taking his eyes off the map.

'Oh, yes, hello,' Reggie added, a moment later.

'Olly popped in here on his way to see his friend Marcus from school, and this gentleman,' Elizabeth pointed at Reggie, 'arrived here looking for you and they started chatting about bikes . . .'

'That was half an hour ago,' Sophie muttered.

I didn't really want them cluttering up the counter. 'Gentlemen, there's a big table in the back room you can spread that map out on, if you must.'

'Olly, don't you dare forget Marcus,' Elizabeth warned him.

'No, okay,' he called back.

'Reggie, was there something you wanted?' I asked in

an attempt to drag his eyeballs away from cycle paths and trackways.

He looked up. 'Well, I came over to see Penny, actually, to return a couple of books I'd borrowed. Anyway, she wasn't at home, so I thought I'd come around here and pester you for a while before I tried again. And you weren't here either.'

'Well, I am now.' I knew I should offer him a cup of tea, but I didn't want Reggie dropping in for a cuppa every time he felt like it, so I resisted the impulse.

'I'd better get going,' Olly began folding the map.

'Me too,' Reggie said. 'I'll try Penny again.'

'You haven't seen my bike, have you, Juno, since I've refitted it?'

'No, I haven't,' I said, feigning interest, and dutifully followed Olly out into the hall to admire it, although it didn't look a lot different to me.

Reggie came after us. 'A real cyclist doesn't need electricity,' he told me, giving me a sly wink.

'I still have to pedal,' Olly told him indignantly. 'It helps, but it doesn't do all the work for me.'

I let them out of the side door into the alley, still arguing. 'How did they start talking bikes?' I asked, once I'd locked the side door and returned to the shop.

Elizabeth smiled. 'By coincidence. They cycled into the lane at the same time.'

Pat paused in the act of threading a bead onto an earring wire. 'They were outside chatting for ages.'

'And then came in here,' Sophie added darkly. 'They

nearly knocked my table over.'

'They didn't wheel their bikes in through the shop?'

'No. Olly came in and opened up the side door. They brought them in that way.'

Elizabeth was frowning. 'I'm rather hoping that they don't decide to go cycling together.'

'Is that likely?'

'Well, Chris Brownlow is back off to university in a day or two so Olly will be losing his cycling buddy. And that Reggie strikes me as odd.'

'He is a bit eccentric,' I admitted. 'But you know, he's a really experienced off-road cyclist. He's been riding about up on the moor all his life. You couldn't find anyone that knows all those tracks and cycleways better than he does. If he takes Olly up there, they are not likely to get lost.'

'Whereas, if he goes with Marcus, they almost certainly will. No, I take your point.' She sighed. 'One shouldn't be prejudiced against oddness. After all, half the world is odd.'

'And the other half don't come in here,' Pat added.

On the journey to Upton Hellions a few days later, I sat in the front passenger seat, next to the Rev. Mary in her tiny car. I didn't have as much leg room as I would have liked but I was better off than Penny and Reggie squashed in the back.

'Stop moaning, Reggie,' Penny told him, about five minutes into our journey. But she had no effect. Reggie spent the rest of the journey ranting over some astrological thing or other. I decided Ranting Reggie would be a good nickname for him. He didn't mention meeting Olly, or anything about bikes, so I didn't either. Instead, I decided I'd better show some interest in the reason for our trip, so I turned to Mary. 'You said the other day that astrological symbols are rare in Devon churches?'

She nodded. We were just north of Crediton, driving a narrow dirt road surrounded by farmland. Here the countryside was more open, more green, more forgiving than the dramatic landscape nearer the moor. 'They are rarer in England than on the Continent,' she told me. 'They always tend to be in older churches. The most famous ones are painted on the ceiling of Waltham Abbey.'

We came to a junction with a fingerpost pointing to Upton Hellions. We seemed to be in the middle of nowhere, but were, it told us, less than a mile from our destination, and it wasn't long before we could see the square church tower up ahead of us.

The hamlet itself was very tiny, just a few desirable properties, mostly thatched. If single mum Lily Marwood really lived here, I decided, then she must be doing very well for herself. St Mary's Church had a pleasing simplicity about it. It was a small, unspoilt and very old, church and graveyard set on a raised bank at the side of a narrow lane overlooking fields. There was just about enough room for Mary's little car to pull up on the verge. The church was reached through a tiled lychgate, a path leading through a cramped and crowded graveyard. Inside the medieval porch I looked up and saw a tiny nest made of mud, built into the corner of the rafters. I smiled. Swallows must nest here in the summer.

We let ourselves through an even older arched doorway, into the church itself.

It must have been one of the smallest churches I'd ever stood in, a pleasing space of plain white walls and simply dressed stone. Despite its small size, it had a light and airy feel, a sense of being left to itself, of unbroken time not interfered with. The little pulpit was just a single enclosed step set against the wall. A fat parson would have struggled to squeeze into it. There was little in the way of fancy carving, and the church was innocent of any flowers.

The one blazing exception to this lack of ornament was the wall behind the altar, decorated by tiles in sumptuous patterns of red, blue and gold. It was here we found the symbols of the zodiac, gold figures on a blue ground, six on each side of the altar.

'They're stunning!' Penny cooed, getting out her phone to photograph them.

They were certainly pretty, although I doubt if I'd have come all this way to see them under other circumstances. But the church pleased me. Reggie was sitting in a pew, drinking in the atmosphere. 'Peaceful, isn't it?' he whispered. 'Or it was until we got here.'

'Aren't you going to look at the tiles?' I asked as Penny and Mary continued to exclaim over them.

He shrugged. 'Seen them before.' Which made me wonder why he'd come on the trip at all. Perhaps it was for company.

After we'd had our fill of the church, and looked around the churchyard, we trooped out into the lane, which was a dead end leading past a pair of fine thatched cottages to the gates of a private drive.

'There's a public footpath, just to the left of that gatepost there,' Mary pointed out, 'that takes us through the field to the Elizabethan farmhouse. In fact, if you look through the gate you can see the back of the building from here.'

'There aren't cows in the field, are there?' Penny asked nervously.

Mary shook her head. 'Just a few sheep. But some of them have newborn lambs, so we'll keep to the path.' She turned to look back at Reggie, who was lingering by the car. 'Aren't you coming, Reggie?'

'No. You know the manor is a private house?' he said. 'You can't go inside.'

'No, but it's lovely from the outside, certainly worth a look.'

'I don't think I fancy the walk, actually,' he admitted.

'Well, we could drive around,' she said, 'there is a road.'

'Are you feeling okay, Reggie?' Penny asked, full of concern. He was certainly looking pale.

'No, I'm fine,' he assured her. 'I might have another look around the churchyard.'

'I could stay here with you,' Mary volunteered. 'Penny and Juno could go by themselves. I don't like leaving you here, Reggie, if you're not feeling well.'

'I'm fine,' he responded, getting irritable. 'Don't make a fuss.'

'Well, it's not very warm.' She held out her car keys. 'Take these. You can sit in the car if you feel chilly. We'll only be a few minutes.'

He accepted them, not very graciously, and we left him to his own devices, whilst we walked the footpath down the sloping field, watched by curious sheep.

The long, white-walled, thatched farmhouse was worth ten minutes of anyone's time, just for the privilege of standing and gawping at it. It was built in 1566, according to Mary, and the oak doorway was original. But it was a private house and after taking a sly picture of it, we felt obliged to take our leave and tramp back up the field towards the church.

Reggie was still waiting by the car, but he was not alone. Standing in the lane talking to him was a woman in jeans and padded body-warmer, her straight brown hair hanging down her back. A golden retriever was sniffing about on the verge a few feet away from her and she was holding the hand of a sturdy-looking, dark-haired boy of about eight. It took me a couple of seconds to realise the woman was Lily Marwood. She turned her head at the sound of our approach. The dog, tail slowly waving, came up to greet us, and I bent down to give him a pat. The little boy escaped from his mother's hold and ran towards him. 'Hello!' Penny called out as he stopped and stood watching us shyly. 'What's your doggie's name?' The little boy smiled, but the sound he made was incoherent, and he raced back to his mother, hiding his head against her legs, more like a shy toddler than a little boy of eight.

Lily Marwood called to her dog and whistled. 'Ruffles! Come here, good boy.' She smiled briefly at us, gave Reggie a nod, and then walked away. As I watched her departing back, I realised I'd missed my chance. If I'd stayed with Reggie and not gone to see the manor house, I might have had a chance to engage her in conversation. Although, what would I have said? *Hi, I'm Juno Browne and by the way, did you murder the father of your child?*

'Chatting up the locals, Reggie?' Penny asked him playfully.

He grinned. 'Just passing the time of day.'

We got back in the car. I'd got the fleeting impression that Lily Marwood's expression when she saw us arrive had been one of relief, but then, if Ranting Reggie had locked her in conversation and she was too polite to tell him to bugger off, she was probably grateful of the excuse to get away. As we turned off to go back to the main road, I looked left and saw her and her son, the dog ambling beside them. They were sauntering along in the middle of the road, in the way of country people who do not expect to encounter traffic. She was chatting to her little boy, and signing to him as she spoke. It's funny how you can form an idea of someone from the briefest glimpse of them. I felt she was someone who was happy with her lot. And I liked her.

CHAPTER TWENTY

'I'm bringing mother back at the weekend.' Our Janet's voice had the long-suffering quality of someone who's counting the days. 'You haven't taken her Christmas tree down yet, have you?'

'No, I haven't,' I admitted. 'To be honest, I forgot all about it.' I'd been into her cottage to check the new central heating was installed and I hadn't given the decorations a thought.

'Thank God for that! She says she wants it to stay up until Candlemass – whenever that is.'

'Second of February,' I told her. 'So, I'll pop in and switch the heating on, Friday night, give the place a chance to warm up. And I'll check out her fridge, get some shopping in.' It wouldn't be like getting in Chloe's shopping, I reflected, no prawns and brioche, no sherry or coffee ice cream, just milk, teabags, a white loaf and a packet of custard creams. And some eucalyptus throat sweets.

'That would be wonderful. Could you make sure

there's some food for the dog?'

I promised I would and rang off, saying I'd see Janet on Saturday.

I looked at my watch. It was barely seven o'clock. The food shops on North Street would still be open. I needed a few things for myself. I could get Maisie's stuff at the same time, if I popped around to her place first to check if there was anything else she needed.

I'd already put Van Blanc to bed. It was cold outside, with the threat of overnight snow, so I'd put my new windscreen cover – one of my sensible Christmas presents, from Pat – onto her windscreen. Keeping it in place was a complicated procedure involving looping bungees around the wing mirrors and down to the wheel arches and I didn't really want to take it off again before the morning. Perhaps I'd abandon the idea of going shopping until tomorrow. Don't be a lazy cow, I told myself, you can walk to Maisie's. And walk I should, after the goodly wodge of cheesy pasta bake that I'd consumed for supper, not to mention the slice of lemon drizzle I'd eaten earlier in the day. It was so good to have Kate and Adam back. They didn't supply me with cooking oil or toilet rolls, though – I'd have to go out and forage for those myself. And there was no time like the present. Much to Bill's disgust, I pulled on boots, coat, hat, scarf and gloves, stuffed Maisie's keys, a torch and a carrier bag into my pockets, and off I went.

Our house is the last property at the end of a cul-de-sac. Our garden backs on to fields on one side, and our neighbour's garden on the other. Outside of the front gate is a rather half-hearted turning circle, surrounded by a mess of scrubby bushes, where I park Van Blanc.

It had not snowed since the night of the wassail and most of what had fallen had already melted, a few vestiges clinging to the verges under the shadow of the hedgerows, and glowing white in the dark. It was cold enough to believe it would snow again, although the sky was clear, stars bright above the rooftops of Ashburton. The constellation of Orion hung just behind the spire of St Andrew's Church. Daniel could name all of its stars, I remembered. He'd traced their pattern among the freckles on my body once. Tears of sadness welled up inside me and I turned away, heading off towards Brook Lane and Maisie's cottage, and didn't look back.

The cold encouraged me to walk briskly, and I stopped only once, to peer over the low stone wall that separates the little river Ashburn from the road, to stare down at its rushing dark waters. The shallow stream was swollen with melting snow, gushing freely, not iced over at all, and keeping up a noisy babble as it raced on into town. I crossed the road, losing sight of the river, and as the houses thinned out, so the space between the old iron lamp posts widened and the lane grew darker. The brook from which the lane takes its name was no more than a trickle filling the roadside ditch, but I had to cross a little bridge, a single stepping stone, to reach Maisie's cottage. I opened the gate, and even through my glove I could feel how cold the metal latch was. I walked up the path to her tiny glass porch, hearing the gate click closed behind me. It was so dark here I needed my torch to find her front door key and fit it in the lock. I opened the front door and my nostrils were assailed by the scent of lemon kitchen cleaner, which failed to entirely mask the faint but more repulsive odour of Jacko. I switched on the lights.

I was in the cottage for only a few minutes. Enough time to make sure the new boiler was working, check out the fridge and dog food situation, and try the fairy lights on the Christmas tree. I watched them twinkling prettily and wondered whether Maisie would still be around to enjoy them next Christmas. Our Janet had not persuaded her to stay with her up in Heck-as-Like, but how much longer she could expect to live in this cottage alone at her age, even with help from me and the care agency, was getting to be a sore point.

I made a list of the shopping I needed and headed for the front door, switching out the lights as I went. Just for a moment I was standing in the dark. Small sounds get lost in the daytime, drowned out by the noisescape of passing traffic outside or the blaring of the television or radio within. But some sounds, however small, are so distinctive, that when you hear them in the silent world of the night, when you're lying awake in bed, for instance, longing to get to sleep, there is no mistaking them for anything else. The closing of a car door is such a sound, or someone trying its handle. Or the click of the metal latch on the front gate when it closes. I heard it distinctly as I stood in the dark behind the front door. Someone was coming in.

I opened the door into the glass porch and peered out between the bowls of Maisie's cacti. There was no one on the path. And there was no sign of anyone in the road. No one had rung the bell, or knocked on the door. Could someone have let themselves out, been in the garden just now, whilst I was inside the house? Or was someone in the garden now? I turned on my torch and followed the path around the side of the building to the garden at the back. If snow had still been on the ground, I would have seen footprints on the path, but as it was, there was no sign of anyone having come that way. I shone the torch around the garden, just in case, lighting up the bird table on the tiny lawn, the bushes around its edge, but there was nothing.

Back inside, I flicked the lights back on and checked the bolts on the kitchen door. All secure. Hearing the front gate closing was probably my imagination. Except, of course, I knew that it wasn't. I locked the front door, went through the gate and let it close after me, standing on the tiny footbridge until I heard it click shut, that sharp, unmistakeable sound.

There was no one in the lane. I turned to go, but had only taken a few steps before something hard hit the sleeve of my coat. I stopped. A white object was lying by my feet and I stooped to pick it up. It could hardly be called a snowball, more like a large pebble of snow, compacted hard as ice. I glanced at the trees above me, but there was no sign of any remaining snow on the branches stretching across the road. This hard pellet could not have fallen from above. More likely it was scooped up from the frozen vestiges of snow lying under the hedgerow. Someone had thrown it at me. I heard rustling behind the hedge, and my eye caught a sudden movement.

'Who's there?' I called out. If some idiot was messing about, thinking it was funny to lob hard lumps of snow at people, they were about to get a telling-off.

'What's going on?' a man's voice called out irritably. A security light came on outside the house next to Maisie's and a balding figure emerged to stand in the driveway, Maisie's neighbour.

'Mr Cooper, is it?' I called out.

'Is that Juno?' he called back after a few moments. He came down to his gate. 'Was that you just now? I saw a light waving about in Maisie's back garden and thought I'd better come out and investigate.'

'That was me,' I admitted. 'But I went out because I'm sure I heard someone come in through her gate. There was no one there, though.' I was still clutching the lump of hard snow. 'Someone threw this at me.'

'Bloody kids messing about,' Mr Cooper tutted. 'Go home!' he yelled down the lane, but there was no response, no shuffling of footsteps, no shouts or juvenile laughter. 'You're all right, are you?' he asked, looking me up and down.

'Fine,' I assured him. 'Maisie will be home at the weekend.'

241

'Oh, that'll be something to look forward to,' he responded sarcastically, 'her and her horrible dog. Mind you, the cat's missed tormenting him, sitting on the wall with her tail just out of reach.' He gave a sudden shiver and patted me on the arm. 'You get home, maid. It's too cold to be hanging around out here.' He frowned suddenly, his hand to his bald head, then held it out, palm upward. 'It's starting to snow again.' He glanced at me. 'You all right to get home?'

'Yes, of course.'

'I'll say goodnight, then,' he nodded, and hurried off back indoors.

I stayed to fasten another button on my coat. Now it had started, the snow was falling fast. I returned Maisie's keys to my pocket and pulled my gloves back on, flipped my hood up over my hat and tucked my hair inside it. For a moment, I glanced back down the lane. Someone was standing there, a dark figure silhouetted by the glow from a street light behind him, the light furthest from me, the last before the lane plunged into the blackness; a shadow, wearing a ragged coat and top hat, the pointed edges of his leafy beard outlined by the lamplight. The Green Man. He raised one arm and pointed at me. For a moment I felt a wave of panic sweep giddily through my body, heard blood singing in my ears. Was he holding the gun? The snow was falling faster, a screen of tiny white flakes making the shadowy figure flicker like an image on an old film. He stood still, watching me. Then he took a step back, out of the lamplight and was swallowed by the dark.

I turned and ran through the snow, my feet slipping in haste, back towards the safety of the town, towards lights shining out in welcome from windows, towards people. Sod the shopping, I ran straight home. I got inside and double-locked the door behind me, standing for a moment in the hall, breathing hard, my chest heaving and my face wet with snow. As my breathing slowed, as I got control of myself, I remembered the snowball hitting me during the wassail. I realised who had thrown it now.

My first thought, after I was safely back inside my flat and had shed my coat and gloves, was to phone Dean Collins. And tell him what, exactly? I pulled off my hat and kicked away my wet boots. Tell him I had seen the Green Man, standing in Brook Lane, seen him for just a few moments through a falling veil of snow, before he disappeared into the dark again? He'd think I'd imagined it. Could I have imagined it? The whole episode seemed like something from a dream, the more I thought about it.

The phone rang suddenly, making me yelp with fright. It was Ricky. 'Hello, Princess, look, we were wondering if you could lend us a—'

'I've seen the Green Man.' I blurted it out before I could stop myself.

'What? Where? What are you talking about?'

'The Green Man,' I repeated. I'd already told him and Morris about the wassail, the day after it happened.

'You sure?'

'I saw him just now outside of Maisie's cottage,' I explained in a shaky voice, 'he must have followed me there.'

There was a moment's shocked silence at the end of the line. 'Have you told the police?'

'No. Not yet. I don't think they'll believe me.'

'Right. We're coming round.'

'There's no need—' I began.

'Shut your mouth. We'll be there in five.'

It was actually nearer ten, by which time I had opened a bottle of brandy – another Christmas present – and pulled myself together.

'He must have followed me from here,' I told Ricky and Morris once they'd settled down on the sofa. Bill leapt up on the arm nearest to Morris and was staring intently from his single emerald eye, trying to assess whether his lap was worthy.

'It's the only explanation for his turning up in Brook Lane like that.' Not a comforting thought, the realisation that he must have been lurking in the dark outside of the house, waiting for me to come out. For one thing, he knew where I live. And he must have been the person who clicked the gate at Maisie's place. Perhaps he'd been standing in her garden all the time I was inside, watching me through the window. Another nasty thought.

Morris was blinking at me anxiously. 'He didn't try to follow you back here?'

'No. After a few moments, he stepped back into the dark and disappeared. The thing is, he threw that lump of snow to attract my attention. He must have hidden himself when Maisie's neighbour came out to speak to me. But as soon as he'd gone back into his house, this Green Man stood in the light. He wanted me to see him.' What I still couldn't work out, was why.

'He's trying to frighten you off,' Ricky responded, 'he wants you to know that he knows you're on to him . . .'

'But I'm not!' I protested. 'I haven't got a clue who he is. Why would he bother?'

'You do have a reputation,' Morris began, almost apologetically, as Bill finally decided in his favour and flowed down on his lap, 'as, well, an amateur detective.'

'You do get up to all sorts, love,' Ricky added, stretching his long legs and crossing his ankles, 'and then end up all over the newspaper.'

'I think *all over* is an exaggeration,' I objected.

'Well, just where it matters,' he argued, getting tetchy, 'on the front bleedin' page! This green nutter wants to warn you off. He wants to scare the hell out of you.'

'Well, he's succeeding.'

'You will have to tell the police, Juno,' Morris insisted.

Ricky took a sip of brandy. 'Course you will. For all you know, he followed you tonight 'cos he meant to kill you.'

Morris nodded. 'He could still be carrying that gun.'

Ricky tugged thoughtfully on an earlobe. 'Although . . .'

'What?' I demanded.

245

'Why the dressing up? If he meant to hurt you, he would have stood a much better chance of getting close to you by dressing in ordinary clothes. He could have been following you in the dark and you'd probably not have taken any notice of him until it was too late. But instead, he throws a snowball at you, and then stands in the light where he knows you can see him. It's like he's showing off, he's saying *look at me*! I think he just means to frighten you.'

'That doesn't mean he's not dangerous, though, Juno,' Morris warned me. 'You must tell the police. He is the man we think shot Don Drummond.'

'If it is the same man.'

Ricky gave a crack of laughter. 'Oh, that's all we need! Green men popping up all over the place.'

I smiled in spite of myself. 'Sounds like an invasion from Mars.'

There was a sharp knock on my living-room door. 'And that sounds like Adam. I hope we haven't woken the baby.'

But the burly, black-bearded pirate to whom I opened the door looked more puzzled and concerned than someone about to give me a telling-off for making too much noise. 'Could I come in a minute?' he asked.

'Sure.' I pointed at the brandy bottle on the table. 'Do you want a drink?'

'No thanks.' He nodded a greeting at Ricky and Morris. 'Kate's got herself worked up about some intruder she thought she saw in our garden, and I wondered if—'

246

I didn't let him finish. 'When was this?'

'Earlier tonight. Well, she saw him just after dark, before I got home. She was here on her own, you weren't back from the shop. She saw him from our living room window, hanging about in the cul-de-sac. She thought he must be a hiker and might be lost.'

Ricky grinned. 'Funny time of night to be hiking.'

Adam shrugged. 'She said he was wearing a backpack. She didn't take much notice of him and went into the kitchen to start supper. But when she came back into the room about fifteen minutes later, he was still there, just standing, watching the house.'

'What did he look like?' I asked.

'She couldn't really see. He had the hood of his jacket up and a scarf over the lower part of his face.'

'It is very cold out there,' Morris pointed out.

'Yeh,' Adam agreed. 'She was on the point of going to speak to him, ask him if he was lost or something, when he saw her looking through the window and hurried off.'

'But she didn't report him to the police?'

'No, and perhaps she ought to have done, 'cos about half an hour later she was sure she saw him in our garden.'

I glanced at Morris and Ricky. 'What was he doing?'

'Nothing. Just standing, staring at the house.'

'What did she do?' I asked, trying to ignore the fluttering of panic in my stomach.

'Well, I was home by then. I went out for a look around but I couldn't see anyone. Kate's okay, I've

247

almost convinced her it was her imagination playing tricks on her but,' he cast an uneasy glance at me, 'I just wondered if you saw anyone hanging about out there, when you came home?'

'No,' I admitted honestly, 'but—'

'Juno was followed tonight,' Morris blurted out before I could stop him, 'when she went out again.'

'Someone tried to put the wind up her,' Ricky intervened before he could say any more. 'Some idiot dressed up in a top hat and false beard.'

Adam frowned. 'Doesn't sound like the same fella.'

'Well, I think you should both ring the police,' Morris said firmly. 'They need to know everything that has gone on tonight.'

Adam nodded. 'I'll go down and give them a call.'

As soon as he'd gone, Ricky flicked a glance at us both. 'Well, what do we think? Is this the same man?'

'With a top hat and false beard in his rucksack, waiting for me to come home.' I thought about this for a moment. 'But he couldn't have known I was going to go out again. I didn't know myself.'

'But when you did, he had to follow you.'

I sighed. 'He wanted me to see him, to frighten me, or . . . worse. Perhaps his original plan was to stay here, stand in the garden and be seen here.'

Ricky's green eyes narrowed. 'What, hang about in the garden all night on the off chance you might glance out of the window?'

'Maybe he'd have thrown another snowball, or

flashed a torch, got my attention somehow.'

'But he couldn't know which windows were yours,' Ricky objected.

'Perhaps,' Morris suggested, 'that's why he was watching the house for such a long time, trying to work it out.'

'But when I came out of the house to go to Maisie's, why didn't he attract my attention then?'

Morris stopped stroking Bill's head and held up a finger. 'Perhaps he wasn't ready. He had to follow you, keep on your tail. Those few minutes you spent in Maisie's cottage gave him the chance he needed for his costume change.'

'I think *Maurice* is right,' Ricky nodded.

'It's all very theatrical.'

'But that's what this bloke is about,' he insisted. 'Theatre. I told you, he's saying, *look at me*.'

'He wants the attention,' Morris added.

I tried a smile, to sound happier than I felt. 'Well, he certainly seems to want mine.'

CHAPTER TWENTY-ONE

'The police have already been here,' Jackie told me with a grim smile as she saw me walking through the showroom towards her, 'asking me if I shot Don Drummond.'

I smiled back. I knew her alibi held up. 'And did you?'

'If I'd shot at him, I'd have killed the bastard. But I was at a friend's house.'

'So I understand.'

She gestured in the direction of a muscular young man, his long dark hair tied back in a ponytail, who I assumed was the apprentice she'd mentioned, his face half hidden by the protective goggles he wore as he bent over the forge. 'This is Ryan.' He paused long enough for us to exchange brief nods of greeting and carried on with his work.

'And presumably,' I went on, still watching him, 'they've also asked you about the Green Man?'

She let out a sigh and when she spoke her voice faltered. 'Bob used to do it, play the Green Man when the Border Morris did gigs in the summer.'

I was surprised. 'Do the police know this? Has anyone told them?'

'I might have mentioned it, but I'm sure someone on the Morris would have done, after what happened at the wassail.'

I felt a tug of annoyance. If anyone had mentioned it to the police, Dean Collins hadn't mentioned it to me. What sort of unpaid informant was he?

'Do you know anyone else who might play it?'

She shrugged. 'Any one of the Border Morris, or from any other Morris team, if it comes to it. It's just a case of dressing in the costume and larking about. Why?'

I told her about his appearance in Ashburton.

She looked genuinely shocked. 'But why would anyone do a thing like that? Is it supposed to be some sort of joke?'

'Well, if it is, it's not funny. You're sure you don't know of anyone . . . ?'

Ryan stopped thumping metal long enough to speak. 'Sometimes Carl Hayward plays the Green Man.'

'Yes, but he's a nice bloke,' Jackie protested.

'He can be pretty scary,' Ryan said. 'He frightens the kids.'

'At performances, yes,' she agreed reluctantly. 'But he'd never dress up and follow a woman, just to frighten her. He'd have to be some kind of psycho. And he certainly wouldn't try to shoot anybody.'

'You don't know where I'd find this Carl?' I asked.

Ryan shifted his goggles up on to his head. I could

see why Jackie had wanted to keep him on. Apart from the muscular physique he had kind eyes and a boyish smile. 'He's got a workshop at the Craft Collective,' he volunteered. 'He carves in wood.'

'Does he?' Don Drummond had mentioned a craft collective. 'Is this place near South Brent?'

'That's it.' He crossed to a corkboard on the wall and handed me one of the business cards pinned to it. 'The address is on there.'

Woodsmen Craft Collective, I read. Jackie shifted impatiently. I got the impression that perhaps Ryan was being more helpful than she would have liked. 'I'm sure it's nothing to do with him.'

'Well, thanks anyway.' I put the card in my pocket. 'I might look him up.' I hesitated and lowered my voice. 'Can I ask you something?' I jerked my head in the direction of the showroom, away from Ryan, and Jackie followed me.

'What is it?' she asked.

'You said you thought the only person who could have a motive for killing Bob was Don Drummond,' I said. 'Did you never consider Lily Marwood?'

'That stuck-up bitch!' she snorted. 'What's she got to do with anything?'

'You don't think she might have resented Bob, for not acknowledging his child?'

Jackie's eyes flashed in fury. 'Look, I don't know who you've been listening to, but her family treated Bob like he was shit! In their eyes he wasn't good enough to be anything to do with their family. He had no chance of getting near that child. It seems Lily Marwood thought he was good enough for a roll in the hay, but not good enough to be the father of his own son. Her family still wanted money for his upkeep, though.' She gave a short, impatient laugh. 'I'll say this for her, Lily Marwood, at least she kept her baby, didn't have it adopted like they wanted her to.'

'So, you're saying she had no ill-feelings towards Bob?'

'I don't know what kind of feelings she had! But Bob hadn't seen her in years.'

She turned and strode away back into the forge. Our talk was obviously at an end.

I carried on through the showroom, stopping for a minute to look at some of the goods on display: the heavy Celtic armlets and crosses, with their woven, endlessly repeating patterns, and on the whitewashed walls, a face, forged in black iron. The Green Man grinned at me, leaves escaping from his gaping mouth.

Jackie and Ryan must have thought I'd gone. I glanced back into the forge and they were standing close together, Ryan's arms around Jackie protectively. For a moment, I thought he was just giving her a comforting hug because she was upset. Then her arms slid up around his neck, she tilted her face towards him, and their lips met in a full-on, lingering kiss. Perhaps, I thought, as I made my way out on tiptoe, Jackie Millard did have a motive for murdering her husband, after all.

* * *

'So Bob Millard's not cold in his grave and Jackie's got a new lover.' Dean chuckled down the phone, 'Unless she was playing away from home all the time.'

'Well, you could hardly blame her,' I said in her defence. 'Not if half the stories I hear about Bob are true. But the point is—'

'The point is,' Dean went on, taking the words out of my mouth, 'we have to consider this Ryan a suspect.'

'Exactly. Jackie might have an alibi for the night of the wassail but she could have sent Ryan to shoot Don Drummond.' Could Ryan have been the Green Man and was that why he'd so helpfully pointed the finger at Carl Hayward, the woodcarver?

'Well, he'd really have to have the hots for her to do a thing like that. Mind you,' he added after a moment's consideration, 'if he believed Drummond was responsible for killing Bob, he might have wanted revenge on him himself. Bob was his boss. Just 'cos he was banging his old lady, doesn't mean he and Bob weren't friends.'

'We don't actually know that!' I protested. 'We don't know Ryan and Jackie were having an affair. Maybe yesterday was the first time they'd ever . . . Anyway, did you know Bob himself used to play the Green Man?'

There was a pause whilst he thought for a moment. 'Yes. It came up in some of the witness statements.'

I almost shrieked. 'Why didn't you tell me?'

'Possibly because it's none of your business, Juno Browne, you *not* being a police officer actively involved in an investigation.'

254

'I share information with you,' I said indignantly.

He grunted. 'Only when it suits you.'

I ignored this, even though I hadn't mentioned Carl Hayward's existence to him so far. I wanted to visit the Craft Collective by myself. 'And how can you possibly say it's not relevant?'

'What?'

'Someone dressing up as Bob,' I said, 'as a character he used to play, to take revenge on his killer. I would have thought it was significant.'

'What were you doing at Jackie's place this morning, anyway?' he demanded, as if he was only just catching up. He's not really slow, but his attempts to change the subject are never very subtle.

'I went to see how she was.'

'Oh yeh? You're not sleuthing, are you?'

'Of course not,' I said piously.

'Well, it looks like this chap who tried to scare you off last night thinks you are, so wind your neck in.'

'I suppose I've only got Kate to thank for the fact you're taking what happened last night seriously.' I'd already been interviewed by Cruella that morning, before I went to see Jackie. She'd made it perfectly plain she thought the Green Man I'd seen in Brook Lane was a figment of my imagination. Perhaps, she'd insinuated with her noxious little smirk, my nerves were getting the better of me.

'No, not just Kate,' Dean informed me loftily. 'Because today, we did some house-to-house enquiries along the route you took to Maisie's place, and although no one reported it last night, when asked, more than one person admitted they had noticed someone behaving suspiciously. Daisy Butler, for a start.'

'Who's Daisy Butler?'

'She's six. She told her mother last night she'd seen a man with a funny beard and wearing a tall hat running across their garden. Her mother told her not to be so silly, but discovered a line of footprints in the snow this morning, which made her take Daisy's story more seriously. Also, a neighbour of hers, who's got a . . .' he paused as if he was consulting notes, 'An *away* garden – is that right?'

'That's right.'

He puffed, exasperated. 'Why can't people around here have gardens joined to their houses like everywhere else, not have them two hundred yards down the lane?'

'It's complicated,' I began, 'it goes back to the time when people used to—'

'Never mind, I haven't got time for a history lesson. Anyway, this neighbour of hers had been working in his shed on his *away* garden, and realised he hadn't locked it and so even though it was snowing by this time, he went back to make it secure. And on his way up this lane, he sees a man kneeling down in the snow, stuffing something dark into a rucksack. But when he called out to him, thinking it was an odd place for anyone to be stopped doing anything, the bloke picked up his rucksack and scarpered. And he fits Kate's description – hood up, scarf concealing the lower part of his face.'

'It could have been the Green Man putting away his costume.'

'It could,' he agreed. 'Anyway, we are taking this seriously. This chap's got a gun, remember. We don't know what his intentions towards you were last night, so until we catch this bastard, will you kindly stop traipsing about on your own in the dark?'

'Yes,' I promised in a docile voice, the very soul of submissiveness. As a matter of fact, it wasn't an experience I was eager to repeat.

CHAPTER TWENTY-TWO

Next morning, I'd just come back from delivering the Tribe and was about to go out of the door, munching a sustaining piece of toast, when my phone rang. I cursed. I wanted to go to the shop briefly and then I was planning a trip to visit the Woodsmen Craft Collective.

'Juno?' It was Penny.

'Are you alright?' She sounded upset, slightly breathless.

'Well, no . . . yes. The thing is, I've just realised something about the murders, something I should have thought of before.'

I groaned inside. 'What?' I asked dutifully.

'Well, I can't say just yet. I've decided to cast a horary. I'll know if I'm right when I've interpreted it.'

I had no idea what she was talking about, except that a horary was some kind of special astrological chart. 'Actually, I'm just about to go out.'

'Could you come around later? To my place? Then we can talk.'

'Well, I'm not sure . . .'

'Juno, please, this is terribly important.'

She sounded on the edge of tears, and I caved in. 'All right. I'll see you this evening.'

'Thank you,' she breathed. 'Thank you so much.'

I put the phone down and sighed.

The Woodsmen Craft Collective took some time to find, largely because I made the mistake of following the directions on its website. *Head for the village of Harbourneford,* it said, so I did, driving down a narrow country road with a sludge of gritty mud down its middle and high hedges, recently chopped back to their bare branches, on either side. It's a small village, nice stone cottages by the roadside, and a red telephone box that actually still contains a telephone, instead of a defibrillator, library or plant swop. There's a handsome farmhouse and an ancient footbridge over a stream, or to give it its proper name, the River Harbourne. I carried on, as advised, and turned up the hill to the intriguingly named Bloody Pool Cross. This was rather disappointing as crossroads go, with nothing to indicate how it had come by its sinister name. But some jolly wag had seen its potential. The sign pointing back to Buckfastleigh had been tampered with, its capital B replaced with an F. It had been altered with a piece of tape, cut to the exact size, so was obviously a premeditated act, and goes to show there's not much going on for entertainment around here.

Just beyond the crossroads I found myself cresting the hill, looking down over the valley of snow-speckled fields, the swell of Dockwell Ridge rising up behind them. I could also see, from a brief glance at my map, that if I'd come straight down the road from Buckfastleigh to Gidley Bridge I'd have probably got here sooner.

I turned sharp right after the low stone bridge and bumped poor little Van Blanc up the wrong *wooded track* before I found the right *wooded track*, as described in the directions, where lo and behold, there was a sign pointing the way that the website had failed to mention.

It pointed me towards a visitors' car park, a clearing with room for about a dozen cars, although the only vehicle occupying it at the moment was a quad bike with a trailer full of sawn logs attached. There was a large noticeboard at one end, full of information about the collective, and basically a repetition of what I'd already read on the website. A group of craftsmen had pooled their resources to buy this piece of mixed deciduous woodland where they could work, carrying on ancient woodland crafts using sustainable resources, and passing on their secrets to those who wished to learn. Courses on a variety of woodland skills were available, as well as training in woodland and countryside management. Full details of these could be found in the Resources Shelter, where refreshments were also available. Whilst visitors were always welcome, they were reminded that the woodland was a working environment where coppicing and tree-felling went on, involving working horses, and were advised to follow the signposts and stick to the designated paths; also, to respect the environment, keep dogs on leads and take any litter home.

I dutifully made my way up along the designated path, following the wooden way-markers. The woods on either side were winter bare, leafless, but the sun shone on the silvery white trunks of birch trees, and on a few brave catkins dangling from the branches of hazel like yellow caterpillars. The woodland floor was a jigsaw of decaying autumn leaves, here and there dappled with snow pockmarked and pitted from the dripping trees above. Ivy clothed the trunks of oaks with green, and my eye caught a bright flash of orange and blurred fans of feathers as two squabbling robins battled for territory among their branches; but otherwise, the wood was quiet, peaceful. No tree-felling going on today, no stamp of horses' hooves or jingle of harness, sadly.

I came upon a low wooden cabin; a man was sitting outside turning an old-fashioned pole-lathe. I watched him working the treadle for a few moments. Evidence of his work, a collection of greenwood chairs, stood on the ground behind him, looking bare and new, as if they had been set out for a meeting and were still waiting for the people to turn up.

'Is it okay if I look around?' I asked.

'Help yourself.' He pointed up the path. 'Just follow the trail.'

'Do you know if Carl Hayward is about?'

He smiled. 'Carl's not here today.'

Just my luck.

'But his workshop is open. It's the one right at the far

end, before you get to the Resources Shelter. We keep an eye on each other's places if someone's away, so just give one of us a shout if you need help with anything.'

'Thanks.' I added casually, 'You don't know Don Drummond, do you? He's a woodturner.'

He shook his head. 'Sorry. I might know him by sight but I'm not very good with names.'

I thanked him again and continued up the trail, past another rustic hut where a woman sat weaving a basket from willow. She called out a greeting. She could teach me to make a besom broom, if I was interested. I quite liked the idea of having my own witch's broom; another day, I told her sadly.

The next workshop, I decided, must be the one I was looking for. Carved benches and garden chairs stood on the ground outside it, along with bird tables and ornaments, the branches of the trees above hung with wooden wind chimes. I raised a hand and brushed my fingers against dangling wooden tubes, setting off a peal of chimes, more clatter than tinkle.

Inside was a dry smell of sawdust and wood shavings. And there were Celtic symbols everywhere. The Tree of Life was carved on to wall plaques, coasters and bookends. Twin serpents devoured each other's tails on bowls and brooches. Of the man who had carved these intricate patterns, there was no sign, but he must be the man Don Drummond had been talking about. A plaque on the wall declared them to be the work of Philip King. Not Carl Hayward, then. This wasn't the last workshop after all. I'd carry on until I found it.

I kept to the trail, but it was a long, lonely walk. It took me to a play area for children: wooden swings, see-saws, ladders and a rope bridge to a treehouse, but no one was playing today. Apart from occasional birdsong, the woods were still and silent, the only sound my own footsteps crunching through snow and dead leaves. I began to doubt myself. Had I missed a wayside marker and branched off along a wrong path? I thought about doubling back when I saw the Green Man standing outside of his workshop. The sight of him stopped me in my tracks. For a moment I stared. And then I drew closer.

It was a life-sized effigy, a dancing figure with both arms raised and one foot lifted off the floor. He was dressed in the top hat and rag jacket of the Border Morris, the wood carved to look rumpled and creased. He was grinning, leaves curling from his mouth to form a leafy beard; his hair was foliage too, bursting through the crown of his battered hat. The hands that sprouted from his sleeves ended in finger-like roots. His expression was jovial, his sightless, wooden eyes creased into a smile. He was the spirit of the wood, a carved robin sitting on his shoulder as he danced. He was not intended to be a sinister figure, yet he made me shudder. I turned and stepped inside the workshop.

The Green Man was everywhere, grinning and gurning like a gargoyle from wooden masks all around the walls. There was nothing else. It was as if this was the only image Carl Hayward carved, an obsession. Those gaping mouths spewing leaves unnerved me, made me want to gag, to get away. I turned to rush out of the door and slammed straight into someone coming in. I yelped, stepped back, and found myself staring into a face I knew. David Fairweather. I let out my breath in shock. 'What are you doing here?'

Concerned, he put a hand on my elbow. 'Juno? You look a bit shaken.'

'Did you follow me here?' I blurted out accusingly.

He frowned, mystified. 'Follow you? Why on earth would I be following you? I didn't know you were here.'

'I'm sorry.' I gave an awkward laugh. 'My nerves must be a bit shredded.'

He smiled. 'I don't see you for years and then twice in a couple of weeks. What are you doing here?'

'I just came for a look around. What about you?'

He looked a bit awkward himself. 'I've just signed Aurora and myself up for a course in greenwood skills. Our professional lives are quite intense, and I thought it might do us good to get involved in something more physical, more grounded as it were, more connected to nature.' He laughed. 'Forest bathing is supposed to be good for the soul.'

I nodded politely, but the Green Man was still freaking me out. 'Do you mind if we go outside? This place is creepy.'

We made our way to the Resources Shelter, a long wooden structure with a sweeping roof and open sides, and sat at a table. This was obviously a new building, and here at last was a sense of organisation, of professionalism. The girl behind the counter stopped preparing lunches for the course students, served me a decent cup of tea and offered me a slice of fruit cake baked that morning. It would have been churlish to refuse. David ordered a Green Forest Smoothie. God knows what was in it. When it arrived, it was the colour of snot.

'Are you really going to drink that?' I asked him.

'Of course,' he seemed genuinely surprised I should ask. 'It's delicious.' He offered me the glass. 'Want to try?'

I shook my head, barely suppressing a shudder as he took a sip.

There were photos around the walls of students learning woodland skills, self-consciously enjoying themselves in the way people do in front of a camera. I noticed a group photo, a gathering of the craftsmen, all smiling. I recognised the man at the lathe and the basket-weaving lady. 'Is Carl Hayward in this photograph?' I asked the girl behind the counter.

She pointed him out and I had to suppress a laugh. Obsessed with the Green Man he might be, but Carl Hayward was not the person I had seen at the wassail, nor the man watching me in Brook Lane. That was a person of average size. Carl was a giant, standing behind all of the others in the photograph and towering over them, ham-like hands resting on the shoulders of the people in front of him. 'He's tall, isn't he?'

'About six-foot-eight.' She smiled. 'He's a real gentle giant.'

I was still staring at the photograph. 'What about the Celtic woodcarver? Philip King?'

She peered for a moment and shook her head. 'No, he's not in this picture.'

He wouldn't be, would he, just because I wanted to see what he looked like.

I turned my attention back to David and he gave me the benefit of his charming smile. *Terrific in bed*, Cordelia had told me, although why those words should flash into my mind at this particular moment I couldn't say. 'Did you enjoy yourself at Penny's the other evening,' he asked, 'meeting up with some of the old crowd?'

I decided perjury would be the best option. 'It was great! No one seems to have changed much. Except perhaps Reggie.'

David laughed. 'Poor Reggie. He hasn't had a lot of luck. He had cancer, but recovered, thank God. I think it's his cycling that keeps him going.'

'He said he'd written a book.'

'He spent years writing it and no one wanted to publish it,' he smiled sadly. 'Then he lost his job. He used to live with an older sister, but she committed suicide. He never seems to have found himself since.'

'That's sad. But you've done very well, at least Seth was telling me so.'

He gave what passed for a modest shrug. 'I'm lucky. I have a strong Jupiter.'

'Ah, so it's all in your chart?'

'And I work bloody hard,' he added more seriously.

'I'm sure you do.'

He stroked his chin, running his fingers over his stubble. I preferred his old, beardy professor look, and wondered if he'd adopted the new style to look younger. 'How does Penny seem to you?' he asked, eyeing me thoughtfully.

'She's hardly changed at all.'

'No, I mean, she's struck me as being on edge lately, not quite her usual self. I wondered if perhaps the move away from Totnes had upset her, but she's had a lucky find with that flat.'

'I think she has a lot on her mind,' I answered evasively. After a moment I asked. 'What's a horary?'

He looked surprised. 'A horary?'

'Penny said she was going to cast one. I didn't really understand what she meant.'

He frowned. 'Did she say what it was for?'

I hesitated. If Penny didn't want to share her theories about murder with David, then it wasn't my place to reveal them, however crazy I thought they might be. I shook my head.

'Well,' he began, adopting a teacherly tone, 'horary is a specialised form of astrology. You ask a question, and you draw up a chart for the time you ask it, and the answer is revealed in the chart.'

It sounded dodgy to me. 'Does it work?'

'It can, if the person drawing up the chart knows how to interpret it properly. It takes a lot of skill. And the question has to be phrased in the right way. It's often used for finding lost objects. I know Penny has used it in the past, in work with the police.'

I nodded. 'She mentioned something about that.'

'She once helped them to find a missing child. The girl had been missing for several days and everyone assumed the worst. The police had no clues and turned to Penny. She drew up a chart and was able to tell them where to look.'

'And they found her?'

'Safe and well.' He gave an ironic smile. 'Not that Penny was ever acknowledged for her work, publicly.'

'No, I can imagine.'

'You ought to come to Totnes, Juno,' David said, smiling. 'Have dinner, chat over old times. Aurora would love to see you.'

Somehow, I doubted that. Old times would undoubtedly mean talk about Cordelia, who was a flame Aurora would probably rather David forgot. I sensed my link to his past might make me a threat. In any case, I don't feel the same about Totnes since Cordelia died. I realised that when I returned to it, years afterwards, thinking I might live there. I knew it would be impossible. I couldn't even go near the place where she had been killed, couldn't bear to see it.

As if he read my thoughts, David said gently. 'It might help to come to terms with things.'

I shook my head. 'You know, not long after Cordelia died, I mentioned to a college friend that she had been knocked down and fatally injured by a van. She actually said to me, in the way people do when they think they're being clever, that if Cordelia was an astrologer, she should have seen it coming.'

David shook his head. 'Crass, and hardly original. But I'm afraid astrologers get this kind of thing anytime misfortune comes their way.'

'I punched her in the mouth,' I told him. 'I knocked her right off her feet, made her lip bleed. I said to her, "You didn't see that coming, did you?"'

He bit back a smile. 'Did she call the police?'

'No, she just cried over all of her friends. I never spoke to any of them again.'

'Unfortunately, or perhaps fortunately,' he responded, 'death doesn't advertise itself with a flashing sign. We can find it astrologically, on a chart – but almost always *after* the event,' he added ruefully.

'You never find it before?' I asked.

'You'd have to be looking. And I doubt if Cordelia was searching for it.' He looked sad. 'She didn't think about death. She was too full of life.'

I suddenly wanted to hug him. And realised it was time I left. David offered to walk me back to my van but the girl behind the counter pointed me in the direction of a shorter path which took me straight back to the car park, bypassing the workshops.

'I'll be fine,' I told him. 'Stay here and finish your smoothie.'

I left him lingering over his glass of snot and bumped poor old Van Blanc down the wooded track in the direction of home.

CHAPTER TWENTY-THREE

'Perhaps not the most intelligent course of action,' Elizabeth suggested when I told her what I'd been up to that morning. We were in the back of the shop and keeping our voices down because I didn't want Pat or Sophie to hear. 'Let's suppose this Carl Hayward had been there and he *had* been the man who followed you to Brook Lane the other night, what would you have done then? In a lonely, secluded place where no one knew you had gone.'

'I don't think it was all that lonely,' I responded defensively. 'There were people within screaming distance.'

She raised a sceptical eyebrow. 'It would have been better to have taken someone with you.'

I hunched a shoulder, a bit childishly, because I knew she was right. 'Well, it's too late now. And anyway,' I added, 'he wasn't there, so—'

The shop doorbell rang just then and a moment later I heard a voice I recognised. 'Just a minute,' I said to Elizabeth and went through to the front of the shop.

Seth was standing there, staring at the painting of the barn owl Sophie had displayed on the wall. She was pretending to concentrate on her current masterpiece, but casting him sly glances from under her lashes.

'I didn't think you'd be back again so soon.'

He grinned at me. 'Hello, Juno! My dad's big birthday is this weekend, so I've come back down for the celebrations.' He nodded at the painting on the wall. 'And I'm going to buy him this. He volunteers for the Barn Owl Trust. He'll love it.'

'Really?' Sophie stretched her dark eyes wide. It was a large painting with a large price tag. She hadn't sold anything so expensive in months.

He laughed. 'Yes, really!' Sophie continued to stare at him, and he added, 'I mean, it is for sale?'

'Well, yes, yes of course it is.' She stood up hurriedly, almost knocking over her water pot in her haste. 'Oh dear, um . . .'

'Shall I take it down off the wall for you?' I offered. She was too short to reach it and in her current state of excitement was likely to drop it anyway. I handed the painting to Seth so he could take a closer look. He held it up and studied it for a few moments. I was praying he was serious about buying it. Sophie had a few reasonable sales before Christmas, but she could do with a boost. 'It's beautiful,' he said softly. He directed a glance at Sophie and grinned. 'Sold.'

She glowed pink with pleasure. 'I'll wrap it up for you. I'll get some bubble wrap and some . . . er . . . cardboard stuff.' She disappeared down under the counter and there was a lot of rustling as if she was an animal making a nest. She came up clutching enough bubble wrap to encase the *Titanic*. She stood for a moment, as if she'd never sold a painting before and wasn't sure what to do next. She seemed overcome with shyness.

Elizabeth had come into the shop behind me. 'Why don't you let me do that, Sophie?' she offered, 'and you can deal with the gentleman's credit card.'

'Oh yes. Good idea,' she laughed nervously, relinquishing the cloud of bubble wrap.

'Juno,' Elizabeth said pointedly,' why don't you make us all a cup of tea?'

'What?'

She jerked her head at Sophie and Seth, who were gazing at one another across the counter, both grinning like idiots. 'Oh, yes,' I said, finally catching on. 'Seth?'

'Not for me, thanks,' he answered, waiting patiently for Ms Sophie Child, painter of the finest, the steadiest and most accurate lines on paper, to stop fumbling with the credit card machine and get a grip.

'Oh sorry! I've keyed in too many noughts. It's not that expensive!' She looked up at him and giggled. 'I'd better void that transaction and start again.'

I ran up the stairs to the kitchen whilst Elizabeth got busy with the Sellotape. I filled and flipped on the kettle, then called to Pat from the landing. She didn't come for a moment, and I called again. She came to the foot of the stairs and scowled up at me, her knitting still in her hands, her ball of wool trailing down the passage behind her. 'What d'you want?'

I put my finger to my lips and then beckoned her to come up.

'What's up?' she asked.

'We're leaving them alone,' I hissed at her.

'What? Why? . . . Oh! Do you think he's not just after the painting, like . . . ?'

'Well, I'm sure Sophie thinks that, which is why she's behaving like such a clot. I mean, I know she's excited about the sale, but it's not as if she hasn't sold big paintings before.'

Elizabeth joined us on the stairs, reeling in the ball of wool like a fishing line, and we scurried into the kitchen. 'He's very charming. Lovely smile.'

Pat frowned. 'He's a bit old for her, isn't he?'

'No, of course he isn't!' I whispered. 'He must be younger than me. And it's easy to forget how ancient Sophie is.' And I'd been worried Seth might be interested in me.

We made tea and drank it. 'We can't hang about up here all afternoon,' Pat complained.

'No, and he's had plenty of time to propose,' I said idiotically. I opened the door and stuck my head out.

I heard Seth's voice. 'So, about seven o'clock, then?'

'Yes, perfect,' Sophie replied, trying not to sound too bothered.

'Right,' I heard the bell jangle as Seth opened the door. 'See you later.'

When I was sure he'd gone, I ran down the stairs into the shop and stood smiling at Soph. She looked up and saw me. 'What?' she asked primly, picking up her paintbrush.

'You can go now if you want,' I told her. 'Get into a bath of scented bubbles, sort out the ritzy underwear.'

'All right, so I'm going out for a drink with him,' she admitted, as Pat and Elizabeth came downstairs. 'There's no need to stand there grinning like that . . . Oh God, you're all at it!' she complained. Then she gave in, threw her paintbrush over her shoulder, clapped her hands in delight, and I gave her a high five.

I lingered in a bath of bubbles myself, wishing I didn't have to go out. Two astrologers in one day were too much, and now I had to go to Penny's place and listen to a third. Do they hunt in packs, I wondered? Had she finished casting her horary by now? I'd no idea how long it took. And what question had she asked it? Whatever it was, she was likely to chatter on about it for hours. It was going to be a long evening. I hauled my body out of the bath, wrapped myself in my bathrobe and heated up a quick supper in the old fling-and-ding. Leftovers again. A goodly chunk of Kate and Adam's curried chickpea pie with spinach. It sounded virtuous, but tasted delicious. I'm sure David would have approved, although he'd wash his down with Snot Smoothie, rather than a glass of red wine.

I must confess I lingered, tempted to pour myself a

second glass. If Penny hadn't sounded so agitated on the phone, I might have tried crying off, suggested I go tomorrow night. But I'd promised I'd go so there was no help for it. Sighing, I got up and dressed. At least it wasn't snowing.

But the temperature had dropped with the nightfall, and it was cold, a clear sky with bright stars and a tipsy moon. Still the Birch Moon, I reminded myself, according to the Celtic calendar. As I walked through the town, past the old weavers' cottages, St Andrew's clock chimed the half hour. It seemed to ring more clearly in the cold air. I shoved my gloved hands into my pockets. There would likely be frost in the morning.

I walked up East Street, past the shops, the smells from the Chinese takeaway on the corner of Woodland Road launching an all-out assault on my senses. Good job I'd already eaten.

I let myself in through the front door of the house where Penny lived, passed the doors of the ground floor flats, and went outside into the area where the bins and bikes were kept. It was dark on the stairs leading up to the garden, an area missed by the light cast from the windows up above, and the steps were uneven. My torch would have been useful, but I'd left the damn thing at home. I took the steps carefully, turning into the raised, walled garden.

The light from the French windows of Loft Cottage was muted because the curtains were drawn, dulling the golden glow of lamplight to a deep blue. I knocked on the glass and waited. Penny didn't come to the door, and I heard no voice from within, so I knocked again.

Perhaps she'd forgotten me and gone out. I tried the door and it was unlocked, so I reckoned I was still expected. I pushed the curtain aside and stepped in, calling a hello. She might be in the bedroom or the bathroom. It took me a moment, standing on the top step, gazing around the lamplit room, breathing in the faint smell of incense, to realise what a mess the room was, to take in the books and papers scattered around, the upturned chair, and looking down at the rag rug, to see what else was lying there. Penny was on her back, perfectly still, her head turned towards me, her eyes wide open, her blue scarf twisted tightly around her neck.

I cried out, dropping down the step into the room, knelt by her side and felt for a pulse at her wrist. But I knew from her wide-open stare that she was dead, from the twisted scarf, the red, ruptured capillaries in her eyes. She'd been strangled. I gave a convulsive sob and tears blurred my vision. On the floor next to her body lay the little figure of Isis, her wings outspread. She must have been knocked off the desk. I reached out and almost touched her, but drew my hand back just in time. I mustn't touch anything. I stared at Penny's lifeless body. There was a scrap of torn paper clutched in her right hand. Poor Penny. She was a Gemini, an inquisitive chatterbox: she lived to learn, to question, to communicate, to speak. And someone had throttled her, choked off her breath. Silenced her.

CHAPTER TWENTY-FOUR

The torn scrap of paper, eased gently from Penny's dead hand, lay on the table between Inspector Ford and me in the interview room at the police station, flattened out, and encased in a clear plastic evidence bag. It was the bottom right corner from a sheet of A4 and was blank except for two curved lines, about a centimetre apart, that ran in parallel, describing a segment from a circle. And between the two lines was drawn a symbol.

'You're saying this drawing is part of an astrological chart?' the inspector asked, gently tapping it with his finger. He paused, his keen eyes searching my face. 'Juno, are you sure you want to go on with this?'

I nodded, wiping at my face with a tissue. I kept crying, kept thinking that if I'd got to Penny's place earlier, when I said I would, instead of indulging myself with a bath and a glass of wine, she might be alive now.

'We can do this in the morning,' he went on, 'if you're not up to it.'

I shook my head, struggled to pull myself together.

'Penny told me she was going to draw up a chart today. These lines form the outer edge of the circle where the signs of the zodiac are drawn.'

'And presumably, our killer has got the rest.' The inspector glanced up at me. 'Could this be the reason he killed her?'

'Well, she was casting a horary . . .'

He gave a wry smile. 'I'm afraid you'll have to explain to me what that is.'

'It's a chart you cast when you want to find the answer to a question.'

'You don't happen to know what the question was, I suppose?' he asked hopefully.

'I don't know how she phrased it, but I think—'

'But surely, sir!' Cruella, sitting next to the inspector, was unable to contain her impatience any longer. 'All this astrology is nonsense!'

'It might be to you and me, Sergeant,' he answered steadily, 'but whatever this question was it seems our killer didn't want anyone to know the answer. And this poor lady is dead because of it.' He turned back to look at me. 'Please go on, Juno.'

'You can ask questions about anything, but horary is often used for finding lost things.' I repeated what David had told me about Penny's work with the police in finding the lost girl.

The inspector looked impressed. 'You don't happen to know where she did this?'

I shrugged. 'Sorry.'

'Look into this, will you, Sergeant? See if you can find which force this lady was working with. And when. Give us some background on her.'

'Yes, sir,' Cruella responded primly, but she didn't look happy.

He pointed at the torn paper, at a symbol drawn for Scorpio. 'Is this squiggle here significant?'

'Not on its own.'

'So, it doesn't help us establish what this chart was about?'

'I think she was asking a question about murder.' I took a deep breath, and launched into an explanation of everything Penny had told me, everything she believed about the deaths of her three colleagues at the university, the drowned psychologist, the toxicologist bitten by a scorpion, and the administrator poisoned by seeds of the autumn crocus. And how she felt they were linked to the murder of Bob Millard and the attempt on the life of Don Drummond.

Afterwards, the inspector puffed out his cheeks in a long sigh, shifting in his chair. 'Now, let me get this right. What you're saying – or rather, what Miss Anderson believed – is that these three seemingly accidental deaths were in fact murders, because the victims were killed in ways too appropriate to their astrological signs for their deaths to be just random. Have I got that right?'

I nodded.

'And she felt the murders of Millard and the attempt

on Drummond's life fell into the same category?' he asked doubtfully.

Cruella gave a twisted smile as if the whole discussion was too ridiculous to be given consideration. I could hear her impatient little foot tapping under the table. I wanted to stamp on it. 'In the case of Bob Millard, and especially Don Drummond, sir, we can think of more down-to-earth motives.'

'Oh, I'm with you there, Sergeant,' the inspector agreed. He folded his arms across his chest and sighed thoughtfully. 'Do you believe all this astrology stuff, Juno?'

'I try very hard not to,' I admitted, 'but I don't succeed.'

He gave an amused little grunt. 'How well did you know Miss Anderson?'

'I used to see her when I came to stay with my cousin in the school holidays. But I hadn't seen her for about twelve years, until very recently.'

'You see, I'm wondering, with the greatest of respect to the lady,' he began slowly, 'whether her enthusiasm for the subject might have led her to see connections that weren't there.'

I had to smile. 'That's more or less what I've been thinking.'

'Yet, she was murdered.'

'The room was in disarray sir,' Cruella pointed out. 'This could just be a case of a burglary gone wrong, a thief who wasn't expecting to find her at home. She tried to raise the alarm and . . .' she shrugged.

'And he tried to shut her up,' the inspector completed. 'Yes, I see. Except if he was out to rob her, he didn't take her handbag with its cash and credit cards, and there was an iPad on the desk which he didn't touch either.'

'As you say, sir, he fled in haste.'

'Ripping the chart from poor Miss Anderson's hand, leaving this little scrap of evidence behind him.' The inspector sat in silence for several seconds, his brows knitted in fierce concentration. 'No,' he said, shaking his head. 'It won't do.'

Cruella looked puzzled. 'Sir?'

'Think about it, Sergeant. There's a struggle over this piece of paper. Miss Anderson is gripping it tightly in her fist, she doesn't want to let go, to let her attacker have it. But then he starts to strangle her, to twist that scarf around her neck . . .' He flicked a worried glance at me, 'I'm sorry, Juno.'

'No, go on,' I urged him.

'What would she do?' he asked. 'What would anyone do in those circumstances?'

'Try to loosen his hold,' Cruella said.

'With both hands,' he nodded. 'If someone tried to strangle you, both hands would go to your throat, instinctively. You'd let go of everything else, you wouldn't hang on to a piece of paper. You'd drop it.'

Cruella's smooth forehead wrinkled in a frown.

'You mean the killer put it there afterwards,' I said quickly.

'Exactly!' he thumped the table with his fist. 'And he tore it off. We were meant to find that scrap of paper. This killer's playing games with us, Sergeant.'

'But, sir . . .'

'Let's hope someone in the rest of the house will have seen or heard something of him. Collins still talking to the people in the other flats?'

'I assume so, sir, yes.'

'Right.' He darted a glance at me. 'Who else knew Miss Anderson was going to cast this horary today?'

'I don't know. There's a group who met at her house recently who all share an interest in astrology. She sees them regularly. But when I asked her if she'd discussed her ideas with any of them, she seemed reluctant. I don't think she'd told anyone else she was casting this chart today.'

'Somebody knew.'

My hand flew to my mouth. 'I told David Fairweather when I bumped into him today. But he couldn't be anything to do with—'

'This is the professional astrologer chap you told us about earlier?' The inspector turned to Cruella. 'Right, Sergeant, we want to talk to Mr Fairweather.' He glanced back at me. 'You don't know his address?'

'Um . . . Totnes, somewhere.'

'Find him. And I want the names and addresses of everyone who was at that meeting.' He glanced at me. 'Can you help us with that, Juno?'

I was still thinking about David, about the

282

impossibility of him murdering Penny. 'Um, I can give you a few names, but I don't know where they all live. David would know them better.'

'One more thing,' he said, leaning towards me. 'Does any of this . . . astrological theory . . . fit in with our Green Man, the chap who took a shot at Drummond?'

I shook my head. 'Penny thought it did, but Don was the wrong victim. He's an Aries. He was shot at the wrong time of year.'

'I see.'

'About the scarf,' I faltered, 'the scarf Penny was strangled with.'

'What about it?'

I thought I'd better say what was on my mind. 'She bought it very recently, from Fizz Drummond.'

He leant forward. 'Don Drummond's wife?'

'Why shouldn't she?' Cruella demanded. 'Her shop is here in town.'

'True. But if whoever killed Miss Anderson – and judging by his tricks, this could be the same man who killed Bob Millard – was also the man who tried to shoot Don Drummond, then there is some link between the victims. We need to know what it is.' He turned to me. 'You don't happen to know if Drummond and Miss Anderson knew each other – personally, I mean?'

'I'm afraid not.'

'You don't think Drummond's our strangler, then, sir?' Cruella asked.

'He'd have to be a bloody fool if he is! We've got a

sample of his DNA and if there's a trace of it anywhere on that scarf . . .'

'Bought in the shop he owns with his wife, sir,' she pointed out. 'He could have handled it there. Defence counsel would make capital out of that.'

He shook his head. 'There was a struggle. If he was in Miss Anderson's flat there will be traces of him somewhere.'

Cruella wasn't put off. 'We've been thinking of Drummond as an intended victim of the killer, sir. But what if our Green Man was really aiming at someone else there at the wassail that night?' she suggested. 'He hit the wrong target. After all, Miss Browne here seems convinced he was the wrong *astrological sign*.' She laid a sarcastic emphasis on the last two words.

The inspector grunted. 'So, what sign should he have been aiming at?' he asked me. 'If Miss Anderson's theory was correct?'

I took a moment to answer. 'Capricorn.'

Cruella gave a trilling little laugh, like ice tinkling in a glass. 'Anyone know any Capricorns around here?'

'Unfortunately, I do,' I told her. 'My birthday's in a few days' time.'

I heard the clock of St Andrew's strike two in the morning, and then again, three. After midnight it does not chime the quarter hours or the half, out of respect for the good citizens of Ashburton and their need to sleep. But sleep wasn't coming to me. Thoughts scrabbled around my brain like creatures in a cage, darting from one subject to another, desperate to find an escape. The tears would come, remembering Penny and Cordelia and how they laughed together, chatting for hours. What question had Penny asked when she'd cast her horary? And if the answer had named her killer, could that killer possibly be David? Not the David I knew, the man who'd been Cordelia's lover, who'd known Penny as a friend for all those years. He couldn't have killed her so cruelly. He didn't have it in him. But if it was David, then I was the one who told him what Penny was about to do. It would be my fault she was dead.

I kept thinking back to what Cruella said about the night of the wassail, about the moment when those shotguns were fired into the apple tree, the moment when Don Drummond was shot by a pistol. I thought about where I'd been standing. The Green Man could not have been aiming at me, not unless he was cross-eyed. But why had he followed me since, to Maisie's cottage, let himself be seen by me? Was he warning me, mocking me, because he intended me to be his next victim? If he wanted to kill me, he could have done it on that snowy night, if he'd been more secretive about it, less intent on showing himself off. It didn't make sense.

I turned over, thumping my pillow into shape. What had Cruella meant when she had said the police could think of down-to-earth motives for someone killing Bob Millard and Don Drummond. *Especially Don Drummond*, she had said. Why single out Don particularly? I must see if I could wheedle out of Dean Collins what the police knew about him. I yawned, wretched, exhausted, my eyes gritty and dry. Gradually I could feel my thoughts relaxing their gridlock, feel myself melting sleepily around the edges. Then a new thought came, and I was jolted awake again. Seth, the astrology student who'd come to the meeting at Loft Cottage. He had turned up in Ashburton again today, on the day that Penny was murdered. He was the first person to mention the Green Man to me. He couldn't be anything to do with Penny's murder. What motive could he have? He hardly knew her. He said. He'd taken Sophie out for the evening. My thoughts were racing again, panicking in my brain. I heard the clock strike four.

CHAPTER TWENTY-FIVE

What is it about dogs? I felt like the walking dead next morning, getting up early after about two hours sleep. But taking the Tribe out cheered me up. Dogs are so pleased to see you, to be with you, to love you. Just watching Dylan, one ear up and one ear down, racing around with Nookie, E.B. and the others, lifted my heart. Dogs don't think about tomorrow. They don't know what their bloody star sign is. They just live in the moment.

After I'd delivered them to their homes, I called in at the police station to sign my statement from the night before. I shopped for Maisie and delivered her stuff to her cottage, putting it all away and setting the timer on her central heating. I wanted to give the place a chance to warm up before she came back tomorrow. She and Janet couldn't arrive before late afternoon, so if I got the chance, I'd come in and flick on the lights of her Christmas tree so it would look pretty when they got home.

After two hours spent on Simon the accountant's pile of ironing, I called in on Mrs Berkeley-Smythe. She had a cruise coming up and we needed to discuss her packing requirements.

'You look very tired, Juno dear,' she observed. 'Are you quite well?'

'Not much sleep last night,' I confessed. I didn't go any further. Why burst Chloe's bubble of contentment with talk of murder? Then a thought occurred to me.

'Did you hear what happened at the wassail over in Widecombe?' I asked. 'A man was shot. Don Drummond, he's one of the consultants at Aigler Wealth Management, the firm your son – the Plymouth One – is in a dispute with.'

Chloe raised her plucked eyebrows. 'He was shot? That's going a bit far!' She chuckled. 'Jonathan is obviously not the only person who's lost money. I'm going to have to help him, you know,' she added, heaving a deep sigh. 'I'm afraid some of my cruising might have to be curtailed in the future.'

Somehow, I couldn't see that happening. 'Your son doesn't know of anyone else who has lost money, does he? You've never heard him mention anyone?'

She looked vague for a moment. 'Not anyone who's likely to go around shooting people.'

'And you've never heard him mention Don Drummond at all?'

'Never.' She returned to the cruise brochure she was perusing. 'And even if he did, I wouldn't remember.'

No, I thought. You probably wouldn't.

* * *

I'd intended to go to *Old Nick's* next. But suddenly I couldn't face the thought of going there, of having to go through the events of yesterday with Sophie and Pat who'd want to know all the details. And I was dead tired. Perhaps it was the shock of Penny's murder, the stress, but I just couldn't face anyone. I went home instead. My heart sank as I let myself into the hall.

I could hear baby Noah screaming downstairs and prayed he'd quieten down. I crept up the stairs so as not to alert Kate to the fact I was home. I didn't feel like talking to her either. Or anyone. I already had a thumping headache. I decided I'd make myself a cup of tea and put my feet up for an hour, maybe close my eyes. But my bottom had barely touched the sofa when my doorbell rang. 'Hell's teeth,' I muttered, and plodded back down the stairs.

Dean Collins was standing on the doorstep, looking anxious. 'I've been trying to catch up with you all day,' he said when I opened the door. 'I've been worried about you.' He reached out and touched my arm. 'I'm sorry about your friend.'

That was all it took to start me off. I began snivelling. I allowed myself to be enfolded in the luxury of Dean's bear-like hug, just for a few moments, before I broke away from him and sniffed. 'Are police officers supposed to do this sort of thing?'

He grinned. 'All part of the service. Can we go up to the flat? I need to talk to you.'

'Do you want a cup of tea?' I asked weakly.

He shook his head. 'I'm okay. You sit down. I'll come straight to the point. The divisional surgeon who was called to the scene yesterday was definite that your friend – Penny – had been dead for several hours before you found her. He thinks the killing must have taken place by mid-afternoon, at the latest. I wanted you to know. The boss said you were beating yourself up about being late arriving at her place. But if you weren't expected till the evening, then she would already have been . . .'

'Thanks,' I said, a bit abruptly. 'Thanks for telling me.' There was an awkward silence, broken by the sound of Bill clawing the back of the sofa. Dean hissed at him and clapped his hands. Unused to such uncouth behaviour, he fled into my bedroom.

'Is there any news about Penny?' I asked. 'Did anyone see anything or . . . ?'

'One neighbour, whose kitchen window overlooks the little garden, saw a man leaving Penny's flat during the afternoon. But she didn't see him clearly. She was looking down on him and he was wearing a baseball cap, just hurrying down the stairs. Dark clothes, that's all she could say.'

'Oh, I see.' Could that have been David? I didn't say anything.

'The boss has gone to Totnes today,' Dean continued, 'to interview David Fairweather, ask him to account for his movements yesterday after he saw you.'

Yesterday seemed like a lifetime ago. 'Look, I think

there's someone else you ought to talk to. A guy called Seth. He was at the meeting at Penny's place the other night and he was here in Ashburton yesterday. He might know something.' I was hoping he wouldn't turn out to be a suspect, for Sophie's sake as much as his own.

Dean was scribbling down the details. 'You don't know this Seth's other name?'

'No. But if you call in on Sophie in the shop, she'll probably know it by now. She went out for a drink with him last night.'

Dean looked up and his blue eyes twinkled. 'Like that, is it?'

I managed a smile. 'Could be.' I waited a moment for him to put away his pen. 'There's no news on Bob Millard, I suppose?'

He shrugged. 'We've talked to all his mates in the Border Morris, and the members of the society he belongs to who restore all that American Civil War junk. Can't find anyone with a motive. There's the woman who keeps suing him for a paternity allowance – I expect she's felt ready to murder him a few times. But, as we know, she's got an alibi.' He pulled a face. 'Jackie might have wanted him out of the way to leave the field clear for this Ryan, but even supposing she had the opportunity to kill him on the day of the fair, there's no evidence. You can't keep stabbing someone with a sharp instrument and get away without any trace of blood on you.'

'What about Ryan?'

'Seems straight. No criminal record, no history of

violence. And if he slunk into the fair under the cover of darkness and murdered Bob Millard, no one saw him do it.'

'Cruella said yesterday you knew of some motive for shooting Don Drummond.' That wasn't exactly what she'd said but it was near enough to draw a response.

Dean grinned and leant across to me, lowering his voice. 'Our friend Don has served time.'

'He's been in prison?' I don't know why I felt so shocked, considering what dangerous vibes the man gave off. 'What for?'

'Fraud. This is years ago, mind. The firm he was working for at the time had encouraged its clients to invest in a property scheme, redeveloping some old industrial site in Plymouth. Turned out the site was contaminated, and the building couldn't go ahead. The investors lost their money. The surveys had been falsified and it seems Don and a couple of his colleagues knew all about it.'

Everyone makes mistakes, Don had said when I talked to him in hospital. Yeah, right.

'So, do we think it could have been one of these investors who still harbours a grudge?'

Dean did not look convinced. 'Yes, but why now? Years after the event. Why wait all this time? I mean, if you're going to shoot the bugger, why not do it straight away?'

'Revenge is a dish best served cold?' I suggested. 'Or perhaps Don's still up to his old tricks?'

He grunted. 'Well, if he is, he's got a bloody sight cleverer at covering his tracks.'

I couldn't help myself, I yawned.

Dean smiled. 'You look like you're dying on your feet. You'd better get your head down for a bit.'

'Thank you, Officer, I intend to do so.'

He stood up. 'I'll go around to *Old Nick's*, see what I can find out about this Seth character from Sophie.'

I thanked him for coming. It was kind of him to let me know about Penny.

'Oh, yes!' he said as if he'd suddenly remembered something, and drew a piece of folded paper from his pocket. 'Your tree calendar. I've taken a copy.' He handed it back to me.

'No need to see me out,' he said. 'You get some sleep.'

I didn't need any further encouragement. I staggered into the bedroom, kicked off my shoes and threw myself on the bed.

I was just sinking nicely into oblivion, Bill purring seductively into my hair, when the cursed phone rang. I moaned. But there was no point in ignoring the damn thing now it had woken me. It was Sophie. Dean had been to see her, told her about Penny's murder and just left. Was I all right, she squeaked down the phone at me, did I need her or Pat to call around? They didn't like the thought of me being on my own. I liked it, I told her, I needed some sleep.

She kept me talking for another five minutes. I managed to slip a word in when she drew breath. Had she given Dean Seth's contact details? No need, she told me in a slightly smug voice, he was sitting there in the shop when Dean called. Was he indeed? That was convenient, I commented. Their date must have gone all right, then. So, Dean was able to ask Seth what he wanted? I asked. Yes. Seth was horrified to learn what had happened to Penny. So were they all. Was I sure I was all right, I didn't need anything? Just sleep, I told her, and put the phone down.

Ten minutes later, it rang again. 'Get that, will you, Bill?' I groaned into the pillow.

This time it was David Fairweather. He sounded genuinely rattled. 'The police have just been here asking me questions. They say Penny's dead . . . murdered . . . that you found her. I can't believe it.'

'It's true, I'm afraid.'

'I mean, how . . . ?' He hesitated to ask the question.

'She was strangled.'

'Oh my God! Poor Penny. And you . . . are you all right? You must be in a state of shock.'

I didn't want to discuss how I was feeling. I changed the subject. 'What did the police ask you?'

'They were pretty blunt. Asked me to account for my movements yesterday, as if I was a suspect. Actually, I was teaching yesterday afternoon, so I have witnesses.'

'I'm sorry, I said I'd seen you yesterday morning. But they wanted to talk to everyone Penny knew. I'm afraid I couldn't help with the names and addresses.'

David gave a short laugh. 'I sent them round to

Reggie. And Clemmie and Maya.'

That'll be fun, I thought. 'Did they ask you anything about the horary Penny was casting?'

'The horary?' He sounded surprised. 'No, why, is it significant?'

'They think so. Penny was clutching part of it in her hand when I found her. The rest of it is missing.'

'Good God!' he breathed in disbelief. 'And you've no idea what it was about?'

'I think I might do. I think Penny was asking a question about murder.'

'Murder? Juno, we need to talk.'

'Yes, but not just now.' I could barely think straight. 'Perhaps we could meet somewhere for a drink? Over the weekend.'

'Of course,' he said. 'Just call me when you're ready.'

I put the phone down, praying it wouldn't ring again. But when you're desperate to get to sleep there is one thing worse than the telephone ringing. The bloody doorbell.

CHAPTER TWENTY-SIX

'Well as I see it, it's got to be that David Fairbrother,' Ricky declared, taking a sip of my brandy.

'Fairweather,' I corrected. He and Morris had gone into *Old Nick's* to top up the items on their vintage clothes sale rail and Sophie had told them about Penny Anderson's murder. They'd rushed around to my place immediately, demanding to know everything. 'And we mean everything,' they had said. An hour later, they were still here. They had refused tea and I'd dragged out my bottle of brandy. If I wasn't to be allowed to sleep, at least I could try to get drunk and pass out. I decided I might as well tell them everything, as at that moment their brains were probably functioning better than mine and one of them might accidentally say something vaguely relevant.

'It's obvious, isn't it?' he went on loudly. 'As soon as he learns this poor woman is performing this horror whatsit . . .'

'Horary.'

'Whatever. He finds that out, and a few hours later,

she's dead. And who else is going to understand this horary thing, anyway, other than someone like him?'

'Except he has an alibi for the afternoon,' Morris pointed out solemnly. 'He was teaching his students.'

Ricky made a huffing noise. 'So he says. That may not have accounted for all of his time. I had a teacher at school used to set the class their work, then nip off to the pub for a crafty pint and get back at the end of the lesson just before the bell rang.'

Morris tutted and raised his eyes to heaven. 'But he would have to have driven over here from Totnes.'

'Wouldn't take long, it's only a few miles.'

'It could. You know how busy the traffic is there, especially around the school run. We've taken ages crawling through there before now.'

'Well, anyway, Princess,' Ricky announced. 'You'd better come home with us. Stay for a few days.'

It took a moment for me to process this. 'I'm sorry?'

Morris blinked anxiously. 'You're not safe here.'

'They haven't caught the green fella yet, and . . . you don't think it's the same bloke, do you?' Ricky asked. 'This Green Man is David Fairweather?'

'No, of course not.'

'Well, you did meet him at that craft place,' Morris reminded me. 'What was he doing there?'

'He told me, signing up for a course.'

Ricky sneered. 'He says.'

'Don't be ridiculous, of course it's not David!' But I spoke with more conviction than I felt. Perhaps I just

297

didn't want him to be because I'd told him about Penny's horary. But what if he'd been lying to me yesterday about why he had gone to the Craft Collective? What if he hadn't been signing up for a course, but had gone there to see someone else, Carl Hayward for instance, or the mysterious woodcarver, Philip King?

'Look, David is a very well-respected astrologer. He doesn't know Don Drummond, let alone have any reason to shoot him. Besides, thanks for your invitation but I've got work to do. Maisie's coming home tomorrow, and I'll need to spend some time in the shop.' I didn't add the fact I intended to spend some time with David. That wouldn't go down well at all. 'But it's sweet of you to worry about me,' I said in an attempt to mollify them.

Ricky tossed back the last of his brandy. 'Just promise us you won't do anything stupid.'

'I won't,' I promised, one person's definition of stupid not necessarily being the same as another's.

There was a knock on the door. It was Kate with Noah on her arm, his sleepy head resting against her shoulder. She had come to show him off. 'I thought it was you two,' she said to Ricky and Morris. 'I heard your voices on the stairs.'

'Oh, it's the baby!' Morris cried in delight. He and Noah had not yet been introduced. 'Isn't he gorgeous? Can I hold him?'

Ricky flicked a glance at me and grinned.

Another ten minutes went by whilst Morris held the baby and cooed over him and Noah stared back at him, sucking on a fist and looking baffled. Morris insisted Noah smiled at him; Ricky said, damningly, he was only passing wind.

'We're too old now, of course,' Morris lamented, staring down at Noah tenderly, 'but when we were young, couples like us weren't allowed to adopt.'

'Oh my God! When *we* were young, couples like us weren't allowed to be couples like us,' Ricky reminded him. 'Stop being such an old fool! C'mon, give him back. We got six hampers of returned panto costumes waiting at home that won't unpack themselves.'

'Oh God. I should be helping you with those. There's that enormous production of *Cinderella* . . .'

'Don't worry about it, Princess. We can cope. Come and help us in a few days, when you're feeling better.'

Morris reluctantly handed Noah to Kate. I'd just about succeeded in bundling them all out of the door when Ricky told her I'd been up to my old tricks discovering dead bodies, and she wanted to know about the murder and I had to go all through the whole thing all over again.

I finally shut the door on them, poured myself another brandy, pulled the phone out of its socket, and headed for bed.

There was only one thing for it, I decided, as dawn was breaking next day, I was going to have to do it myself: cast a horary. My knowledge of astrology is little more than surface deep, comprising a ragbag of information I'd picked up from Cordelia. I wouldn't be able to interpret the thing properly, of course, but I might glean something from it. I knew Cordelia possessed a book on the subject amongst the boxes of stuff under my bed, and I dug it out. It was heavy, as thick as a house brick and would have made a useful doorstop. There was obviously a lot to learn. I made myself a mug of tea and then settled down at the kitchen table with the laptop.

Luckily for me, I didn't have to go through hours of mathematical calculations to set the chart up. These days, there are any number of astrological websites on the internet offering to calculate charts for free. David Fairweather's for one. And although it's interpreted entirely differently, horary is calculated in the same way as a birth chart. Both require a date and a place and a time. The only difference is that for an individual's chart it's the time of birth you want to know, and for a horary, it's the time you ask your question. The question in this case being: who killed Penny Anderson?

Once I had David's face smiling confidently from the screen, I input the necessary details: the date and time, the place – I was offered a drop-down of major towns or I could input the latitude and longitude. Ashburton was too small to appear on the drop-down, so I had to stop everything to look up its coordinates: Latitude 50° 30'56.12' North; Longitude 3° 45'20.59' West. Bill came along to help and leapt on the table, watching the screen earnestly. 'Put one paw on this keyboard and you're dead,' I warned him as I input the last of the coordinates and pressed 'enter'.

A moment later, David's smiling face was replaced by the chart: a circle divided into twelve segments, each containing symbols for the planets. I stared at it for several minutes. I had absolutely no idea what it meant. I turned to Cordelia's book. Chapter One. *The sign on the Ascendant symbolises the querent*, I read. Well, that was me, I was the querent, the person asking the question. And the chart showed the sign on the Ascendant was Capricorn, which is my birth sign. This definitely represented me. So far, so good. What next? Next, the book told me, I should look for my ruling planet, in this case, Saturn. I could see the symbol for it clearly in the twelfth house. The House of the Unconscious Mind, Penny had called it, but the book on horary called it something different: *the House of Secret Enemies*, it said, *the House of Self-Undoing*. Cheery stuff, this horary. The twelfth house symbolised *things not yet known to the querent*.

I went back to the book again, but soon found myself lost in an astrological fog, reading words I didn't even understand. I was supposed to look for *significators*, for the *sole dispositor*, whatever that was. And the eighth house, the House of Death, had far too many planets gathered in it for my liking. It would take months to understand everything I needed to know. I decided to give it up as a bad job and closed the laptop.

'A little learning is a dangerous thing,' I told Bill solemnly, wagging my finger at his nose. And whilst this couldn't be called a prediction, it did turn out to be true.

CHAPTER TWENTY-SEVEN

Saturday is my usual day for manning *Old Nick's*. Sophie or Pat may come into the shop if there is something they need to do, but basically, it's their day off, especially at this time of year when things are quiet. Pat would be busy up at the farm. Sophie had a waitressing shift this morning. And this evening, she'd been invited to Seth's dad's big birthday party. Seth told her there would be someone there that he wanted Sophie to meet. I just hoped it wouldn't turn out to be another girlfriend.

If I'm lucky, Elizabeth may come in to help. She likes to keep the book exchange ship-shape, the volumes arranged on the shelves in strict alphabetical order of author. It does make books easier to find but I think the real reason she does it is that she can't help herself; it's the old schoolteacher coming out in her. Except I'm not really convinced she ever was a schoolteacher, but as it's one of the few parts of her murky past she's prepared to admit to, I have to take it at face value.

As it turned out, I was lucky. She arrived shortly after

I had opened up. Olly had gone to an orchestra practice, so she decided to come into town, lend me an hour or two and do some shopping. And visit Tom Carter, I added privately.

'And I thought I might call in on Tom,' she mentioned casually, 'see how his hip is coming along.'

Why she had to be so secretive about the fact she and the sexy-seventy-something Tom obviously fancied the hell out of each other, I don't know. Perhaps it was to protect Olly's adolescent sensibilities. The possibility of an active sexual relationship between OAPs was something that had probably not yet drifted into the realms of his juvenile imagination. She didn't want to shock him.

'So how is love's young dream?' she asked.

It took me a moment to cotton on. 'Oh, you mean Sophie and Seth! Apparently, he was hanging around the shop yesterday and he's invited her to the family birthday party tonight.'

'My God!' she laughed. 'This is more serious than I thought.'

We were both still laughing when the shop door opened and in walked Inspector Ford. The laughter died on my lips. What had I done now?

'Morning, ladies.' He was smiling, which was a good sign. If he'd looked like thunder, I'd have hidden under the counter. 'Juno, I wonder if I might have a few words with you? Don't worry, this is not an official interview, more of a little chat.'

'Good morning, Inspector,' Elizabeth smiled graciously. 'Would you like a cup of coffee?'

'Well, only if you're making one anyway, Ms Knollys. There's no need for you to absent yourself on my account. As I say, this is just an informal chat.'

Elizabeth glanced at me and crooked an ironic eyebrow. 'I'm sure we could all use a cup. Milk?' she asked him.

'And two sugars please,' he added as she slipped away upstairs. He pointed to Sophie's chair. 'May I?'

'Please do.' We were being very formal and polite this morning.

'How are you feeling?' he asked. 'Collins says you weren't too good yesterday.'

'I just needed some sleep.' He hadn't come only to enquire about my welfare. 'What can I do for you, Inspector?'

He didn't answer directly. He sat down and crossed his arms across his chest. 'In the last twenty-four hours,' he began ponderously, 'I have interviewed some very unusual people. Mr David Fairweather, who despite his line of work, seems normal enough, gave me a list of Miss Anderson's friends. I began with his wife – partner, I should say, Aurora. Interesting lady, into the study of past-life relationships, apparently.' He shook his head and sighed. 'Then I called on a Mr Reginald Ryecart. D'you know him?'

I smiled. 'Yes, I've known Reggie a long time, although I hadn't seen him for years, until recently.'

'He struck me as a bit of an oddball. Tried to tell me about the work of some French statistician. I forget the name . . .'

'Gauquelin,' I supplied for him.

'That's the fellow. He tried to get astrology accepted by mainstream science, apparently. Mr Ryecart seemed quite fixated on the subject.'

'It is a passion of his. He wrote a book about it once. Poor old Reggie, he is a bit eccentric. To tell you the truth, I think he's lonely.'

'Well, I didn't stay long with him. He didn't look too well.'

I remembered he hadn't looked good on the day we'd visited the church at Upton Hellions. I hoped he was all right.

'I called in on a very pleasant lady vicar,' the inspector went on, 'and went to see two ladies who live with a lot of cats.'

'Maya and Clemmie.' I'd loved to have been a fly on the wall with that one.

'Well, the one with the purple hair said she could see my aura and the other one tried to sell me a Native American amulet to protect me against evil spirits. Little thing, it was,' he made a circle with his finger and thumb, 'about the size of a coin. I told her, some of the evil spirits I have to arrest need something a damn sight bigger than that.' He paused, frowning. 'See, the thing is, Juno, all this astrology and horary and what-not, these Celtic symbols, they're a bit muddled up in my mind.

I'm trying to work out if there's really any connection between them, I was hoping you might help me out. You understand this stuff, don't you?'

'Some of it,' I admitted. 'But what you really want to know is whether there's a connection between Penny's murder and the others.'

He nodded.

'Tell me something first,' I said. 'Penny's work with the police in finding the lost child, did you find out anything about it?'

'We found the county force concerned,' he admitted. 'But they were very reluctant to talk about it. They simply confirmed Miss Anderson had been of great help to them in their investigation.' He gave a wry smile. 'They wouldn't say how.'

'I see. Thank you.'

'Now, how much do you understand about this horary she was engaged in?'

'Nothing.' I told him about the chart I'd cast earlier in the morning and how I'd failed dismally to understand more than a fraction of it.

'You see, Juno, I want to understand better what was going on in Miss Anderson's mind that could have got her killed. I'd really like to know what was going on in the university with the deaths of her three colleagues. But I can imagine what my superior officers might say if I suggested opening up murder investigations on three historic deaths, judged by the coroner to be no more than accidents, on the say-so of a dead woman claiming there were astrological similarities.'

Elizabeth returned with the coffees at this point, put them down on the counter and retired discreetly to attend to the bookshelves, where she busied herself with her books. She might look as if she wasn't listening, but she could hear every word.

'This Celtic stuff, these elderflowers left on the body of Bob Millard,' the inspector went on after he'd thanked her for the coffee, 'and the leaves dropped at the scene where Mr Drummond was shot. There was nothing like that left on Miss Anderson's body.'

I was about to say no then took in a breath as realisation dawned. 'The figure of Isis.'

The inspector frowned. 'What?'

'The statuette on the floor, next to Penny's body. Isis was the professional name she used when she was an astrologer for a magazine. The statue used to sit on her desk.'

'But when you found her body, it was on the floor?'

'I thought it must have been knocked down there in the struggle with her attacker, with all the papers and books and things. I remember feeling surprised it hadn't broken. But it was on the floor. What if her killer placed it next to her body deliberately?'

'But Isis is not a Celtic deity,' the inspector objected. 'She's Egyptian, isn't she?'

'Yes, an Egyptian goddess. She ruled creation.'

'Isis had the power to destroy with a single word.' It was Elizabeth who spoke, and we both turned to look at her. 'Isn't that what Penny would have done, if she'd been able to name her attacker?' she asked. 'She would have destroyed him with a word.'

'And to stop her,' I said, 'her killer silenced her.'

The inspector was silent himself for a while, looking thoughtful. 'If the placement of the little statue is symbolic, then do we conclude our Green Man is at the back of it, even though it's a symbol from a different culture?' He gave a short laugh. 'He's a bit of a cherry-picker, this one.'

'If he left the scene in a hurry, perhaps he was improvising.'

'And the figurine was to hand,' Elizabeth pointed out, 'sitting there on the desk.'

'Sounds as if our killer hadn't come as well prepared as on previous occasions.' Inspector Ford said slowly.

'What if he didn't mean to kill her at all?' I asked. 'But he knows the chart could incriminate him and panics.'

Elizabeth looked sceptical. 'He was sufficiently in possession of himself to place the figure of Isis on the floor.'

'It doesn't really help us much, does it?' I thumped my mug down on the counter in frustration. 'I feel like we're going round and round in circles.'

The inspector gave a sympathetic smile. 'So do I, Juno,' he said.

'My old granny used to read the tea leaves,' Maisie told us as Our Janet poured the tea. They'd been home about twenty minutes. I'd missed their arrival, occupied in closing up *Old Nick's*. When I got to Maisie's the Christmas tree was already twinkling away, and more importantly, the cottage felt cosy and warm. 'Course, you can't do it now,' she went on dismissively, 'everyone uses teabags.'

Jacko, who had greeted me with a volley of yapping, followed by a welcoming growl, was busy with his snout in his doggy bowl, pushing it around the kitchen floor. 'Let him out into the garden, will you, Juno?' Maisie asked when he'd hoovered up the last scrap of food and driven the bowl into a corner, and added pointedly, 'He wasn't allowed in the garden at Our Janet's.'

'Mum, that is not true!' Janet protested. 'The only time he wasn't allowed in the garden was when little Poppy wanted to ride her tricycle.' She shook her head at me. 'He took exception to it, kept snapping at the wheels.'

Maisie sneered. 'He was only playing.'

'He frightened her.'

Maisie tutted, as if her three-year-old great-granddaughter ought to toughen up.

'I've been in touch with the agency about Mother coming back,' Janet told me, 'but I'm going to be staying here for a little while, so we won't need you for a day or two.'

I gave a silent cheer. I'd missed Maisie and I was glad to have her back, but grateful to have a few more hours to myself. 'Are you sure you're happy to walk the dog?'

I knew this heroic task had been delegated to Janet's son whilst Jacko was in Heck-as-Like.

She nodded and gave a long-suffering sigh. 'I'll manage.'

'I don't know what the fuss is about,' Maisie remarked. Janet and I exchanged a look. As Maisie hadn't walked him herself in years, she probably didn't.

'He's no trouble,' she insisted. 'If people wouldn't ride their bicycles on the pavements and wheel their damn trolleys and baby buggies along 'em, he'd be as good as gold.'

'It's not just wheels,' Janet objected, 'it's other dogs. He goes for anything on four legs!'

'He does not!'

'He's having a go at them all the time.'

'He's only defending himself.'

'Defending himself? Mum, he's aggressive!'

This was an argument I knew would run and run.

'Let me know if you change your mind,' I whispered to Janet and slipped away whilst I could.

CHAPTER TWENTY-EIGHT

Did I trust David Fairweather? I'd found some old photographs in a box of Cordelia's things, taken during the summer when she and David were an item, before he moved on.

I must have been about twelve at the time. The three of us were on the moor together. I'd forgotten the day, but there was no mistaking that ragged, rocky skyline, the stacks of weathered granite, cleft and criss-crossed by wind and rain. We were on Hound Tor. There was a picture of me standing on a high stack of rock, waving at the camera, my red hair flying out like a flag. Cordelia was standing on a stack just below me, wearing her favourite yellow jumper, pointing up at me and laughing. There were more pictures of the two of us clambering about, and then one of David, on a rock just below me. I had climbed up high and got myself stranded and he was helping me to climb down. His hands were clasping both of mine, and he was encouraging me to jump. The next photo was of the two of us, standing safely on the ground, both grinning, David's arm around me in a fatherly hug. I trusted him then. And if I wanted to find out any more about the horary Penny had been casting, I would have to trust him again. I picked up the phone and called his number.

I didn't want to go to Totnes, and I didn't want him to come to Ashburton. I didn't trust him that much. I wanted neutral territory, somewhere public. I suggested we met up at the Abbey Inn, a riverside pub on the road to Buckfast, a shady spot where trees grow down to the water's edge. There's a terrace there where people can sit outside on a summer's evening and enjoy lovely views of the River Dart, looking downstream to the stone arches of the old bridge. But on a dark January evening we'd have to make do with the traditional old-world charm of the interior, the original fireplaces, the oak panelling painted to give the place a lighter, more modern feel.

On my way out, I bumped into Kate pacing up and down the hall, looking weary and frazzled, a red-faced, grizzling Noah in her arms. I told her I was off to the Abbey Inn to have a drink with one of Cordelia's friends. 'You wouldn't like to take a grumpy baby with you, I suppose?' she asked.

'Not just now,' I said. 'But thanks for the offer.'

I got there early; I'd already grabbed a table and a glass of wine when David arrived. I saw him come into the bar, looking around for me. He looked shocked and sad and anxious, and I felt wicked for having suspected him for a moment. I called his name, stood up and let him enfold me in a big hug. He stared into my face, concerned. 'Juno, this is awful. Are you okay?'

'I'm fine.' I glanced at my glass on the table. 'I don't know what you drink, so I didn't order.'

'No, of course not. I'll sort it out. Another?'

I shook my head. He came back from the bar a few minutes later with a pint of some kind of organic real ale and sat down. 'Do you mind talking about it?' he asked, drawing up his chair. 'About Penny?'

'It's okay.' In a way, I needed to talk about it, to go through it all again in my mind. I described for him what I'd discovered, Penny's body lying on the rag rug, the blue scarf twisted around her neck, the little statue of Isis on the floor next to her, the torn scrap of paper clutched in her hand. I watched him closely as I spoke, searched his eyes for any tell-tale flare of recognition or guilt, but all I saw was horror and pity. And sadness.

'Who could do such a thing?' he breathed when I had finished. He took a sip of ale. 'This horary of Penny's, you said on the phone you thought it was something to do with murder?'

'That's what she told me. I had spoken to her earlier in the day.' I hesitated, then decided to plunge in. 'David, had Penny ever spoken to you about the deaths of some colleagues of hers?'

He looked shocked. 'You don't mean Cordelia?'

'No, no! These were people she worked with, or at least was acquainted with, when she worked part-time at the university. Their deaths were treated as accidental,

313

but Penny was convinced they were murdered.' I told him how her friends had died and the astrological connections she saw that convinced her their deaths were not accidents. 'What do you think?' I asked at the end of it.

He let out a long, slow exhalation of breath. 'I don't know,' he admitted.

'Do you think her theories are credible?'

He shrugged. 'I suppose . . . Well, yes,' he said after a moment. 'Yes. I mean . . . they seem bizarre but . . . astrologically, yes, they make some kind of sense.'

'This all took place after Cordelia died. You and Penny were still friends. And she never mentioned any of it to you?'

'No.' He shook his head. 'Never.'

I wondered why not.

'It gets worse,' I warned him. 'She thought the killer responsible for the university murders had also killed Bob Millard, the blacksmith, and tried to shoot Don Drummond.'

He frowned. 'Why? There's nothing to link these recent crimes to those killings years ago, is there? No tangible reasons, I mean.'

'There's nothing to link the victims, beyond the astrological connections that Penny made. But there's an added complication.' I mentioned the Celtic symbols left at the scene of Bob's murder and Don's shooting. 'Do they have any significance in mainstream astrology?'

He shook his head. 'The Celtic lunar calendar is a

thing of its own, unique to its culture.'

'It's almost as if whoever did this is showing off the breadth of their knowledge,' I said.

'Well, they say serial killers are narcissists.' David took a thoughtful sip from his pint. 'And also that they want to be caught.' He considered for a moment, his fingers idly touching the stubble on his chin. 'You think Penny was looking for an answer to all of this when she cast the horary? But a horary can only answer a specific question. How she worded it would be crucial. You don't know what her question was?'

'No. She didn't tell me on the phone. She was planning to share with me what she'd found later. She'd asked me to go to her place in the evening so we could talk.' I hesitated, then thought I might as well come clean. 'I tried to cast a horary of my own,' I admitted, 'asking who killed her.'

David raised his eyebrows in surprise. 'Did you?'

'I couldn't make head or tail of it. All I found out was that I was the person asking the question, and I knew that before.'

He gave a wry smile. 'Horary is a very specialist subject. It's complicated, to say the least. I could have a look at it for you, but I'm no expert. You did this in Ashburton, I take it?' He took a notebook and pen from his pocket. 'Do you remember the exact time?' I did and he wrote it down. 'And what was the exact question?'

'Who killed Penny?'

He slid an anxious glance at me. 'The chart won't give you a name, you realise?'

'Of course not. But I thought it might give me some clues.'

'Well, I can't make any promises, but I'll bring the chart up on the computer and see what I can make of it.'

'Thanks, David.'

He smiled, and leant towards me confidentially. 'I don't know what they're up to,' he said, dropping his voice to a whisper, 'but there are two old guys sitting at that table over there behind you – no, don't look round – they came in just after I did, and they've been watching the pair of us like hawks. Whenever I make eye contact, they look away.'

'Two old guys?' Suspicion reared up like a cobra inside me, but I resisted the temptation to turn my head.

'Well, elderly.'

'I wonder, would one of them be tall and distinguished-looking with a fine head of silver hair?'

David raised an eyebrow. 'That's right,' he muttered.

'And the other a short, fat man, bald, with little gold spectacles?'

He grinned, bemused. 'Do you know them?'

'Ever so slightly,' I responded. I stood up and smiled politely. 'Would you excuse me for a moment, please, David?'

'Of course.'

I felt as if someone had struck a match, lit the blue touchpaper. I had become a fizzing fuse, an angry firework about to explode. I strode over to where Ricky and Morris were sitting and thumped my fists on the table. 'What the hell are you two doing here?' I whispered fiercely.

'Well, you see—' Morris began, looking flustered.

'Don't tell me, you just happened to come here for a drink?' I asked sarcastically.

'We called in to your place, to see how you were,' Ricky retorted, 'and Kate told us you were coming here to meet up with . . .' he glared fiercely in David's direction. 'Well, we guessed it would be him. David Fairbrother!'

'Fairweather,' I corrected between gritted teeth. 'Now, look, David and I are just having a drink. Okay? I do not want you two following me about . . .'

'It's not safe!' Ricky argued. 'He's a suspect.'

'I do not need a nursemaid,' I hissed, my cheeks growing hot with a fusion of anger and embarrassment. I glared at Morris. 'I certainly don't need two!'

'Something wrong?' David was suddenly beside me, standing there, smiling.

'I don't think you've met Ricky and Morris,' I began awkwardly. '*Old* friends of mine.'

'How do you do?' he asked politely, shaking hands with each of them.

'Why don't you join us?' Ricky invited him.

'Ah, no, thank you. I think it's time I was going,' he said, glancing at his watch. 'Juno, I'll do that little job we spoke about, and I'll let you know what I find. In fact, I might show it to Aurora, if it's okay with you – get a second opinion.'

'Of course. Good idea.'

He kissed me lightly on the cheek and nodded a goodbye to Ricky and Morris.

'Aurora?' Ricky repeated incredulously, long before he was out of earshot. 'Is that his woman? Blimey!'

'It's just a name,' I said furiously, pulling out a chair and thumping myself down on it.

Ricky grinned. 'I bet it's not her real one.'

'Would you like another drink, Juno?' Morris asked timidly.

'Yes, I bloody would!' I fumed. 'Honestly, you two! That was so cringingly, fucking embarrassing. I suppose I should be grateful you didn't decide to wear a false moustache.'

Ricky nodded at him. 'I told you we should have done it in drag.'

Morris stared at me anxiously over his little gold specs. 'We're only thinking of you, Juno, love.'

Ricky suddenly rounded on me, pointing a finger in my face. 'You promised us you wouldn't do anything stupid.'

'What's stupid?' I protested. 'This is a public place, there must be twenty people in here.'

'And out there,' he responded, glowering, 'right down by the river, is a dark and lonely car park. He could be waiting for you out there, right now.'

'That's ridiculous.'

'Then what about the green bloke? He followed you once, he could follow you again.'

I opened my mouth and shut it again. 'Well, you've got a point, I suppose.'

'Don't you move, I'll get you another drink.'

'I've changed my mind,' I said childishly. 'I don't want one.'

'Up to you. But *Maurice* and I are having another, and you are not leaving here before we do.' He stood up. 'No wonder Daniel decided not to stick around when this is what you get up to.' He walked off to the bar.

I felt as if he'd slapped me. In the stunned silence that followed, Morris tried to take my hand. 'Take no notice of him, Juno, love. He didn't mean it.'

'Yes, he did.' There was a lump in my throat so big I thought it would choke me.

Morris fidgeted with my fingers. 'We worry about you.'

'There's no need.' He was gazing at me like a scolded puppy and I relented. I couldn't stay angry with him. 'I know you worry. But I wish you wouldn't.' I reached out and patted his arm.

He brightened up, tried to change the subject. 'It's your birthday on Monday. We want to take you out to lunch. Unless you have a better offer.'

Suddenly two arms came round me from behind my chair and a face pressed up against mine. 'Sorry, Princess,' Ricky whispered, planting a kiss on my cheek. 'I spoke out of turn. Forgive me?'

'Oh, just naff off!' I told him. I couldn't stay angry with him either.

He returned to the table a moment later with three glasses.

'I was just telling Juno,' Morris told him as he sat down, 'we'll take her to lunch on Monday.'

'If she can stay alive that long.' He passed me my glass. 'Don't you want to live to be forty-three?'

'Thirty-two.'

He chuckled. I'd fallen right into that one. 'Cheers!' He held out his glass and after a moment I clinked it in a desultory fashion.

'Cheers!'

'Put a smile on it, Princess.'

I stifled a laugh. 'You are abominable!'

He didn't respond, he was staring out of the window, peering with narrowed eyes into the darkness outside. 'I believe it's snowing again,' he said.

'Really? I can't see anything.'

'Neither can I,' Morris confessed. 'But he's always been very long-sighted.'

I got up and knelt on the window seat, cupping my hands around my eyes to cut out the reflections of the room behind me, and peering through the glass into the night. Tiny white flecks were landing on the wooden tables on the terrace outside, and falling out of sight, disappearing into the river below. It didn't look like much, probably just a shower.

Half an hour later, when we got up to leave, it was still falling, faster and heavier. There was already an inch on the ground. Linking arms, the three of us trod the slippery way to the car park, Morris hastily pulling a woolly hat from his pocket and jamming it on his bald head. We must have been the first to leave since David had gone, because the snow in the car park was pristine, an unblemished coverlet of white. Except for one set of footprints, which came into the car park from the road in a single line, straight to the passenger door of my van, then curved slightly, around to the back doors, round again to the driver's side, then back, out of the car park, down towards the riverbank.

'Someone's been having a nose about.'

Could those be David's footprints? I wondered, but he had gone before the snow had started. If he had gone. Ricky detached himself from my arm, went to the back of the van and tried the doors. 'There are some marks on the back here, looks like someone's tried to jemmy them open.'

'Bloody hell!' I went to join him, slithering on wet snow in my haste. 'Have they damaged my doors?'

He shook his head. 'Nah! Whoever it was, they didn't get in.'

'Perhaps they got scared away,' Morris suggested.

'By what?' he asked. 'No one's driven in or out.' It was true, there were no tell-tale tyre tracks in the snow, no other footprints except for our own. 'Give us your keys a minute, Princess,' he said. 'Let's make sure these doors still open.'

I elbowed him aside. 'I'll do it.' I fitted the keys, turned them in the lock and swung the doors open.

Ricky wrinkled his nose. 'Blimey! It pongs of dog in here!' Meanwhile Morris had taken out his phone and was using the torch to peer through the trees at the riverbank.

'See anything?' he called out to him.

'No, there's no snow here under these trees. I can't see where the footprints end.'

I was about to shut the doors again, to see if they still locked properly, but Ricky stopped me. He leant into the van and whisked aside the old doggy blanket, as if checking no one was hiding underneath.

'You don't seriously think I might have had a stowaway on board?' I asked.

'Only if he's got no sense of smell.' He banged the doors shut and held out his hand for the keys. He locked the doors, closing my keys in his fist. 'Tell you what,' he suggested, as Morris came back to join us. 'Why don't I drive Van Blanc back to Ashburton? You go with *Maurice* in the car.'

'Why?'

He shrugged. 'Just to be on the safe side.'

'Oh, for goodness' sake!' I muttered. 'I'll be perfectly safe.'

'And if you hang back a bit,' he went on, ignoring my protest, 'you'll be able to see if anyone tries to follow in another vehicle.'

'It's a good idea, Juno,' Morris said, nodding.

'You're overreacting.' I sighed loudly. The two of them were so bloody exasperating. 'All right!' I consented. 'If you must play cops and robbers.'

'Well, that's effing rich, that is!' Ricky responded, opening the door on the driver's side. 'Coming from Miss Amateur Sleuth of Ashburton.'

Before I could retaliate, Morris grabbed my arm and began steering me towards the place where they had parked their old Saab. 'Take no notice of him, Juno,' he whispered.

We waited ages whilst Ricky fiddled about adjusting the seat and the mirrors and flashed the lights and finally got his seat belt sorted and was ready to go. Anyone who might have been lying in wait would have given up and gone home by now. I said as much to Morris, waiting behind the wheel of the Saab and he chuckled. 'Oh, here we go,' he said as Ricky finally made it out of the car park.

We followed, slowly, at a discreet distance, leaving room behind the van for any pursuing vehicle to close the gap, for a sinister shape to slide sneakily into the space, its rear lights glowing red in the dark. None did. The short ride back to Ashburton was entirely uneventful, as I knew it would be. Even the snow stopped falling. I couldn't dissuade the two of them from walking me right up to my front door and staying whilst I opened the door and we checked there was no Green Man, nor anyone else, lurking in the hall.

'Goodnight,' I said, kissing Morris and Ricky in turn. 'And thank you.'

'Our pleasure,' Morris assured me, dimpling.

'Goodnight, Princess,' Ricky added. 'And just remember, until this murdering bastard's been caught, no messing about.'

'No sleuthing,' I nodded obediently. Anything to shut him up.

That night I dreamt. I was driving my van down a long road, through a dark tunnel of trees, their twisted branches reaching out to twine each other overhead. I drove through snow, my windscreen wipers swishing away the falling flakes of white, my wheels hissing as they turned the snow beneath them to slush. Something in the van behind me moved, the blanket stirred, a dark shape rose up slowly and the face of the Green Man loomed in the rear-view mirror, grinning.

I woke up in a panic, sweating, heart racing, sitting upright in bed. It was a minute or two before I calmed down, before I felt safe, knew for certain it was only a dream. I lay back on the pillows, paying attention to my breathing, keeping it steady. And I began to wonder, if the Green Man was indeed Penny's astrological killer, what manner of murder would he plan for a Capricorn? Capricorn the goat: hardworking, ambitious, climbs high. A vision of the old photograph flashed into my mind: me as a child, standing, waving from the top of Hound Tor. A fall, that would be most likely, I decided, a fall from a high place. So, no clambering about on high places, I warned myself, as I drifted back off to sleep, not for the time being.

CHAPTER TWENTY-NINE

The snowfall of the previous evening had just been a tease, enough to get me excited at the prospect of snowmen and toboggans. But by morning, there was barely enough left to scrape together a soggy snowball. The weather had warmed up in the night, and only patches of white were left lying on the green fields, soon to be washed away by the rain that fell steadily from a concrete-coloured sky. I wasn't tempted to go outside. Perhaps later, if the weather brightened up. For now, I was happy with tea and toast in bed with Bill, listening to various famous people discussing the Sunday newspapers on the radio. My bedroom was a tip, I observed as I munched, trying not to drip melted butter on the duvet. It needed a proper tidy-up. Apart from the items of clothing I had abandoned on taking off, leaving them to find their own way to the wardrobe or the laundry basket, I still had piles of Cordelia's books arranged around the floor, waiting to be returned to their boxes and shoved back under the bed, including that slab of a thing on horary. I wondered if David had replicated the chart I had cast yet, if he'd found out anything. Probably not. It was barely ten o'clock. He was probably still on the morning yoga, or sex with Aurora, followed by a revolting green smoothie, or orange juice and croissants and some ridiculously expensive ground coffee whose beans had to be passed through the digestive system of some wild creature before it was fit to drink. I was only jealous, I realised with a sigh. Not of the repulsive smoothie or the pretentious coffee, or even the sex, but of being in bed with your loved one on a Sunday morning, knowing you had the whole day to cuddle up together if you wanted to. And maybe, if I hadn't been so wantonly reckless in the past, so heedless of danger to my life and limb, I might be cuddling up with Daniel right now. Bill took me to task, nudging my arm with his head and reminding me that regrets are useless, *he* was here and I wasn't paying him due reverence and attention. I tickled the black velvet fur between his ears for a while, then got up, showered and got dressed.

The tidy-up took longer than expected. The scattered garments were easy enough to gather together and deal with, but the books took ages. I sat down on the bed and pondered. Did I really need to keep them all? I had kept them because they belonged to Cordelia, and I felt a pang of sorrow at giving away anything of hers. But if I hadn't read them in the twelve years since she had died, was I really likely to start reading them now? I had no desire to follow in her footsteps. Perhaps I would just keep one or two basic ones, offer the others to Seth. He might find them useful. I picked them up one by one, leafed through them, and began to sort them into piles.

At first, I was reluctant to give away anything where she had scribbled her own thoughts in the margins, but this applied to most of the books and I decided to toughen up the rules. Then there were old copies of the charts she had drawn up. Hours of work had gone into them; it seemed a terrible waste to throw them away. They might be useful to someone for study purposes. I worked my way to the bottom of the box, undecided about the contents. I found an old diary, not a book of Cordelia's daily musings, but simply an appointments book, where she had scribbled down things she wanted to remember. I found my birthday noted, just *Juno* scribbled by the date. There was another name there too. I smiled. I didn't realise I shared my birthday with someone else she knew.

The last item in the box was an envelope about three inches thick. I realised it contained the original draught of Reggie Ryecart's book, the one he told me he had sent to her all those years ago. I supposed I ought to return it to him. I noticed the envelope had been readdressed to him, in Cordelia's writing, so presumably she had finished with the manuscript and was intending to send it back to him herself. Why hadn't she? The flap was open, and I pulled the whole thing out, including a letter from her lying on the top of the manuscript. The reason she hadn't got around to posting it was all too clear. The letter was dated the day she died. She hadn't had the chance.

Dear Reggie,

Thanks so much for allowing me to read your manuscript. I feel very honoured to be the first person to read such an excellent and scholarly evaluation of the work of Michel Gauquelin.

I have written my comments and notes in the margin of each page as you requested, and I've also pointed out any spelling mistakes. Quite a few of those! I think this is a brilliant book, my dear friend, which is why I am begging you to do one thing. Get rid of the introduction. Frankly, it's awful. It's much too personal and passionate. I understand the resentment you feel, and I know you blame certain people for the misfortune in your life, but to begin your book with a direct attack on them ruins the objectivity of the work itself, and anyway, is probably libellous. Throw it away, Reggie. I'm sure any publisher would advise you to do the same.

I'm going to post this to you so that you have a chance to think about what I'm saying before we next meet. I know you won't like my saying it, but we both know brooding about the past never did anyone any good. You've got a chance to start a new chapter in your career with this book, Reggie, just turn the page on what happened before.

Written with love,

Your friend Cordelia

Fascinated, I put down the letter, picked up the manuscript, and began to read. And it was all there. The answer I had been seeking had been under my bed all the time.

It was there in the introduction: the resentment, the vitriol, the venom, page after page of it. I sat staring at it for a long time, wondering what to do. I looked at the envelope Cordelia had written. Did Reggie still live at the same address? I hunted for his phone number, and found it, scribbled in the inside cover of her diary. It was a landline. Surely, he had a mobile by now? If he had, I couldn't find it. I phoned the landline, but there was no reply. He must be out. Reggie's rather querulous tones asked me to leave a message, so I did. I put the phone down. There was nothing to do now, but wait.

I had plenty of time to think long and hard about what I had read, and during the afternoon, I decided to make another call. I dug out the business card she'd given me from my bag, and phoned Charlotte Webb.

'I hope you don't mind me calling you on a Sunday,' I began, but as soon as Charlotte recognised my voice she began gushing like an open tap.

'Juno, I've been hearing amazing things about you, and you never said a word when you came into the shop! I was telling Sally Mitchell . . . you remember Sally, she got expelled for smoking pot . . . about how you'd come in the other day, and she told me she'd read all about you in a local paper and that you're a famous amateur detective . . .'

'I wouldn't exactly describe myself in—'

'It's so exciting!'

I inwardly cursed Sally Mitchell for being even more of a blabbermouth than Charlotte, but then realised I might be able to turn this to my advantage. 'Actually, Charlotte,' I said, 'that's partly the reason why I phoned you.'

'Oh my God! Are you investigating something?'

'Sort of,' I admitted. 'As coincidence would have it, the other day I found myself in Upton Hellions, and guess who I saw whilst I was there?'

'Not Lily?'

'Lily Marwood,' I confirmed. 'I didn't get the opportunity to be properly introduced, but I was wondering if you wouldn't mind answering a few more questions about her?'

'Oh, fire away!' Charlotte responded, bursting with curiosity.

So, I did.

It wasn't until late in the evening that Reggie picked up my message and phoned me back. 'You have my original manuscript?' were his first words. His voice sounded shaky.

'The one you sent to Cordelia, all those years ago,' I told him. 'I thought you might like to have it back.'

'Very kind of you, Juno.' There was a long, thoughtful pause. 'Have you read it?'

'I've read enough.'

He gave a slight, nervous laugh. 'I know what she wrote, you know. I was so impatient to find out what she thought about my manuscript, I phoned her on the night before she died, to ask her.'

'And did you take her advice, ditch the introduction?'

'I did, with some reluctance. But it didn't make any difference,' he added bitterly, 'no one was interested in publishing it. Gauquelin was no longer considered fashionable.'

'Couldn't you have published it yourself?'

'It wasn't so easy then as it is now. And in any case, it still costs money. And time. As it turns out, I don't have either.'

'I could come over to Totnes tomorrow,' I told him. 'And bring the original back to you. Do you still live at the same address?'

'No. No, I had to move out of the family home after my sister died.' He gave me the new address, directions on how to find it.

'I'll see you in the morning, then.'

'Yes, why not?' he asked. Again, the nervous laugh. 'We can wish each other happy birthday.'

'Indeed, we can.' I put the phone down. Then I picked it up again and dialled another number. Lots of people die on their birthdays. I didn't intend to die on mine.

CHAPTER THIRTY

The ancient town of Totnes, which dates back to Saxon times, is a bigger, busier, more bustling town than Ashburton. It boasts its own castle for a start. Not a romantic ruin, the picturesque setting for a fairy tale, but a chunky Norman fortress, a solid ring of stone sitting on a steep, grass-covered mound, a stronghold so heavy and impenetrable-looking, any marauders intent on siege were likely to have thought twice and taken their giant catapults home at the very sight of it.

I parked in a car park at the bottom of the town, and walked along Ticklemore Street to the bottom of Fore St. Here the castle was hidden from view, the long, steep shopping street leading its way up the hill, beneath the graceful East Gate Arch, once the gateway into the medieval town. It was at the very top of this hill, in a place called The Narrows, that Cordelia had her shop. It was also the place where she died. The closer I got to it, the more difficult I found it to take each step, as if my feet were turning to lead. Fortunately, I didn't have to go that far.

Just after the arch, I turned right off the steep hill, along a thin ribbon of pavement, around the back of St Mary's Church, towards the old Guildhall, along Ramparts Walk. Here I wound my way around a maze of curious, narrow turnings until I found the row of terraced houses where Reggie lived. I knocked on his door.

'Come in!' a voice called out. 'The door is open.'

I stepped inside. There was no hallway; the door led me straight into a single room that was both kitchen and living room, dark enough to need lamps lit even on a sunny morning. I stood still, blinking in the dimness and waited.

'Come in! Come in!' Reggie's voice repeated brightly. It took me a moment to see him, standing by the kitchen stove, his hand on the kettle. 'It's a lovely bright morning. Better than yesterday, eh? A bit chilly, perhaps, but I see you're well wrapped up.' He grinned.

'I thought we might celebrate our birthday with tea and cake in the garden. What do you think?' He waved an arm in the direction of a glass door opening on to a paved courtyard where I could see a round garden table and two chairs. The garden finished in a low wall, and beyond it, a view of the steep, green mound, leading up to the stone castle on its top.

'You've got a great view of the castle,' I said.

'Go on outside,' he invited airily. 'Take a proper look.'

His voice seemed overloud, his forced jollity a cover for nervousness. I was glad to escape the dark confines of the interior and walk out into the sunshine. I went to the end of the courtyard, gazing up at the castle. When

I reached the wall, I peered over. I was on the edge of a steep drop, perhaps thirty feet to a paved courtyard below. I took in a shocked breath. The wall was no protection against a fall, barely above knee height. Reggie might have warned me. But then, I realised with a sickening feeling of dread, he wouldn't do that. The neighbours on either side had erected fences on top of their walls, to safeguard the owners of the tiny scooters and toys I could see scattered about, to stop them from clambering over the edge, from falling. But not Reggie.

'Ah, the little Capricorn goat, how sure-footed she is! How high she climbs!' I heard his voice behind me and turned. He was standing in the garden doorway, a ghastly grin on his face. Seeing him in the daylight, I was shocked at how haggard he looked, how drawn. He was obviously ill. 'I'm afraid the old fence collapsed a year ago, and I haven't got around to replacing it.' He nodded at the envelope I was carrying. 'I see you've brought it with you. You said you'd read it.' And then after a moment he added, 'So you know.'

I put the envelope down on the wall. 'I know you were a lecturer at the university.'

He laughed bitterly. 'A junior one.'

'And you tried to introduce a new course.'

'A ground-breaking course!' His eyes flared up, his gaunt face suddenly alight with passion. 'It would have been the first of its kind in this country, the only place in the UK where you could study psychological astrology to degree level.' He took a few steps towards me. I instinctively shrank back, edged into the corner of the wall, with the neighbour's fence behind me. He noticed my movement and gave a tiny smile of triumph. He was enjoying the feeling I was nervous, that he had me in his power. Well, stuff that. I straightened up.

'What happened?' I demanded.

'You've read it! It was the interdepartmental committee.' His face twisted in a mocking grimace. 'They reviewed all proposed new courses. They blocked it, said it wasn't a suitable course of study in a place of serious learning. And they didn't stop there. The very fact I had suggested such a course meant that in their eyes I was no longer considered an appropriate person to hold a university post. A year later the university let me go, said it was all to do with budgetary cuts, but I knew.'

'So you set about murdering the members of the committee.'

'Not all of them,' he answered, matter-of-factly. 'Just the ones who'd blocked me.'

'Starting with Professor Gideon.'

He laughed and shook his head, holding up his hands as if to show they were innocent of bloodshed. 'No, ironically, that was nothing to do with me. It was an accident. Honestly. Gideon was just an idiot who went out sailing when he was stoned. He must have fallen overboard. But the way he died gave me the idea for how to deal with the others who had blocked me, starting with Gordon.'

'How did you manage the scorpion? Did you steal it from the laboratory?'

'I didn't have to.' His smiled was exultant. 'Even then

you could buy just about everything on the internet. I had to pay a lot of money for a Deathstalker.' He pulled thoughtfully on the lobe of one ear. 'It came through the post in a little plastic box, I remember, like a sandwich. I had to do a bit of breaking and entering to get into Gordon's flat, but that was quite easy. He lived in a basement apartment, you know.' He paused, waiting for my reaction, when none came, he shrugged. 'I see the fact is lost on you. Pluto, ruler of Scorpio, God of the Underworld, rules everything underground, you see, from sewage pipes to Hell itself, so his living in a basement flat . . . but even dear Penny didn't pick up on that one.

'I just took the lid off the plastic box *very* carefully, put it on the floor in his bedroom – where I imagined he would be most likely to wander in bare feet, and left the rest to the scorpion. I thought it might take some time for the ugly little brute to get him, but it must have stung Gordon that very night.'

'Didn't anyone at the laboratory notice they *didn't* have a scorpion missing?' I asked.

'Oh yes,' he nodded. 'A junior researcher, but like all juniors, she was shouted down.'

'And what about Dorothy?'

'Bitch!' he pronounced venomously. 'She worked in the vice chancellor's office. She was the one with the most clout, the most influence. If it hadn't been for her . . .' He took a breath, gaining control of his anger. 'So, after she retired, I began to follow her about, got to know the places she frequented. I bumped into her *accidentally* in her favourite cafe. Do you know, the shrivelled old crone actually invited me to her place for dinner? "Let bygones be bygones," she said, the sanctimonious cow, as if she wasn't responsible for destroying my life.'

'But how did you get her to ingest seeds of autumn crocus?'

'When I arrived for dinner, I wasn't sure how I was going to do it,' he admitted, smiling. 'I was hoping that fate might grant me an opportunity to somehow sprinkle them on her food without her noticing. But in the end, it was simple. Whilst she was still at the kitchen stove, concocting her witch's brew, which I have to say, turned out to be revolting, I slipped them into the pepper grinder on the table. It was one of those you upend, you know with the grinder mechanism in the top? Which means the last thing you put in there is the first thing that gets ground onto your dinner. Or onto hers. I told her it was so delicious it didn't need any further seasoning. When I left, and she was already starting to look a bit green around the gills, I simply slipped the thing into my pocket and disposed of it on my way home. As far as I know, no one has ever questioned that there was no pepper on the table. Why would they?' He held up a finger. 'Our tea ought to be brewed by now. I'll go and fetch it.' He smiled when he saw the look on my face. 'Oh, don't worry, Juno! I'm not going to poison *you*. That wouldn't be fitting.'

No, I answered silently, you've got something altogether more appropriate in mind for me.

I could escape at this moment, rush through the garden

door into the kitchen and out through the front door. I doubt if Reggie, frail as he seemed, could overpower me. But whilst he was in a talkative frame of mind, there were other things I wanted to hear him say.

He came back outside, bearing a laden tray and set it down on the table. 'Here we are!' he said brightly. 'Do come and sit down.' I stayed rooted to the spot and he raised his eyebrows. 'No?'

'But the course you proposed wasn't the only reason you were dismissed from your university post, was it?' I challenged him. 'In fact, it wasn't the real reason at all.'

His smiled faded. 'What do you mean?'

'You were a lecturer, with a duty of care towards your students. You had an inappropriate relationship with a first year, Lily Marwood. She left.'

'I loved Lily. I wanted to marry her.'

'And you killed Bob Millard because you were jealous of him.'

'Jealous? How could I have been jealous of that imbecile?' His lips tightened into a grim line. 'He wasn't fit to touch her. He polluted her, got her pregnant, ruined her career, saddled her with that little monster. I always swore I'd get him for it one day.'

'The child is not the monster here, Reggie,' I told him.

He flushed slightly. 'Even so, I would have been prepared to marry her.'

'But she didn't want to marry you, did she? She left college before you were sacked, went her own way, started again, a new life.'

'I never stopped loving her.'

'Is that why you hung around outside St Mary's Church, just hoping she might walk by?'

It was sad, pathetic, as pathetic as me driving up to Halshanger Common, hoping Daniel would be there. 'How many times have you waited for her there over the years?'

'That's none of your business,' he hissed.

'But why did you wait so long to kill Bob?'

'It was just after the child was born, eight years ago, that I became ill for the first time. I had a course of chemotherapy. After my treatment, my sole focus was on getting myself well again, getting fit. A lot of good it has done me,' he added bitterly. 'I had no thoughts about killing Millard. Then, at my routine check-up a few months ago, I discovered I hadn't cheated cancer, after all.'

'I'm very sorry.' I meant it. Fate was cruel. 'But how did you know Bob would be at the fair?'

'I didn't!' Reggie gave me a radiant smile, pouring tea as if he was playing hostess in some polite society salon. 'I came to the fair so that I could reacquaint myself with *you*. You see, you were already a person of interest to me, Cordelia's beloved niece turned amateur sleuth. And a Capricorn to boot! You were perfect. I decided, when I started reading about your somewhat foolhardy exploits in the paper, it had to be you.'

'What had to be me?'

He didn't answer. 'I followed you around the fair for most of the day, you so busy with your little clipboard,' he added mockingly. 'I stood right next to you at times, but you didn't recognise me, didn't even see me.'

'Had you come to kill me?'

He looked genuinely shocked. 'Good Lord, no! That wouldn't have been appropriate at all.'

He grinned. 'But I've followed you many times since, watched you.'

The thought made me shudder, wondering about the times he might have been watching me and I never knew. I remembered him coming into the shop with Penny. *Look who I found lurking outside your shop*, she'd said. And then, when he met Olly outside with his bike. And I had told Elizabeth that he would be safe if Reggie took him cycling up on the moor. I felt ice cold at the thought of it.

'But then I saw Millard, there at the fair, boring on interminably about his wretched war wagon, and he mentioned to the crowd that it was his birthday . . .' He laughed. 'Well, it was too great an opportunity to miss. I hung about in the dark until he was alone and then stabbed him with a pritchel. I couldn't have killed him with it, but I took him by surprise. He stumbled backwards and fell.'

'Then his murder wasn't planned?'

'Just the gods smiling on me.'

'What about the elderflowers?'

'Oh those! Picked them off a hedgerow months ago, discovered I still had them in my pocket. I thought they might spice things up a bit.'

'And you decided to continue with the Celtic symbolism when you tried to kill Don Drummond.'

'Exactly.'

'I think I know why you tried to kill him.'

He looked amused, as if he was humouring a child. 'Tell me.'

'Your sister committed suicide, after losing all her money.' Ryecart is an unusual name, easy enough to find. I'd read about her online yesterday when I was waiting for Reggie's call, in an old newspaper article. 'Aigler Wealth Management were her financial advisers.'

Reggie's face darkened. 'It was Drummond who encouraged her to invest. Arrogant young prick! He was only a junior consultant at the time, but he thought he knew everything. But he wasn't prepared to accept any responsibility for my sister's losses when the scheme failed. I read in the paper he was going to be at the wassail. So, a few days beforehand I cycled up to Cold East Farm, did a reconnoitre, discovered that convenient back lane where I could hide my bike, make a quick getaway if I needed to.'

'But the wassail was at the wrong time. The sun wasn't in Don's sign.'

'I'm running out of time,' he cried impulsively. Then he gathered himself once more. 'I can't wait for the Sun to be in Aries. I won't be here.'

'I'm truly sorry for you, Reggie.' Sorry for that old friend of Cordelia's, sad that failure, resentment and bitterness, the illness ravaging his body, had turned him into the creature he now was. 'Why Penny?' I asked.

'She could have stood up for me, for my course. She could have spoken in my favour at the university. But no, she kept silent, to keep her job.'

'But she was just a part-timer working in administration, typing up notes,' I protested. 'She told me herself she was little more than an office junior. She had no influence.'

He was shaking his head. 'They might have listened. But she never even owned up to the fact her real job was concocting horoscopes for stupid magazines.'

'And that's why you killed her?'

He shook his head, and for the first time his face showed a trace of sorrow. 'If only she hadn't tried to cast that horary. I didn't know she was doing it. I just paid her a visit and there she was working on it. I panicked. knew the chart would point to me, knew she'd work it out. She was so good at it, so clever. And it wasn't the right moment, you see. She wasn't the right person to discover the truth.'

'But I am?' I felt sick inside. 'You could have killed me the night when you followed me to Maisie's cottage, when you dressed up as the Green Man, but you wanted me to see you.'

'I stood in your garden. I was going to throw stones at your window. Very inconsiderate of you to go out.'

'But before then, on Boxing Day. It was you in the grounds with your torch. What were you hunting for?'

'Nothing. I was just keeping tracks on you.'

'And you followed me to the Abbey Inn? Tried to get into my van.'

'I wanted to leave you a present.'

'Another bunch of birch leaves?' I asked.

'No.' he fingered a silver chain at his neck and pulled

out a tiny pendant, holding it up, the head of a horned goat. 'Capricorn, you see.' His eyes gleamed with excitement. 'I wanted to keep you interested.'

'Why? Why me?'

'Because we share the same birthday!' He came towards me then, and I stiffened, fumbling for a hold on the fence behind me. He stopped and laughed. He was standing against the wall, a few feet from me. 'You're a Capricorn. And it has to be you,' his voice dropped to a whisper, 'because I killed Cordelia.'

Just for a moment my heart caught in my throat, my fists clenched. But I knew he was lying. 'No, Reggie,' I breathed out slowly. 'That isn't true.'

'I did. It was my fault.'

'No. Penny was there, you weren't.'

'Penny couldn't see me from where she was standing. But Cordelia spotted me. I waved to her, beckoned her across the street. I was the reason she stepped out into the road. I killed her,' he repeated. 'I killed Cordelia.'

He was edging closer to the wall. And suddenly I knew what he wanted me to do. He wanted me to rush at him in rage, push him over the edge. And it didn't matter whether or not I fell to my death, as long as he did. He hadn't picked me to be his next victim, but to be his executioner. 'I'm not the Capricorn you're trying to kill, Reggie,' I breathed in horror. 'You are.'

He leapt up suddenly, balanced on top of the wall. 'I killed Cordelia.' He tried to sound mocking, provoking, but couldn't conceal the desperation in his voice. His feet danced on the stones and I wanted to cry out, reach out, stop him.

'Please come down from there,' I begged him. 'You'll fall.'

'You're not listening.' He stretched out his arms on either side, as if he was crucified, offering his body for me to push him. 'I tell you I killed her.'

'I don't believe you. Please come down, Reggie. You don't need to do this.' I did not dare reach out, try to grab him, because I knew he'd jump, drag me over the edge with him. I shook my head as I backed away, my eyes filled with tears. 'I'm sorry Reggie, but I can't help you.'

As I turned to walk away, David burst through the open door into the courtyard. For a moment he stared aghast at Reggie on the wall. 'Don't!' he cried out, as arms outstretched, Reggie took one step backwards off the parapet and fell, silent as a stone.

I rushed to the edge, compelled to look over. Reggie stared up at me, his broken body splayed out on the hard paving below, his limbs at odd angles, darkness spreading in a pool around his head. He had got the death he wanted. I felt David by my side. 'Oh God,' he muttered. We both turned away, David leaning his weight on the table for a moment, resting his hands on it, taking in what he had just seen. He breathed out a long sigh, then turned to look at me. We hugged each other in sadness. 'I hoped you might have got here a few minutes earlier,' I told him.

I had phoned him the night before, to tell him where I was going, emailed him a copy of Cordelia's letter and the introduction to Reggie's book, just in case anything happened to me. It was practically a confession in itself.

'I've been banging on the front door for the last five minutes.'

I left it on the latch. Reggie must have locked it after me.

'I've called the police. A neighbour came out to see what the fuss was about. She knew Reggie was ill, might need help in here and she let me have his spare key.' He shook his head sadly. 'At least I was here to be a witness when he jumped.'

I reached into my pocket and pulled out my new phone. 'I've had this set to record. With any luck, I'll have most of his confession.'

He frowned at me. 'Why did you call me last night, instead of the police?'

'Because I trust you,' I answered. 'And the police would have tried to stop me. They might have arrested Reggie on suspicion, and I know he would have clammed up. They would have got nothing out of him. I guessed he'd talk to me. But if anything happened to me, I knew you could explain everything to the police.'

He reached an arm around my shoulders. 'Let's wait outside.'

We could already hear a siren in the distance. 'Did you do the horary, by the way?' I asked. He nodded. 'What did you discover?'

'That you were the question,' he said. 'And the answer.'

CHAPTER THIRTY-ONE

I stood at the edge of the pavement on The Narrows, at the top of the hill where the road curves around, standing in the same spot where Cordelia had been standing all those years ago, the moment before she died. I looked down towards East Gate and the town, then up and across the road. Reggie had been lying. There was no possibility he could have been standing there and not been seen by Penny. He could not have beckoned Cordelia to her death unseen. In a way, he'd tried to beckon me to mine, but really, it was only his own death he had been craving.

I was wearing Cordelia's amber earrings, the ones she left me in her will, and held a bunch of early narcissi, tied with yellow ribbon, her favourite colour, her favourite flowers. I touched the cool petals to my face for a moment and inhaled their sweetness. Then I did what I should have done years ago, I laid them against the wall outside her shop, marking the place where she had died. The shop was a boutique now. The current owner wouldn't know why the flowers were there, but it didn't matter. *To Cordelia,* the card read, *forever in my heart.*

I turned to David, standing close by. 'Thanks for coming.' I gave him a hug.

'I wanted to,' he said.

'Why don't you join us for lunch?'

He looked at his watch. 'I'd better not.' He gave a wry smile. 'Aurora, you know.'

I smiled too. 'Yes, I know.'

'Look, the monthly astrology meetings will be carrying on at our place, so if ever you feel tempted to join us . . .'

'Thanks,' I said. 'But I don't think I will.'

He nodded as if he understood. He stayed for a long moment, looking at me. Looking down the years, I felt. 'I'll never forget her, you know,' he said.

There didn't seem anything else to say. 'Goodbye, David.'

He smiled. 'Goodbye, Juno.' He set off up the road, turning to give me one brief wave before he disappeared around the curve in the road and was gone.

Ricky and Morris were standing a little way away, waiting. I had missed out on my birthday lunch last Monday, so they were taking me out today, exactly one week later. I turned towards them, walking between them and catching each of them by the arm. We walked in silence for a few yards.

'So, how's the love affair coming along?' Ricky can never stand silence for long.

'You mean Sophie? Seth introduced her to someone at his father's birthday party who publishes natural history books. He saw her owl painting and came around to the shop to see her other work. He's talking about giving her a commission to illustrate a book on the hedgerow. She's so excited.'

'That's wonderful!' Morris beamed, his face lighting up. 'She deserves a chance like that.'

'It would certainly solve some of her problems for a bit.' And mine, I added privately.

Ricky chuckled. 'She's smitten with this Seth, then?'

'Oh, she likes him a lot. But he's gone back to Wales. He'll be there until Easter now. They've talked on the phone a few times, but to be honest, she's worried she's not clever enough for him.'

'Sophie's very clever,' Morris protested.

'Yeh,' Ricky agreed. 'But I expect she's worried he might fall for some brainy Welsh undergraduate.'

'Well, if he does,' Morris said with a definite nod of his head, 'he's not worth worrying over.'

'Absolutely,' I agreed. Secretly, I think if Soph has her heart set on Seth, then she's stiff competition for any woman, brainy or not.

'So where are we going for lunch?' Morris asked. 'How about we drive over to Dartington, try the White Heart?'

'Oh, I love it there.' The old pub is attached to a medieval hall, part of the ancient Dartington Estate, and set in lovely gardens. It was too early for the crocuses. The earth would be brown and quiet, a few green shoots, perhaps, the first brave snowdrops. But the days were beginning to lengthen now. There might be cold weather to come, but we had escaped the dark of midwinter.

'It's Monday, though, isn't it?' Morris added with a frown. 'I wonder if it's open on a Monday? Not all places are,' he gave a worried shake of his head, 'especially at this time of year. We could try—'

'Look, let's just stop standing around on this bleedin' cold corner, eh?' Ricky complained. 'This wind is like a knife and I'm going to need the loo before very much longer.'

I tapped him on the arm, gave him my best serious look. 'You are going to go and see the doctor, aren't you?'

'Oh, don't worry, Princess! *Maurice* has booked me an appointment for next week.'

'Good for *Maurice*,' I said approvingly.

'If the White Hart isn't open,' Morris carried on, 'we could always drive over to—'

'Oh, let's not try to second-guess it!' Ricky protested. 'We'll find out when we get there. If it's not open, we'll go somewhere else.'

'That's right,' I said. 'It doesn't matter. Let's live in the moment. Let's just go.'

ACKNOWLEDGEMENTS

I would like to thank my dear friend Claire Caldwell, without whom I would never have got to know and love Ashburton. Come back again soon. I'd also like to thank Patti Wigington for work on the Celtic Tree Calendar. My usual thanks go to Fiona, Susie, Fliss, Libby and the rest of the team at Allison & Busby, and in particular, my wonderful agent, Teresa Chris. I'd like to thank my good friend Sue Tingey, Di, my sister Rosie and my husband Martin for all their love and support and for keeping me sane, just about.